The World Is Round

THE

WORLD

IS

ROUND

Iva Pekárková

Translated by David Powelstock

FARRAR

STRAUS

GIROUX

New York

Translation copyright © 1994 by David Powelstock

All rights reserved

Originally published in Czech under the title

Kulatý svět, copyright © 1993 by Iva Pekárková

Printed in the United States of America

Published simultaneously in Canada

by HarperCollinsCanadaLtd

First edition, 1994

Library of Congress Cataloging-in-Publication Data

Pekárková, Iva.

[Kulatý svět. English]

The world is round / Iva Pekárková ; translated by David

Powelstock. — 1st ed.

p.   cm.

I. Title.

PG5069.P44K8513   1994   891.8'635—dc20   94-653   CIP

Acknowledgments

I'd like to thank all the people who helped this book to happen: Lisa Ross, Elisabeth Dyssegaard, David Powelstock, Radim Valák, Jitka Neuberg-Dvorak, Kaca Henley, and many others. My special thanks go to all my campmates in Trais-kirchen, who—willingly or not—shared their life stories with me, talked to me, ignored me, or pissed on my head, and also to the United States of America, which accepted me as a refugee in 1986 and, therefore, changed my life.

*When I consider the brevity of my life, engulfed
before and after by eternity, the small space which
I fill, or even so much as see, surrounded by the
infinite enormity of spaces which I do not know
and which do not know me, I am amazed that I
myself am located here and not there, now and
not then.*

PASCAL, *Pensées*

Where then should I have gone—know ye not?
Bare were my feet.
And prickly all the paths
With thorns of loves I have left
And friendships time has torn apart.

FAIZ AHMED FAIZ

The World Is Round

I don't think Angela could have lived anywhere but East Berlin, in an attic room a hundred meters from the Wall. She was only a couple of years older than I, but she knew people and the world with an unerring sixth sense that I could never develop in myself; by some sort of miracle she was studying philosophy—and with the help of her insufficient English and my lousy German she divided humanity in two for me with the English words *good* and *red*.

Almost all her friends lived their lives nearly the same way: in the back courtyards of dusty, abandoned East Berlin tenements, in attics atop narrow, creaky, worn-out wooden stairs.

She lived without running water or a toilet, with an illegal electrical hookup cleverly tapped into the main line. She had a narrow bunk in her place (into which she and her Franz could barely squeeze themselves), an Oriental rug, and on the windowsill a bottle filled with tradescantia that in winter were always myrtle-green and in summer darkened to a brownish red.

She also had a map of Berlin tacked to the wall right next to the window with its wooden bars: the hewn-out, halved, almost dead capital, disemboweled like a chicken. The map depicted the streets and squares and intersections, a forest-green Lenin Park, and a great orange blotch imprinted with black letters spelling out WEST BERLIN.

As if the mapmaker were trying to convince the people that over there, on the other side of the barricades, there was actually nothing but a gaudy, orange, shameful blemish on the collective face of the Good Socialist Germany of the East. As if out there, beyond that gray wall, there was only a loathsome orange-colored desert. Impenetrable and lifeless, dangerous and forbidden. A desert you would never learn much about.

·

Angela had lived that way for a long time—but not always in the same garret. Young lunatics like Angela were regularly evicted from their illegally occupied apartments; now and then someone tipped off the police that they had seen a light on at night in the attic, now and then the police conducted raids on their own. And as a precaution against the police Angela had long kept in readiness a large canvas bag, into which everything—books, her clock, her bedding and clothes, paintings by friends, and her unfinished dissertation—could be thrown in an instant. Then she would live for a while with a friend while searching for another attic hole: one as yet undiscovered.

That was the way Angela lived, as did most of those who meant anything to her: one lived on the seventh floor, another on the fifth or sixth; some had just one window beneath the slanting garret ceiling, while others had two or even three. But all of them, every one, had at least one window that looked out onto the Berlin Wall and beyond. They gazed day after day at the real orange fleck of WEST BERLIN, and because they were higher up, they saw farther than others.

Hundreds of cars with Western plates passed beneath the striped barrier at the checkpoint daily, bearing people who spoke the same language, people of the same nationality, people who nevertheless grew more differentiated every year. Between East and West Berlin there were no public telephone lines, and only the rare letter or package managed to make it just those few blocks.

The orange patch of the forbidden hovered over the West, as if the comrades were tripping over themselves to rewrap a sweet, aromatic tangerine in its peel. Its orange-colored peel, through which we would never bite.

●

Angela was studying philosophy: the jubilant, blood-soaked Marxist kind, it's true, but one couldn't study any other kind. She told me that at least this way she had access to the library, at least she could work on her own, at least she didn't have to spend the years enthusiastically constructing blossoming Ostberlin.

Every day, equipped with her special pass, she penetrated into the university; every day in the lobby she spat lightly under her breath as she passed by the enormous quotation from Lenin chiseled into marble, which said, PHILOSOPHY TEACHES US HOW TO THINK, BUT MARXISM TEACHES US HOW TO LIVE; and every day she looked out of her garret, across the roofs of the buildings, at the Wall.

It was a wall like any other: rough and gray and plastered, with barbed wire strung along the top. It was a wall that challenged you at least to touch it; to convince yourself it was real —like the wall of a park or a garden, like the wall of a Garden of Eden filled with glistening tangerines—to convince yourself it existed.

Except that if you touched this wall, the shooting would start. The Wall was shielded by fear of death and the unknown, like the repelling field of a magnet.

This magnetic force field enticed Angela. Angela did not seek death on the Wall, the West did not lure her, the glistening tangerines of West Berlin did not call out to her for peeling: Angela did not want to live anywhere else. But the Berlin Wall, with its force field, permeated Angela's entire life; it formed and changed her. Angela had learned how to live with the Wall—in the end, perhaps, even coming to need it, the way a reservoir requires a dam. Behind East Berlin's impenetrable human dam Angela gathered creative force just as a river collects its waters above a weir, forming a deep and mighty lake.

Angela wrote poems in German . . . poems I didn't understand, but I knew they were magnificent and just and wise. They were poems about anguish and bondage, about freedom and walls, about the unfettered sky filled with stars that revolved in great circles above the world—of which she saw more than anyone else because she was higher up.

Angela sensed the walls around her, she fondled them. She sought out the connecting beams, embrasures, and joints in the walls. She groped around for the knowledge that pervaded her entire life.

·

On the eastern side of the Berlin Wall there had arisen a whole brotherhood of Wall worshipers, a brotherhood of attic-dwelling girls and boys, men and women, firmly cemented together by the repelling force of the orange fleck. The members of this brotherhood helped one another; they put each other up when they had just been thrown out of their garrets; they slept with one another, tenderly and amicably; they recited one another's poems; some painted pictures and hung them up on the others' walls.

And so one apartment came to resemble the next; in each of them hung pictures inspired by the Berlin Wall. A friend of Angela's painted them: the world cut in half. A road winds through open fields, suddenly and absurdly blocked by a senseless barricade. A red-and-white-striped barricade: a cylindrical piece of pipe or log, encircled by two intertwined serpents, guarding the gates of paradise. Angela's friend painted worm-eaten apples and the unbroken skins of tangerines. The orange-colored fleck of WEST BERLIN.

·

There was shooting by the Wall. Rarely at people, since very few would-be fugitives were still that foolish. But now and then some stray East German cat would fail to read the warning signs, walk up to the Wall, and rub its soft coat against the rough surface. Then the whole neighborhood would roar with machine-gun fire. The attic-dwellers just sighed and cringed a little: again.

Above the Wall circled only flocks of pigeons of undeclared citizenship—and their wings fluttered their way into Angela's poems. Wings in the shape of freedom. Freedom in the shape of flight.

●

When I was there for the first time, the acacias were blooming on Angela's street. The clusters of blossoms shone through the yellowish luminosity of the slanting evening sunlight—and the scent of acacia blossoms flowed down like honey into the millions of grains of dust that sparkled in the atmosphere, settling in our bronchial tubes, making the air undulate, and falling on pedestrians' heads and intoxicating them.

We watched it from Angela's window. The setting of the sun had already cast a shadow in front of the Wall, and we knew that its other side was now tinted orange like that blotch. We knew that on that evil, other, orange-colored face of the Berlin Wall, intoxicated by that same scent of acacias, people were painting flowers, words of protest, and doves of peace . . . and we longed to paint, on our own Wall, at least one spray of acacia.

That, I believe, was in 1982: the twentieth anniversary of the Wall's construction stirred up a great commotion among the West Berliners, while almost no one spoke of it in the East. I was preparing to get out soon—to get out of Czechoslovakia, to go far away, for good—to head for the orange flecks of Yugoslavia, Austria, America. I didn't know a thing about the world, but my hands were itching to peel its secrets like tangerines and bite into them. I was preparing for the orange blotches, lands where the sun set later than it did here. Or earlier.

I took Angela by the hand and told her all about it. I knew that she couldn't go with me. I knew that the East Germans were far worse than even our authorities when it came to traveling; that year after year Angela spent whole days in unbelievable lines to get visas for Hungary, Romania, and Bulgaria; that they would never allow her to go anywhere else; that the entire rest of the world would remain for her nothing but a splotch of orange.

I was preparing to leave at the time and I said: "Angela, I'll find someone for you in the West, you can get married or I don't know. First I'll get out, and the minute I get my head above water, then I'll . . ."

Angela said: "Do you think I couldn't get out of the country? I've got friends in the West, you know, I know how to get out of here, it's just that . . ."

The narrow barred window of the garret pointed toward the northwest, a beam of sunlight illuminated millions of grains of Berlin dust, and the shadow of the Wall crept farther and farther into the East, licking at the heels of passersby.

"I won't go," Angela said, and it sounded as if I didn't understand a thing. I can still remember that bitterness in my throat—the bitterness that crept down deep inside of me—and it's never left me.

·

We understood each other about seventy percent of the time —with an Anglo-German, Czech-Russian grab bag of words that cropped up in the course of each sentence as the most likely means to mutual comprehension. Whenever one of us was speaking, the other would frown with concentration and say guiltily: "*Co? Was?* What?" A long series of these "whats" was always picking away at the connections. We knew that we could have understood one another deeply, to the last drop, if not for the language barrier, which we therefore resolved to destroy.

In order to destroy this barrier, we went to bed together. And we touched each other: at first clumsily, timidly, because touch burned and so much damage could be done. After that it got better all the time. I held Angela's body in my arms, a woman's body just like my own—and it was like feeling myself, the understanding entering me through my hands. The late spring sun tinged the flower on Angela's windowsill with a reddish glow, the intoxicating scent flowed thickly from the acacia blossoms like honey—and the venom from their roots poisoned the earth. The two halves of the world still existed, but the bitterness of the barriers dissolved within us: better and better all the time. And afterward, when we were both breathing hard and had forgotten about speech, it was like a private victory for the two of us. Or more precisely, for the one of us.

Then I leaped out of bed as if bitten by a snake: "Jesus Christ, Angela, what are we, some kind of lesbians?" Angela put her hand through to my crotch from behind and tenderly, as if playing with herself, pulled me back: "Don't worry. We're not lesbians!"

•

I came to Berlin two or three times; Angela wrote me in Prague and always let me know whenever she changed addresses. She wrote in that Anglo-German mix, of which I could understand about seventy percent. I held these letters up to the light, felt them, sniffed them . . . and from them I could sense Angela's supple hands, the aroma of her sweat, and the restraining dam within her. The orange-colored fleck of WEST BERLIN.

Then the letters stopped coming. I went to Berlin. I looked for her at her last address and at all the old ones. Angela was nowhere to be found. And I didn't run into a single member of the brotherhood of the Wall, even though I wandered for hours through the attics of East Berlin. I haven't found out what happened to them, and I probably never will. Maybe they were arrested and locked up; maybe they got wise, grew up, and moved away; perhaps the brotherhood fell apart. In any case, I was sure of one thing: Angela was still in Berlin. East Berlin.

She had never crossed that Wall; she had never wished to cross it. She remained in front of the Wall, on its gray side, and I knew for sure that she was getting stronger all the time: that she was like a river pouring against a dam, gathering depth and force.

•

So now (even though the Berlin Wall has long since been destroyed, chunks of it sold to tourists for ten marks apiece, the world unexpectedly a better place), I dedicate this book to them: To the brotherhood of the Wall. To the ones who stayed.

1

"This year I'm finally going to file for a travel visa," I said to Standa.

"You didn't file last year."

"Last year, no. They probably wouldn't have given me one anyway. We talked about that a year ago, remember?"

"They say this year it's even harder."

"They say the same crap every year."

"And so you think this year they'll give you one? Just like that?"

"I'll have to get a doctor's note, saying that I need to go to Yugoslavia for health reasons. That I've got a screw loose, or something like that. I'll ask my uncle, he'll know who I can pay off to do it. And how much. You know I'm no good at these things."

"Yes, I know. But why all of a sudden, peanut? Yugoslavia? Don't you realize I don't have enough vacation time to stand with you in those lines at the passport office—or even to go with you? Even if they gave me a visa."

"I know that. You've never gone anywhere with me."

"You know I haven't got the time. I haven't got the money either, I've got—"

"—two kids to support."

"I've got two kids to support. That's the way it's always been, peanut. You're living with an old divorced guy with two kids to support."

"Well, so I'll go without you. I'll take care of everything without you—and I'll go without you . . . finally . . . to see the world. I'm going to make sure I get that visa this year."

"Why all of a sudden? You're not trying to get rid of me by going to Yugoslavia, are you? You're not planning on *staying* there, are you, peanut?"

I raised myself up onto my elbows on Standa's enormous, bare mattress on the floor (on which we'd been screwing around for two years, because we didn't have the means to buy so much as a chair), ran my finger over the lower margin of his manly whiskers, which pricked like clipped copper wire (because I knew that this would tick him off), and said, looking him in the eye from up close, "That, Stáník, is precisely what I'm planning to do."

Standa's face twitched, first with irritation, as his puffy mustache tickled his nose, then with surprise: with the kind of disbelief we experience when something we have long feared in silence really materializes after all. And then he said, offhandedly, as if nothing had happened, as if he could dispel the whole thing with a show of good cheer: "You're not serious, of course, peanut."

"But I am serious."

"But it's so sudden."

"I've been thinking about it for a long time."

"But you haven't said a word about it until now."

"But I have. Don't you remember how we said what fun it would be for both of us to go traveling around Italy. To ride around in a gondola in Venice. To go swimming in Naples . . . How we would see all of Leonardo's original paintings and Michelangelo's sculptures—you really don't remember? Or how we would have a farm somewhere in Texas, raise horses, and you would rope them with a lasso. You really don't remember how we planned all of that . . . ?"

"Planned! How the hell could you think we planned something like that?! We were *dreaming* about that, peanut! That was just a *game!*"

"I thought maybe we were planning it."

"Did you really think I was going to take off with you to some godforsaken backwater to raise nags? Did you, Jituš? Have you gone completely out of your mind? Again?"

"No, Stáník, no I haven't," I said soothingly, because after two years I knew full well where these confrontations of Standa's realism and my antirealism led. (Perhaps we had only been dreaming, like children, about those other things—love and a life together and the future—but I didn't want to think about that.) I ran my hand under the down quilt. That still worked. The little bundles of muscle on his stomach stood out beneath my fingers—and I knew again that he was my man, my protector, my guardian angel. Standa was frowning. I pushed the quilt up from below and gave him a good, long kiss on his manhood. That worked even better.

Then I said cruelly: "If they give me a visa, I'm going to stay over there, angel. Whether you go with me or not. I just can't live in this hellhole anymore."

Standa's sex-tinged smile faded on his lips. "Do you really mean to leave me, peanut?" And suddenly he was mine again, my Standa, Stáníček, the little boy undone by his own mistakes and misjudgments, a medley of screwups from which I was always supposed to extricate him. Simply because I was with him. Simply because I wasn't capable at the moment of imagining being with someone else.

I stood up and walked across the thick green carpet of Standa's studio apartment to the window. It was on the very outskirts of Prague, and tall fences of corrugated sheet metal shielded narrow pedestrian walkways from the construction sites. The housing developments of Prague were sprouting and spreading before our very eyes. Like tumors, they devoured the land, stealing it from the fields, forests, and meadows. In the fields covered with the first thin dusting of snow sat the rooks, blacker than black, that migrated here every November, and the halfheartedly blue sky reflected from their wings. Through the resonant corrugated metal of one of the fences could be heard a bus, that rare herald we had spent over two years desperately awaiting at the stop whenever we wanted to get downtown. You could hear it conquering puddles and potholes and sloughs—every bend I knew so well—and when I rested my hand on the windowpane I could feel it make the earth shudder.

Standa had told me a thousand times that I shouldn't show myself off naked in front of that curtainless window. But of course I didn't give a shit about that. I bent down a little in order to look to the west, where the sky was already turning orange. My breast pressed against the window and that touch cooled like the caress of water. The west was orange because the sun set there.

It was Saturday evening; half the weekend was already down the tubes. And I would have been glad to tell him about the orange-colored spot of WEST BERLIN, but I didn't know how.

Standa came over to the window and pressed up against me from behind. He rubbed the skin on my breast in order to warm it up. In a voice that didn't suit him at all he whispered in my ear: "This is an incredibly stupid thing to do. What is it you plan to do there, peanut? What if you can't handle it out in the world? What if I lose y—" He choked and corrected himself. "What if you get lost in that big world out there? Then you'll be sorry, till the end of your days you'll be sorry that you were so reckless." Recklessness was not one of Standa's vices. At least that's what he thought.

"You're talking like a book. Like the newspaper. As if you'd fallen for all that propaganda, too. Because if I don't do it, then I'll just go on stewing in my own juices *here*, for a *change*. And until I'm old and gray, until the day I die, I'll regret that I didn't have the guts to get my butt out of this country. Don't you understand that a person has to live *somewhere*? Either I live here, or I live there. You've got to decide."

"But you were *born* here . . ."

With his free hand Standa covered my hand, the one I had pressed against the windowpane. The sun now glanced into the studio at an angle, making visible the omnipresent brownish dust (dried-out clay raised, even in late fall, by windy vortices from the denuded construction sites and ploughed-bare fields) and rendering our hands translucent. Against the window in that light my fingers were slight, delicate and rosy, like a nest of baby mice unearthed beneath the plough. Standa's hand was illuminated around its rough nails, and its calluses and bumps stood out, as if in proof that Standa was a hardworking man.

We were starting to get goose bumps as we stood there naked—and I moved my left hand across the sill right up against the window, into the few cubic millimeters warmed by the sun. My right hand was pinned between the cold windowpane and Standa's hot, loving hand. It was like those two worlds: the cool, distant, evening world out there beyond the window and a person right here, a person who desires you. In that instant it struck me that to the end of my life I would be resisting the temptation to remain in that warmth—protected—while with my hand I would reach out, touching those other worlds: cool and pitiless, orange and alluring. That was the way it would be for me until the day I died. For me and a million others.

The earth is blue like an orange, said the French poet Paul Eluard.

The orange sun played in fleeting reflections over Standa's handsome masculine face with its stiff captain's whiskers. My head inclined, I looked into his eyes from up close.

"Peanut, it's cold here. We'll catch a chill."

I nodded. And a flock of black rooks of indeterminate citizenship landed, scattering across the damp and puddled clay and the remains of the first snow that had melted into rusty-brown blotches like continents. The rooks cawed with their throats strained forward. Their wings shone blue with the reflection of the distant, round world. Yes, the world was round for them, because they had probably flown around it. For me the world was still flat.

●

"It's the same with the world as it was with that can left over from the American war rations," I philosophized. "The one your father found in the cellar. Almost forty years old. You can't know if the food's gone bad until you open it. In the end it turned out there was perfectly good mutton inside."

"Why does it have to be *now*, peanut? Why not last year? Why don't you put it off until next year, say? Maybe in a year or two I could . . . Why does it have to be precisely now, for Chrissake, that you get it into your head to . . . ?"

"Last year I wasn't ready for it. But I thought about it."

"And now you want me to believe that all of a sudden you're . . . ready?"

"Yes, I'm ready now. It's like when you left Ilona. You told me how it came over you: how you always loved her, but that she got on your nerves more and more—and nothing happened, nothing, all the time nothing, until one day it all fell apart and you could leave. Well, it's something like that for me now."

"What does Ilona have to do with emigration?"

"You emigrated from her. You escaped. And you can't just simply go back."

"I don't want to . . . but I could."

"You could. But you'd have to compromise yourself in a big way. And it would never be the same again. Exactly as if you had returned to Czechoslovakia from emigration. Exactly."

"Why are you bringing Ilona into this, huh? Ilona means so little to me now that I can just chat with her normally. Every time I go to pick up Pet'ulka we sit down and have a cup of coffee and she tells me how he's been behaving all week."

"Yes, I know."

"Or is it . . . Maybe you're getting all sulky on me because you think that—"

"Oh, please!"

"So what's your problem with her?"

"I haven't got any problem with her. You're the one with her two kids."

"You could've had a kid with me, too. I can't help it if you gave it up."

I gave a start, but just a little one, because Standa didn't even have a clue. It seems men have no idea that in every woman there remains a small scar from every child she decides not to have. It's as if somewhere inside, somewhere you can't even see, you cut out a little piece of yourself. The scars remain in there and reproach you, and trying to hush them up with talk of what a cruel world it is only works after a little while. My scar was barely a couple of months old.

"Perhaps not all your admirers want to bear your child, angel," I remarked. "Perhaps two children is your limit. And what's more . . . if you recall . . . you sure didn't say anything to me about keeping it; in fact, you kept bitching about how you had two kids to support. Maybe you didn't want to have a child with me at all; after all, it wouldn't be any new thing for you."

"Maybe I didn't, peanut, or maybe I did. I was just a little afraid that I could see myself marrying you or something . . . because you're so sweet. These whole two years I haven't even wanted to be unfaithful."

"But you were."

"Yeah—but I explained that to you. That I wasn't . . . we weren't as together then as we are now. Men are probably different about that, peanut, and I—"

"It really doesn't matter."

Standa reached under the quilt and with that familiar, *familiar* movement he pulled me toward him. As the nipples on my breasts danced before his eyes, he caught them with his lips. That worked, too . . . it was mutual. I gave a little sigh and ran my hand down his manly, muscled body. "Standa," I exhaled like a perfect specimen of a girlfriend, and I snuggled up under him. There was sweetness and longing and surrender in this, but very little, so very little of the untamed excitement remained, perhaps because this was already our third fall together. Perhaps because I knew him so *damned well.*

My heart was like a hammer pounding away in both of us at the same time—and it was terrifically pleasurable. Coupled with him I could not imagine that I would ever be with anyone else, that I had ever *been* with anyone else. Standa was not my first man, and I was far from his first woman, but when we were together it seemed like it should be that way all the time.

Or perhaps it seemed that way only to me: only to me, because Standa had already been so terrifically together like that with someone before. Maybe I just didn't understand it all yet, maybe I hadn't grown up that much yet. Perhaps I wasn't jealous of Ilona only because I had no idea what it had been like . . . between them.

Sex was terribly important between us, it had to work in order for the whole thing to work, because beyond that there weren't many things we could do together. We could talk on and on about the same things—about the apartment, about faraway places and karate, about love and the two kids that had to be supported. Sex was enormously important between us, because in that sector of the world where it had been our fate to be born there was already very little left for us to discover, and we were still young.

I pull him closer to me, arching my whole body up against his. And in the dark velvet tunnel I savor his bliss with my bliss. He is gentle, careful; he knows that everything is messed up inside after the abortion; he knows that it hurts sometimes. But I plunge all of him into me, I wrap him in myself like clematis wrapped in paper. I snuggle under him like a good girlfriend. I know every curve of his body, every little hair. I know the secret places, from which precise and infallible wires of pleasure run deep inside him, so that I can make him whimper and sigh, make him mine . . . It has worked like this for more than two years. I draw him in with a rising tide of slow waves and I know exactly the moment when he will close his eyes and squeeze my head between his hands.

"It's so beautiful with you, peanut!"

"Does it feel good inside me, Stáník? Do you like visiting inside me?"

"It's smooth, like honey."

"It's you who is sweet. It seems like I could stay like this forever. Forever, you know?"

"I'd like to die this way. But without losing this feeling. That's how I'd like to die!"

I bit his shoulder. The neighbors, turned off their television and we automatically lowered our voices. The paper-thin walls of the building teach you to control yourself in a hurry. At least they had taught us.

As the time began to approach I panted quietly and apologetically in his ear: "We have to be careful! These are bad days again, you know."

The pleasure was growing. A white star was burning deep in my belly. I bit his shoulder again. I knew that this worked for both of us at the same time. I could feel the enormous, glorious pain inside, but the scar still hadn't healed completely. Standa's hammer was pounding away at it faster and faster. "You've got to be careful!" I yelled in desperation.

"What if we had a baby? What if that's exactly what you need?" Standa forced out between his teeth.

"You've got to be *careful!*"

The visitor was instantaneously transformed into a venomous cobra. Standa could hurt me just like that; he *wanted* to hurt me and I had to clench my teeth, everything hurt so much inside. I tried to push him away: "Do you understand me! Be careful!" Standa held me harder, and even through the fog of coupling I started to feel like a whore, like a vulnerable marble surface beneath a vandal's defacing diamond. I dug my heels into his groin and, using all my strength, managed to free myself. I could smell my scent coming from him and from me . . . Neither of us said a word for some time—and two pairs of hate-filled eyes met for an instant across Standa's broad bed.

"You wanted to get me in trouble on purpose," I exhaled finally.

"Don't be afraid of me, I'll be good, let me in," Standa muttered, and I crawled away from him on the bed as if he were a poison-filled syringe.

"Do you want me to kiss it?" I asked perfidiously.

"Don't pull away from me! Are we living together or not? Have

I ever said I didn't want to have a kid with you? I'm completely crazy about you, understand; and we've gotten so wonderfully used to each other! And now you want to leave me . . . all of a sudden?! Wait, hold still, will you!"

"Standa, if something happens, I'm not supposed to have more than one abortion in a year! I can't risk any more fuckups! Do you want to get me in trouble? Do you want to ruin everything for me?"

Standa dug his nails into my sides: the hard, short, grooved nails of those working hands. Those hands that had two kids to support. They extracted a trace of blood. I hissed and pulled myself free again.

"I'll give it a great big kiss. A *huge* kiss. Do you want me to?"

"But I want to be inside you. I want to *be* with you, I want to stay with you, Jitka, don't you understand?"

"Then go with me—if you want! And don't make problems for me, Standa, *please!*"

"I'm not going anywhere. I'm used to it here. I'm too old for that!" Standa blurted out—and as his cock went soft I was less and less afraid of him.

"Look, we'll just say this: we'll be together until I leave. And then—then we'll write. We'll always write . . . I'll definitely write you," I promised. And it already sounded idiotic.

"I know," Standa sneered. " 'I'll write you. I really *will.*' I've heard that so many times, peanut, are you going to do it to me too now? Jitka, *I love you*, don't you understand? I don't want to find anyone else. We're so beautifully used to one another . . ."

"I'm surprised you've never said it to me like that before."

"Because we never needed to! Because now, when I'm about to lose you, I'm so incredibly aware of it! How much we need each other. How much I need you!"

"Standa, you're carrying on like a fallen nun. After all, you were together with Ilona for such a long time."

"Because I thought it was love."

"But it wasn't."

"It wasn't. But you're it! And now all of a sudden you're running off, my princess is sick of it all, she says! Do you know what a pain it is—to find oneself a decent woman? In this hellhole?"

"I'm going to have to find a man for myself, too. In time."

"And then you'll find out just how lucky we were, you and me. I've had an awful lot of women, peanut, an *awful* lot—and only two of them were worth anything: Ilona and you!"

"And I've had an *awful* lot of men, too!"

"Tell me about it, baby! Until I took you under my wing, you didn't know which end was up. But you're a quick study."

"I'll find another man, and you'll find another woman. After all, that's the way it always is in life. And this, what we have . . . what we had between us—we'll remember it until the day we die. That's the way it always is, and don't tell me it's not."

"You've got no idea, peanut, absolutely no idea, what it is to look for someone new. You're young, maybe it will be easier for you. But me—I'm already twenty-nine! I'm already so damned dried up, so *dried up*, peanut, sapped, and you were the last one I wanted to try to get it together with. You've never really broken up with anyone. You don't know what it's like. But me—I split up with so many girls. When I split up with Ilona I thought I'd never love anyone ever again. Because it gets harder each time: you haven't found that out yet, peanut. I thought I would never *feel like that* again. But you broke through. And even so, it wasn't right away. If I split up with you, now, then I just don't know anymore."

"That's a load of crap, Standa."

We talked until it was pitch-black out; only long, anemic beams of light from the windows of the opposite apartment units reached us, projecting our monstrous shadows on the wall. Standa and I debated. We whispered. We begged. We shouted. The neighbors had already turned the TV back on, so we had no reason to control ourselves.

And Standa kissed me all over my body, long, windswept kisses. He kissed me on the neck and on the breasts and behind the knee. He kissed my groin and begged: "Let me in, please let me in, into your beautiful honey-sweet pussy! I'll be good, I'll be good! I promise I won't screw up! I promise!"

"Go buy yourself a rubber!"

"Hey now, peanut! Come on, let me in for a little visit. I need you so badly. I want you so much!"

Gradually I gave in. I let him get between my knees and opened the gate for him. But now I didn't trust him anymore; the pounding pleasure deep inside me had an aftertaste of arsenic. As soon as he began breathing hard I kicked him away.

"But, peanut," Standa twittered. "Come on, let me in!"

"No, no more," I answered firmly. "But I'll kiss it for you!"

And Standa rolled over on his back, with his manhood raised toward the ceiling—so that the band of light from the opposite building projected its enormous, throbbing shadow. Suddenly I felt passionately sorry for him. Standa clutched a pillow and bit into it. I knew he felt like sobbing: it was always that way when he lost at something. And then, through the pillow, he murmured resignedly, as if he had now reconciled himself to everything, as if he had finally understood everything, as if he were trying to drain his horn of plenty to the very last drop:

"All right, then, blow me!"

2

It was some time around then that the dream appeared in its true form: substantial, truthful, and clumsily undreamlike, like someone coming to step on your throat every night.

It was just one dream, in essence, although it wasn't always the same. It was a whole series of nightmares that surfaced and submerged and melted away in concert with my sleep—but they terrified me with the same, universal hand. Despite the dream's variety and inventiveness, a common denominator could be derived. As if each night I was reading one or two or three chapters from a single enchanted book, all of them communicating something to me.

I suppose the whole thing had its origin somewhere in childhood . . . the time when my feet had not yet touched the earth, the time when the globe was me and I was the globe: the globe of the belly that gave birth to me. The dream must have accompanied me from the time when my mother placed her hand on her swollen mysterious belly and felt with her own insides that primary animal law, that the earth is round because it gives birth to us.

It was an intrusive and ubiquitous dream, and only the animal warmth of an embrace could save you from it.

It was *the* dream.

The dream that ever and always without cessation brought it home to you that you were a speck in the universe. An utterly meaningless, hobbling clown in the circus that, God knows why, is called Earth.

It had been clear since November, but still the manner of parting caught us by surprise. The truck squealed, pulled over to the shoulder—and from his hiding place behind the concrete divider bounced Standa, in order to embrace me one last time. His hair smelled of April showers and I could feel the safety of his hands when, like twin bowls, like a cuirass, they cupped those absurd protrusions of the female body. I had known for a long time that this was my man, the one I trusted—and yet I had never before felt so strongly the sweetness of his embrace as now, when it had to be for the last time. I knew that Standa did not carry within himself my longing for the forbidden hemispheres of the globe, while I was already cultivating within myself the enormous sensual space where I would store that whole world. Once I had traveled across it. Once I had come to know it. Once I had stuffed it into my memory as a kangaroo stuffs her baby into her pouch. And because the driver of the truck that would carry me off into the distance was already losing his patience, gunning the motor and even creeping forward bit by bit, I raised one finger of my left hand, turned it to point at myself (to make it clear that we didn't both want a ride), and said in universal pseudo-German, "*Ein Moment, bitte,*" while with the fingers of my right hand I felt the raised muscles on Standa's stomach, narrow ridges hard as leather, warm as a glowing stove top. Standa was giving off warmth. He had always given off warmth. And because only a little of Standa's warmth was left to me, there grew inside me that cold empty space that would remain when his hot, hard hands were gone—and I knew that I would have to fill that space, compensate with the great unknown world into which I was striding at that very moment. That empty space was already torturing me with memories: of childhood; of Standa, whom I was kissing; of abandoned plans and of hopes. This sadness did not want to leave me and I understood that it was good that way. So I gave a deep sigh, in order to hide it far down inside, and uttered that stupidest of all sentences: "Do you know that I love you, Stáník?" And Standa whispered: "You know I do, peanut, I love you too!" And it wasn't such a stupid goodbye after all. The driver stepped on the gas again and, really, what a vulgar display: the poor guy stops for a hitchhiker, then on top of it he has to wait until she's done necking with some other character. The tips of my nipples were pressing against the inside of my bra and Standa obviously had a pressing problem elsewhere. "You're taking all of this away with you!" he said reproachfully. I pushed up against him and felt with my lap the last allotted tactile sensations. We continued to hold on with our hands, our fingers, our fingertips—and finally all there was left to do was blow him a kiss through the open cab door of the Scania, smile absently at the driver, and stare into the rearview mirror for a time, until Stáník's figure shrank to a single solitary vertex of infinity that would accompany me on the long road.

It was ugly out, so the highway seemed grayer than ever, and
the little woods and thickets, the villages in the valleys, and the
fields with red deer did not emerge from the gray mist. All you
could see was the high wire fence that was supposedly intended
to keep animals from running across the highway.

In some language or other the driver complained about the
sun, how it wasn't shining for us. I nodded. And I watched my
homeland disappearing past the wide windshield of the truck. My
homeland, to which I would never, never be allowed to return.

And so it seemed a little unfair to me that my last vision of
this landscape should have to be so gray. After all, my country
ought to have offered me a proper farewell. The sun should have
been shining, the birds singing, the meadows glowing green . . .
My country should have said farewell to me with fair sunny
weather. The same kind of fair sunny weather Standa and I had
created for ourselves in private, so that we would think fondly
of one another afterward. When I was gone. But the highway,
which I had actually known from happier days, threw a monkey
wrench in my plan, projecting grayness on the microfilm behind
the retina.

Fortunately, however, I knew from every large truck I had
ever climbed into that you could look only forward, never backward, so that the landscape that escaped to the rear of the truck
could never be seen again, even if you stuck your head out the
window. This is the law of long-distance travel: you move and
live only forward, you can never look back. So that now—even
as we hurtled into the insipid gray—I was convinced that the

body of the rig, like the zipper of an enormous sleeping bag, was opening in the landscape a flowered grandeur, soaked with golden sunlight.

I knew that I would never again see my homeland, that flowered grandeur, even if I stuck my head out the window. But that it would remain within me.

We were approaching the Komarno border crossing and I realized that I was crying only when my eternally smiling driver handed me a neatly folded tissue.

●

He was taking me as far as Belgrade. The trip took three days and three nights. I remember the nervousness at the border; the scowling, corpulent woman who stripped me down to my panties; the dutiful customs officer who held the metal tubes of my backpack up to the light to see if I had perhaps hidden Western currency or friends' addresses in them. Of course I had absolutely nothing. Not even the ten marks that Standa had lovingly bartered for on the black market and instructed me to conceal in a tube of toothpaste.

I remember flat Hungary, the vast open stretches with windbreaks and lone horses. I remember the painful inner fear, the loneliness, and the impatience to get out of there once and for all. And also the red-blue-and-white-striped barrier at the Yugoslavian border, whose three colors danced before my eyes like the three serpents guarding the gates of paradise when the customs officer raised them for us. He did this entirely without formalities, only wagging his finger at the driver, a gesture meant to demonstrate his vicarious pleasure at the driver's good fortune.

Of course I slept with the trucker. His name was Ramazan, from Turkey. We lay down together in the truck that very first night: it was not a means of payment for the ride or for the pistachio nuts he fed me. There was not even the fear that he would dump me in some wilderness in the middle of the night. I simply couldn't have cared less, and Standa was somewhere far away.

I had told myself before leaving that I wanted to remain faithful to my Standa for a little while: at least two or three months. But there really was no reason; Standa and I had made no promises to each other, and Standa didn't even know about my vow of faithfulness. It had been for self-protection, for myself alone. After all, Standa had etched himself into me over the years, and as long as no one erased him he would go on protecting me. At least for a while, I would have him there on my skin. Then all of that went out the window that very first day. And I had no choice but to change my outlook on things.

Ramazan had magnificent Turkish genitals, incredibly hard and supple, like a deerskin glove, and a clear consciousness of his size reflected in an enticing restraint. In the morning he let drop a remark about how he didn't know what was wrong with me. "You fuck very well," he said in English. "But no pleasure, no pleasure . . ." But it was just because it depressed me that first night how he was exorcising from my body the last molecules of Standa's love for me, the remnants of his warmth and protection. It felt damned good when Ramazan gently filled me with his circumcised gift, but that was exactly why I felt like crying when it occurred to me that he was flushing out two years, almost three years of my love, expunging Standa from me—making of me once again the clean, white, blank, *erased* sheet of paper that I had not been for years and did not want to be. I began to hate him: for taking my Standa from me, for carrying him off to Turkey somewhere, for destroying the precise dimensions of the little tunnel I had once known, and for impersonating Standa. I was mad at Ramazan because his foreign smell was replacing Standa's smell, because he was rubbing out my memories—and because even if he had known that, he probably wouldn't have given a shit.

And I guess I had started to cry. Because Ramazan winked at me and handed me a neatly folded paper tissue.

By the second night all this had ceased to trouble me, and after the third night (spent in a fenced-in rest stop near Belgrade, where we went together to the men's shower to wash, and where enterprising Yugoslavian hookers circulated around the parking lot until dawn, pounding intrusively on our windows), Standa had already receded somewhere into the past and held no power over me whatsoever.

My dream drew me from Belgrade to the West, to the Austrian border, where they caught me trying to cross, locked me up for two days among the whores in the Maribor jail, and then wanted to "deport" me: they used their official authority to force me to buy a ticket to Hungary and then led me under police escort as far as the train. But when I succeeded in getting off the train in Belgrade, my dream reached even fuller fruition than I had expected. Namely, it threw me into the path of an English sailor who by sheer coincidence was driving a truck along the tedious highway from Belgrade to Zagreb. Tricolored tattooed snakes undulated on his arms, he offered me a swig of Scotch from a bottle, he spoke authentic British English to me at a charitably slow pace—and the equatorial ring in his ear intimated that he had some knowledge of the world's roundness. I put myself in his hands.

"To Austria? You sure?" he said doubtfully. "That means crossing the mountains. And if I'm not mistaken," he added, "they keep a keen eye out over there. Why not give Italy a go? By way of Trieste. I'll take you there."

And so the Brit stopped for me a couple of kilometers from the border. It was a moonless night—actually it was raining a little and the moon was hidden behind thick clouds. Fortunately, the curtain of mist reflected the lights of the border post, making it possible for me to see at least a little. The Brit pointed all this out and explained where I could walk and where it was best to crawl. "You go along the side of this hill above the border post," he said, pointing. "And once you see its lights beneath you, you're on the Italian side. The border makes a little bend here. Beyond the border post, turn to the left, toward the south. About a kilometer beyond the border there's a sort of little Italian hotel, and I'll be waiting for you in the parking lot. To make sure you've made it all right."

Everything happened just as he had said. It was not even difficult. True, I had to climb through some barbed wire, but this was not the barbed wire of an international border but low barbed-wire fences erected by the villagers around their fields to keep the goats out. I passed above the border post, precisely as the sailor had prophesied, and when I found myself once again on asphalt, there were aluminum bottle caps pounded into it. I knew that I was saved.

And when the Brit and I had found each other again, the dream was no longer leading me: the world had become the dream. The sailor really was parked where he had promised. He climbed down from the cab and walked around it. He had been waiting for me and this moved me: I had someone waiting for me in the West. And not just anybody: a British sailor! I crept out of the thorns and brambles: with scratched legs, punctured body, and an enormous duffel bag on my back. "*I am here!*" I shouted in English. Then I cast my pack off into the dirt and threw myself around his neck. The equatorial ring swung before my eye. Through it, as if through an opera glass, I gazed into forbidden worlds. I hung on to the Brit and embraced him, so that he had no choice but to make the tricolored serpents on his arms ripple and keep pulling me closer. He stroked my back in the most proper way and waited with patient English composure until I had finished blubbering. Suddenly it occurred to me that this was an adventure for him, too. "So welcome!" he said to me. "You must come visit England sometime!"

With blubbered-out eyes I gaped through the glittering equatorial ring into the worlds that had opened before me. Deep down inside, within me, beneath the tears, there lurked a blissful, euphoric joy. The British sailor and I hugged—and suddenly, out of nowhere, the whole world lay at my feet. My smelly feet.

6

Later I unrolled my sleeping bag in a ditch. So that in the morning, when the first rays of the sun awoke me, they tickled my nose with their pleasant orange color. And suddenly it all came back to me.

7

Italy was freedom. Euphoric, boundless, and somewhat threatening. Fairly unpleasant, actually.

It was also a sea so blue that it colored my dreams. That one dream, actually. The sand was freedom, as were the sea and the air; all that space was such an enormous freedom to run amok in that you finally found yourself huddled by a cornerstone, not knowing which way to turn. I was unbearably, disgustingly free, and poor as a church mouse.

Western Europe was nothing at all like the orange blotch the comrades had tried to convince us it was. It teemed with the stultifying power of goods and colors and people. The earth was a wagonload of seas and continents and languages and fear and men and everything. Everything I should have seen before, but which now took me by surprise.

In Venice there were black gondolas and a blinding sun that glanced off everything—the surface of the water, the masts, the paving stones of the squares, and the wings of the pigeons—directly into your eyes. Venice was the Grand Canal, along which boats traveled like buses: boats so expensive that I had to sneak on without paying. Venice was architecture that gave you a crick in the neck, swarthy Italians who tried to pick you up, and flexible drinking straws with blue-and-white stripes. The Piazza San Marco with its sharply toothed walls, on which flocks of tourists fed flocks of pigeons golden corn. Venice was the tabs from cans of beer and soda trodden into the heat-melted asphalt. Venice was freedom and helplessness and hunger, timid glances at trash baskets buzzing with wasps, into which oversated tourists tossed half-eaten pizzas.

Venice was a turmoil of moods, confusion and heat and euphoria and panicked fear of the unknown: fear that you simply could not squeeze your way into this gigantic, wide world, that you would lose your way here and become lost.

·

And Venice was also wooden pilings driven into the bottom of the sea, on which sat albatrosses.

The guy who (in miserable English) informed me that they were albatrosses was named Dana and was a student from Kurdistan.

"Kurdistan?" I said, amazed. "That's somewhere in Africa?"

"It's not in Africa," Dana said, laughing with the superior air of a world traveler. "It is a small land between Iran and Iraq, you see?"

"I've never heard of it."

With a long, dark finger Dana drew it for me in the sand of the Lido.

"So you're an Arab?"

Dana seized me by the throat. "I am no Arab!" he shouted, nearly strangling me. "I am a Kurd. And if you ever say again that I am an Arab I will kill you!"

"Oh," I said and disengaged myself. This round new world was overflowing with mysteries. And the scent of wisteria, compact and intoxicating, so much so that when Dana took me home it was all a bit like a dream again. They lived in a really nice apartment on the Lido: three Kurds, all friends, and a thickly painted girl from England who offered me two fingers with a certain reserve, stating her name as Betsy.

"Hi, Betsy," I said. "My name is Jitka."

"I-ka?" she ventured with that same reserve.

"Okay, Ika it is."

One of the friends, his name was As, went out to buy some white wine: to celebrate my escape from the Communists. They said it was a great thing, breaking free like that—and that I was too good for the East. They were glad I was here. "All of us admire you terribly much," the Kurd As said to me in studied English. Consequently, I became a hero. But what next? The Kurd Dana ran down to the kiosk to buy a pineapple for us all —enormous and alluring, scaly and chilled. Even through the skin it smelled like the last one I had eaten: in Prague, at Christmas, when I was five. After that they had supposedly stopped importing them.

We cut up our pineapple and each of us took a slice. Except Betsy, who said that pineapple scratched her throat.

"You need some lubrication," the Kurd As put in.

And as we got steadily drunk in honor of my newly acquired freedom, it ceased to matter on whose lap I or the English girl sat. The world was small and light, like a balloon filled with hydrogen, and I used my claws to hold on to my little round slice of Earth by the edges, gazing boldly into its sweet mysteries.

•

Dear Dana and I suddenly found ourselves alone in bed, and it was hard to say where exactly our clothes had ended up along the way. Dana's kiss tasted of the exotic, of wine and pineapple: it was the prescribed, inevitable kiss with which decent boys begin. Then he stretched out my legs and shoved it into me. I screamed. "Sorry," he said. "I'll be more careful." And he was. He sounded the depths quite courteously. "I'm going to cut myself a piece of pineapple," he said to me afterward.

"Dana, are you back already?" I asked the unkempt shadow in the doorway.

"No. My name is not Dana. My name is As."

"Where is Dana?"

"I don't know. Probably with Betsy."

"Oh," I said, and As closed the door behind him. His kiss tasted almost like Dana's, also exotic, but a little different. "Go get yourself a slice of pineapple," I said to him afterward.

I don't remember the name of the next shadow. I pulled him silently into the room and knew beforehand that his kiss would have yet another, slightly different taste.

•

In the morning Betsy called England. She did this twice a week. "You absolutely can't imagine how terribly expensive it is in Italy!" she squawked affectedly. We were all sponging off Betsy's filthy rich daddy.

•

And so we lived quite peacefully there—three Kurds, myself, and an English girl—and the world, round and supple as a kitten, purred obligingly at our feet.

●

Later I packed my worldly possessions into my faded backpack, and my uplifted thumb cut me a path northward across incandescent summertime Italy. Toward a legal, organized freedom that led somewhere. Toward a freedom where God only knew if there remained some small place for me.

9

Freedom begins with a double cordon of cops and a door with thick bars, behind which they lock us all up. *Flüchtlingslager Traiskirchen bei Wien*. Suddenly we are all *Flüchtlinge*, refugees. *Nummer. Name. Passport*. Trochees. *Tschechoslowakei*. Not very cleverly, I wipe the fingerprint ink all over my face with my hands. Czechs, Poles, Hungarians, Iranians. Finally we are all registered. To which country do we wish to go? We all have to see the doctor for an examination. Form an orderly line in front of the office door. One line for men One line for women Children stay with your mothers. Does everyone here understand Polish? The Afghani interpreter will be here next Thursday. *Deutsch? Verstehen?* Do you understand? *Nichts?* Does everyone here understand Polish? Each of you has the right to medical treatment free of charge. You must tell us now whether you have had any of the following illnesses: viral hepatitis, gonorrhea, syphilis . . . Whoever requires it will receive medical attention. Does everyone here understand Polish? Anyone who is ill, please step out of the line.

The isolation ward is a long corridor on the third floor of the building. A row of green doors opening into the rooms. Apparently, the camp was once a military garrison. Now it is ours. But it still smells of the army: greasy mess tins, coarse camp soap, the menthol toothpaste that we are also issued, the horse blankets that slip from between our hands. *Zimmer achtundneunzig*, says the Austrian. *Schlafen*. You will sleep there. *Verstehen?*

Two million languages, sweat, bustle, and children crying. Windows without bars open out onto the courtyard, conveying the

last trembling scents of linden blossoms. Smell is the only sense
I am able to employ in the slightest. Several pairs of curious eyes
peer out the open door of the room. You're new. Where from?
What language do you speak? Where is it you want to go, what
do you want, what sort of person are you? But none of that is
important. The main thing, my dear girl, is that you don't steal.

●

I crawl into the top bunk by the window and form a nest from
the two sheets and military blanket. The sheets are fresh, laundered, enormously clean-smelling. I concentrate on making my
bed. Sleep is indispensable and extremely important. In a minute
I know the names of the others and where they are headed. Now
we are all refugees. The room smells of wet plaster, a flaking
canvas painted by moisture seeping down from the upper corners:
we are on the top floor, it probably leaks in from the roof. The
water has decorated the ceiling and top halves of the walls with
golden maps. The charts according to which Columbus guided
his boats. Maps of lands, seas, and oceans. Maps of the continents
that we will someday reach.

●

And, of course, the dream returns the instant I am without a
man, a dream borne from a childhood so distant that it brings
back the pain of sprouting wings. A dream from the illustrated
book of Saint-Exupéry; a dream in which you touch and smell
and live with your very own self—and at the same time you see
yourself as a tiny orange fleck on a blue planet, beyond which
sets a violet star.

●

At five-thirty in the morning an Austrian cop bangs on the
door: "Breakfast! Brea-a-akfa-a-ast! *Essen! Essen!*" The two gay
Hungarian girls on the bunk below me come untwined and start
blabbering. Or at least the Czech who keeps endlessly reminding

us that he is the head of a family calls it blabbering because he cannot understand it. We have no language in common with the Hungarian girls.

And so from the very first days, we are divided into *us* and *them*. We are the Czechs. The Slovaks, to a lesser degree. The Poles, marginally. We are *us* inasmuch as we can understand one another, even though the most important thing is that I am myself. All the others, of course, are riffraff.

"*Essen!*" The cop pounds on the door and throws it wide open. One of us gets up, rubs the sleep from his eyes, and goes for rolls and weak coffee. The coffee goes into an enormous water can that has to last all day.

The corridor comes alive with bustle. A couple of hungry souls go dashing off to breakfast. The low sun already gilds stripes of dust in the corridor. A stripe creeps from each window. Families scold their children and hunt for them in the corridor. An Afghan woman breaks pieces off a roll. She has on a sari with a veil up to her nose, and she keeps turning away, toward the wall, in order to stick another little chunk into her mouth beneath the veil. From above the veil peer her exhausted chestnut eyes. I try English on her. She doesn't understand—or is she just not reacting? Perhaps they too have divided everyone into *us* and *them*? I want to know. But there is no one to ask. Even though, of course, everyone knows everything.

I play dice with some Poles. Tadeusz makes the dice out of pieces of bread: he rolls them for a long time between his fingers, spitting in his palms, then flattens the sides on the edge of the table and uses a match to impress into them the one two three four five six. Then he dries them in the sun that slants beneath the window. Tadek always knows what to do with himself: he has learned this in prison. He was one of the first members of Solidarity. That sounds interesting. I sleep with him. Tadek has a wife and two children at home. He is headed to Canada, they will come after him. He will have to work hard in order to pay their way from Poland. But hopefully in a couple of years . . .

"Doesn't it bother you to be unfaithful?"
"Not at all. Does it bother you?"
"I've got no one to be faithful to."
"At least there's no one for you to miss."
(No one to miss. No one to miss, Standa?)

·

In the dream a stark-naked fool steps on the Earth and it spins like a centrifuge, with dizzying speed, dizzying, more and more dizzying. I press myself against Tadek. I don't want to see the fool smash his face in.

·

Breakfast, *essen, essen,* a couple of unfinished sentences, euphoria, joylessness, and fear. Why are we stuck here? Because we are waiting for a hearing. A hearing? Yes, from the Austrians, sure, they call you for your hearing after all this has driven you nuts, but before anybody tells you what you should say to them. They ask you what country you want to go to and what reasons you had for leaving. Reasons? Reasons, of course, after all it's basically a request for asylum. Asylum . . . sure. In those papers they gave you to sign there's also an application for Austrian asylum. You can't stay in Austria without it.

Noon, chow time, pink meal tickets and a line in the mess hall, where Middle Eastern–looking cutthroats throw everything in a mess tin and cover it with gravy. Food is enormously important, because it helps a person to think. Eat a lot of fish. It's good for you, they say. Perhaps the poor things died for our sake. We chow down in the mess hall, choking on the bones. How can they possibly serve carp in gravy, the Czechs fume. Now, now, young man, this isn't home, is it? You're in the sticks now. We dig away with our spoons, seated around rickety tables. We are not allowed to take food upstairs. We would be feeding the roaches. And they are fat enough already.

•

The stark-naked fool attempts to drag a bunch of balloons across a Nevada desert filled with cacti. The balloons break and are as pained as pierced souls. The cacti grow together into an impenetrable wall, gray, tall, and senseless, which from now on separates me and Standa. And white, hot bodies try to press through the barbed wire. While from their stabbing wounds, lacerations, and gunshot wounds pour streams of green despair.

•

Smells, dust, longing, filth, and euphoria. Why are there so many of us on this earth? It is crammed full of people with the same destiny, stepping on one another, fighting, shouting one another down, each one desperately alone.

•

EVERY FRIDAY BETWEEN EIGHT AND NINE IN THE MORN-ING, IT IS NECESSARY FOR EVERY REFUGEE TO TAKE A BATH, declares the announcement written in seven languages on the wall of the isolation ward. Some of us need it. A trip under escort across the yard. One line for men One line for women Children stay with your mothers. A mass of stenches, steam, children yelling. The overwhelming, omnipresent smell of coarse soap. An Afghan woman raising her sari and bathing her ankles under the shower. Children of every color and type splashing one another. Hygiene is enormously important. Because it helps a person not to be a pig.

It is noon on Friday, and those of us who do not have their own soap smell of the officially issued camp soap. The scent of menthol toothpaste wafts from many a mouth. There are an awful lot of us here: us, the uprooted ones.

•

Tadeusz is writing a letter to his wife. One more for the pile that will never be sent. I take the ballpoint pen from his hand

and kiss him: Teach me some Polish! We are playing dice with the other Poles. Someone has smuggled in a bottle of Wodka Wyborowa. The sun lurches drunkenly through our cell. I am writing a letter to Standa, one I will never send. In it I am faithful to him. Total bullshit. Different rules apply here and now, the rules of contact and new acquaintance, the rule of grab whatever you can, the rule that it is good to drive away the dream. The rule that we need one another, because otherwise we are all alone in this big, wide world.

●

There are a million things I don't understand. In the isolation ward I am learning the camp like a foreign language: slowly, falteringly, without a textbook. And it is so damned easy to get things wrong.

●

Beneath the windows of the isolation ward stand those who were released a few days earlier into the free camp, craning their necks and shouting up at us. By means of strings we lower down to them they send up chocolate and cigarettes and Wodka Wyborowa. The camp below smells of freedom. The scent of linden is almost entirely gone by now.

●

And when the lights go out in the evening, the glow of Vienna's lights beyond the window illuminate the water paintings on the plaster ceiling. Those golden brown outlines that—if you forget almost everything you know about geography—remind you of the continents.

Europe.

Asia.

America.

With half-closed eyes I fashion their shapes above me. They are mixed together, confused, just like we are. They are thrown around like cards on a table. Pick a card, any card, don't hes-

itate, any card at all. Will it be the ace of hearts or the old maid?
Any card at all. Any card. Don't hesitate. No *time* to think it
over. And you must take a card!

•

Sleep is enormously important, because you don't have to
think. About the continents on the ceiling. About Europe. Or
America. The Hungarian girls below me are at it again. The Czech
clicks his tongue: Tsk! Tsk! And since my bunk is connected to
theirs, the tall metal bars convey to me the tremblings of their
heavenly love and their tender Hungarian blabberings. I already
know why this bunk has been left for me.

But I also know that I don't actually want to sleep, that the
dream is lurking just behind my eyelids: that it will be here
immediately, the instant I take my eyes off my continents. My
continents, to which I long to travel.

Europe, Asia, America, Africa, Australia, Antarctica. I gaze
at my continents. They might just as easily be clouds, or irises.
What if I thought about irises? Anything would be better than
that dream.

•

America.
Canada.
Australia.
Pick a country to apply to. Supposedly no one else would take
you. You could also stay in Europe, but that doesn't pay these
days. You say you need information? You say you need time?
Well, forget about it, you're buying a pig in a poke. For that matter, why didn't you know before you took off just where you were
headed? Did you think that everyone here was waiting around to
take care of you? Did you think that everyone here loved you?

Didn't you realize that this world existed before you arrived?

•

—So, young man, you've got an uncle in Australia and he wants
you there, well, whaddya know. By all means, go there,

but watch out! These uncles aren't always just dependable old milk-cows, mark my words, these uncles are liable to bleed you dry, my dear boy. Haven't you heard about the Czech guy in America who worked for his darling uncle for a dollar fifty an hour—for eleven years?! A dollar fifty an hour! The average hourly wage in the States is twenty-two dollars and thirty-seven cents, so just watch out, make sure they give you more.

—But that was in America . . .

—Sure, that was in America, but the same thing can happen to you in Australia, young man, do I really have to—

—The hourly wage there is not twenty-two dollars! My aunt wrote me that it's more like five!

—Well, I don't know where your dear old aunt got her—

—I heard it's eighteen.

—You see that, eighteen or twenty-two. If you're working for less, you're getting exploited, mark my words.

—You'll get exploited no matter what.

—I heard that in Canada—

—Forget about Canada! They won't take an unmarried man, don't you know that? Nothing but families with children, if that.

—But didn't they accept that locksmith? My husband says—

—Sure, a locksmith, young lady, a locksmith, maybe. But an unmarried *intellectual* they would never take. Besides, you can easily wait more than a year for Canada. They've got good security, *social security*, understand, so they're scared people will go over there to, say, study or something. Living on that security. You can kiss your Canada goodbye. They've got security over there.

—Supposedly it's even better in Sweden.

—Yes, it's better there, young man, plus they've got cute little whores and dirty Swedish movies, but as soon as you get there they sign you up for Swedish classes, and if you can't get that gibberish into your thick skull, they lock you up.

—That's ridiculous—

—Lock you up, I tell you, they used to cut your hand off for stealing over there. And if you—

—The Swedes haven't been taking anyone for a long time.

—Sure, I'm telling you, they already have a load of émigrés. And those Swedes don't like foreigners much. You'll be an immigrant till the day you die.

—That's what we'd be here, too.

—That's what you'll be everywhere—and they'll never let you forget it, either. Here in Austria, for example—

—Supposedly it's even worse in Switzerland!

—Oh, sure, in Switzerland! You'll never get to Switzerland, young man, even if you cut yourself up into little pieces and mail yourself there. Supposedly they want to maintain the purity of the population, goddamn yodelers. You haven't heard about the guy who lived there peacefully for *five years*, they kept promising him asylum, then, finally, after five years, they sent him off to Prague in handcuffs? The Swiss will—

—They did the same thing to some Poles!

—What they did to our Polish brothers over there doesn't interest me one bit, let them do whatever they want with the Polacks, we're already up to our ears in them here and the whole place stinks of piss. They're doing this to *us*, to Czechs, understand! The minute you set foot in Switzerland you'll never be sure what will happen, till the day you die! And listening to those damned bells of theirs, and all their sacred cows! Don't you know anything: even once you've got asylum it takes twelve years before they'll give you Swiss citizenship. Twelve goddamn years!

—Supposedly it's only four years in America.

—There you are mistaken, young lady, in America it takes seven! They don't pamper you over there, either.

—It's five in America! After all, I know when my own aunt got her citizenship.

—Maybe it *used* to be five, or maybe your dear aunt married into it. Because in America—

—They say in Australia it's only three!

—Forget about Australia! Ferchrissake, you wouldn't even want

to live there, with rabbits and kangaroos and descendants of
those thugs who've been gnawing on cactus over there for two
hundred years. Who would want to live in that godforsaken
armpit of the world. Even the stupid plane ticket costs five
thousand dollars and it takes you three days to fly there!

—My uncle flew there for twelve hundred. The flight took twenty-
nine hours.

—Well, they must have given him a discount. Just so they could
get your dear uncle to come in the first place. And with women,
what a situation . . . Well, would you want to turn your daughter loose over there, madam? There are seventeen times more
men than women. And can you imagine what they do to earn
their daily bread, every last one of them? Sure, when a lady
is ugly as sin—

—I heard there isn't a word of truth to that thing about the
women.

—Well, go see for youself how much young meat you turn up.
I'm telling you, there's nothing over there but thugs and ma-
laria and Christmas in the middle of summer, and skin cancer,
because everybody's always lying around on the beach. You
might just as well stick your head in a kangaroo's pouch and
croak, really, I'm telling you—

—South Africa's the place, that's where we're headed! As soon
as they let us out of isolation. We're applying right away. It
isn't all that hot down there, decent hygiene—most of all, the
blacks don't use the same toilets as you. I'd go to America, but
they say the blacks there are taking over, they've already got
their own newspaper and they want their say in everything.
South Africa's the place! Down there—

—Well, go right ahead and give South Africa a try. But they
haven't been taking anyone for five years. I'm tel—

—My brother got in there two years ago.

—Well, I don't know about your dear brother getting in there,
but it's getting worse and worse every year, every day, every
hour, that I guarantee you! And besides, the population is

eighty-six percent black, eighty-six percent stinking niggers. And those tropical diseases! Those black girls, all nice and ready for you—and they've all got lice. You start up with some black wench and within two days you've got pus dripping out of your thing, this I guarantee you.

—Olda, don't talk like that! Not in front of the children . . .

—I, personally, plan to stay in Austria. It's not far home, to Brno, when I feel like visiting in a few years. Nice temperate climate I'm already used to, we'll somehow learn this German, too. Am I not right, Mařenka? And the kids will get a decent, Catholic education. These Austrians are good at observing religion—start in the crib. I'll stay here, in Austria, with our neighbors. We only emigrated for the sake of the children anyway. And to go dragging them halfway around the globe . . .

—Don't even think about Austria. These chestnuts'll make your life miserable, all right. See, they don't even want us here temporarily, they're just waiting to ship us off to some backwater. When you tell them you want to stay in Austria, they'll make it hell for you. You'll get the lousiest pension house, the most rotten food, dear madam, just to get rid of you. Finally, you'll be lucky if you can make it to Germany. The Austrians won't give you asylum!

—But we want to try it anyway—

—And so what is it you want to do here in Österreich? Pray in the little churches? Listen to the babbling brooks? Yodel along with them, world without end, hallelujah? Or get drunk on half-fermented wine at some idiotic festival? The overwhelming majority of the population here, young man, are quite simply nuts. Just look around at these cops, just look at their bloated Austrian mugs, the way they twirl their billy clubs, the swine. And the way their eyes pop out of their heads every time they get a load of one of our girls' butts. Just make sure to keep them at arm's distance, young lady. That's the only reason they go into the service in the first place, so they can fuck around, after all what's it to—

—Olda . . . the children . . .

—Someone told me they're here as a punishment.

—And does that surprise you? Who else would put up with this place, among these beasts from Arabia, these Gypsies from Romania . . . Who else could take all these Albanian cutthroats and whores from Hungary and Poland or whoknowswhatall stupid trash? Who else could take it but a convicted cop? Who else would put up with this hell, with everybody fighting and beating each other up and twittering godknowswhat stupid gibberish?! And everything's going to hell, to boot. Just yesterday I saw this kind of Gypsy or Iranian or whatever kind of whore, wrapped up in her stinking rags, her tits flying all over the place—

—Olda!

—That's just the kind of trash we have around here. And it comes crawling here from every godforsaken corner of the earth, like cockroaches to stale beer. To us, to Austria! As if this colored scum couldn't just stay back there where it was spawned! They just throw their children over their shoulders and the whole kit and caboodle comes crawling here! As if Austria didn't have enough riffraff as it is. They don't even know how to open their stupid beaks, all they do is crow their heads off in that gibberish of theirs and sleep around and multiply. And believe it or not, what's more, these stupid chestnuts give them asylum! Mark my words, they give it to them . . . if they're from Iran or Afghanistan or whoknowswhat godforsaken Arab shithole. And the good, honest Czech white person they send up shit creek without a paddle. They leave us to grovel around Europe and no one wants us anywhere. It's disgusting!

●

I stagger out of the stifling room like a phantom and go to get some fresh air in the corridor, which smells of summer and lindens just past blossoming. I think secretly of my Kurd Dana. Call him an Arab, Olda. He'll kill you.

I am playing dice with the Pole, Tadeusz. He smiles at me over the table, strokes my hand—and his eyes, with their look of solidarity, of Solidarity, *Solidarność*, wink at me from the cloud of smoke pluming from his densely packed *papierosa*. He teaches me the Polish for "book" and "I like you very much" and "It doesn't matter." "Are you coming over tonight?" I nod and go to shower. There is even a shower in the bathroom, but the faucet on it doesn't work. I wash my body with a long hose connected to the sink tap, previously installed by someone for this purpose. I step in the suds, the smell of laundry soap; I step in the filth from other female bodies, preparing myself to be touched. I wash my underarms, my back, my throat; I splash around, happy as a seal pup. I wash my crotch in the stream of water, and the water voluptuously suggests everything I have planned for that night. In the line of those also longing to wash, two Czech mothers lean together. They watch me sloshing happily, their eyes revealing certain suspicion. One whispers something to the other. I sleep around, they say. So be it.

Then I go to Tadek's, take the ballpoint pen he is again using to put together a letter to his wife. "I'm lonely, Tadek. But I see some new people have moved into your room . . . with kids . . ."

"It doesn't matter. *To nie przeszkadza.*"

Tadek and I sit on his bed, and several newly arrived Polish parents observe us reproachfully. What are these two going to do? Right here in front of the children? As soon as the lights go out I forget everything. I get undressed quickly beside him under the blanket.

The smell of soap, shaving cream, and a strong Polish *papierosa*. Each man smells differently. Each one has a slightly different taste, too, and each one has a different way of chasing the dream away. Nevertheless, each of them chases it away. I open myself to Tadek in the dark. I know that today we have to be quiet, there are children here, there can't be even the slightest squeak of the bed, and this fact transforms longing into passion and passion into ecstasy. It seems to us that we love each other.

.

Breakfast. Coffee. Dice with Tadeusz. He tells me about Solidarity. It sounds like a Russian fable about the Revolution. When will he give it a rest, this Tadeusz, as if the whole world were nothing but *Solidarność*. He carves an indecent portrait of Jaruzelski into the table. Another act of resistance, I think. Lunch. Pink meal tickets. Blue and white meal tickets, too. The white ones are for Moslems and the blue for nursing mothers. Gradually I am beginning to perceive the things around me. First, I see colors. The colors of faces, hair, clothes, meal tickets. The Austrian cook punches the meal tickets with a hole punch. Pink, white, and blue confetti rains onto the mess-hall floor like an illusion of colored wind. A tanned individual dumps an undercooked slice of leg roast into your tin. They have good stuff to cook with, but they don't know what they're doing. Or else they are saving the best for themselves.

.

A couple of unfinished conversations. Dice with Tadeusz. "Dinner! *Essen!*" Pink meal tickets and a hunk of Hungarian sausage. Salad of sliced Chinese cabbage, only slightly rotten, a source of vitamin C. We live like cabbage, greenly, vegetatively. The earth is green, blue, and orange. Mostly blue. Like a tangerine.

.

Why did you leave? Did you have reasons? Reasons? Right, *political* ones, good sound political reasons? Were you oppressed in your homeland? What resistance groups did you belong to? What do you have to show for yourself, hero? Do you have any scars, bullet wounds, burns, marks on your body, an eye patch? Did you have reasons for leaving, hero? Then name them for me:

one two three four. You say you've never thought about it before? Well, it's time you started, hero, because the Austrians will be asking you about it pretty damned soon at your hearing . . .

•

—You say you got out by way of the Yugoslavs? So you seriously think that makes you something special? Get your nice little visa to go to Yugoslavia, arrive by train in Belgrade like a fine gentleman, then take a nice moonlit stroll over the hills into Austria. You say it was raining? But no one will be asking you whether or not you wore holes in your shoes. You took the easy way out—

—The easy way out, oh sure! Maruška and I had so much stuff, all of it in plastic shopping bags, the children are always running off on you, getting scared, crying . . . and you're terribly scared yourself. Don't you know that the Yugoslavs have been shooting at people down there? They even wrote about it in the *Kronenzeitung*—

—Well, I don't know what these chestnuts are writing in the *Kronenzeitung*, I don't understand their gibberish and I have no desire to understand it. *You*, young man, were not shot, otherwise you wouldn't be here, so what do you have to show for yourself? Soiled trousers? Look at those Slovaks who sailed into Vienna on a pleasure cruise with first-class berths—and now they are giving some sob story about how the Communists oppressed them. If you were pissing in your pants along the way, young man, nobody's going to notice it. There are some people here who hijacked an airplane in order to get across the border, and even they didn't get asylum. There are others here . . . right behind us in the *Familienhaus*, there's one guy, a Slovak, he flew a balloon made of crêpe paper over the Danube near Bratislava, the border guards shot through the balloon, he fell to Mother Earth in Austria, broke his face, they gave him *temporary* asylum in three days, and since then not a word, hasn't even got work papers, they say he's gone brain-dead from that fall of his, so you see—

—That's not true, my brother in Vienna said—

—Well, young man, I'm not interested in what your dear brother said in Vienna, I'm telling you what *I* know. And there's another guy here who served on the border, and when he thought he had it all figured out, he crossed a marsh in the Šumava mountains and his buddies shot at him. They shot off a quarter of his left ear and he shat his pants real good and so in Germany they put him in a mental institution where to this day he's filling up his pants with—

—Olda!

—And haven't you heard about that family of crackpots who forded the Mur? Half of them drowned and the two-year-old baby got asylum. How does a little brat like that come by it? I'm telling you: here *I* am finally, the head of a family, and I'm going to look out for myself. Aren't I right, miss? If *I* kick the bucket, who's going to take care of those little ones? My feeble wife? Yes, life for the head of a family is harder than hard in the West . . .

—But the Austrians have to understand: it wasn't at all easy to leave everything behind. I left my old parents . . . We had a summer cottage, with a vegetable garden, that the Standard Farming Cooperative hadn't stolen from us yet . . . After all, we all had to *make a big decision* to leave . . . we were all *oppressed* back there, you couldn't even breathe . . . the Austrians have to understand that it's not easy to take off and leave everything behind—

—And so you think you're a hero. Bullshit! Believe me, these chestnuts don't give a damn. Listen to what *I* left behind over there: my childhood and youth, my old loves, my first wife and two boys, my hopes and my dreams! D'you think these chestnuts care about that? They sit here on their fat asses—and if you don't like it, you should have stayed at home. And they're running a pretty whorehouse here, too, Viennese bastards, don't know how to work themselves, and instead of their honest Czech neighbor they let in Turks and Arabs and Idontknowwhatall sorts of colored half-niggers, the whole lot comes streaming in: why that rabble doesn't just stay in the desert, I'll never understand. Meanwhile a decent person can't get asylum. These Austrians, they only see you through those blinders of theirs: what *reasons* did you have for leaving?

—We had good reasons: we are a Catholic family—

—Well, now, you can always hang it on God Almighty, these chestnuts are damned religious bastards. This is the way it is: there are three kinds of reasons—economic, political, and religious. If you bank on economic grounds, you'll never get asylum, not on your *life*. There was one family here, these Slovak shepherds, from Záhorácko. The Austrian at the hearing says: 'Why did you leave?' 'We-e-ell, you see, Mr. Officer, we wanted to give our chi-i-ildren yogurt every day—an' in rece-e-ent years there hasn't been any yogurt to gi-i-ive them—'

—But that's a perfectly good reason!

—And you know what, young man, the chestnuts didn't buy it. They don't know crap here about what it's like not to be able to give your children a little yogurt. Their shops are overflowing with the stuff.

—But if that was the main reason, what were they supposed to do, lie at the hear—

—Now now now, when were you born? Yesterday? You're in the West now, you've got to lie like a politician, otherwise you'll never get anywhere, not on your life. There are only three types of reasons: economic, religious, and political. You can cross economic reasons right off the list—

—Then we've got great grounds, real ones, not made up. Both of us, my wife and I, had to sign Party applications before we could get employment! We are a Catholic family—

—Well, don't you go bragging about that at the hearing! Party applications! You think the chestnuts are holding their breath for the chance to give asylum to Commie bastards? Did you just land from outer space?

—But as my husband said: we *had* to. And I always say: it's *best* to tell the truth. You have a clear conscience and no one can catch you in a lie. It pays to tell the truth in the free world. After all, that's also why we emigrated, because that ocean of lies all around you there—

—Ha! So the young lady fancies she's in the *free* world! This world is free, all right, but not for us immigrants. You'll see how they tie you down with this freedom, until instead of free-dom you'll be scrubbing the stairs in the *Lagerleitung* with no asylum in sight! Or slogging away for chickenfeed as a *Gas-tarbeiter* for these filthy rich bastards!

—But the salaries are good in Austria . . .

—Good, good you say, that's not saying much, and most impor-tant, they aren't good for you. They'll think twice, boy, before they give any decent *Arbeit* to a *Flüchtling*. There's a lot of bloodsuckers here—and I don't just mean the Austrians. There are Hungarians, Poles, Yugos, even some of those Turkish bastards—and every last one of them wants to bleed you dry! Trust the Czechs least of all: if it's some Pecháček or Horáček or Tajtrlik, run in the opposite direction as fast as your feet will carry you, 'cause they'll have you digging your own grave for life with that kind of *Arbeit*. They've got it all worked out—

—Why did you run away?

—Now see here, take my advice and don't go around asking people about that. These Austrians'll be asking you about that plenty, until you're soft in the head, at all those hearings. Besides, I have nothing to fear. We, dear boy, were dissidents, and I'm going to shout it out right in their faces: Sirs, we were dissidents—and I—

—But real dissidents don't have to go through the camps at all. They get asylum right in Vienna.

—Oh sure, you're talking about the Charterists! Those Chart-erists, as soon as they get here they have everything all set up for them by their comrades who got here before them. Apartments and social security and German courses—and asylum, young man, within three days, so they can start lounging around on that social security and bullshitting right away. They're all just a bunch of thieves.

—Charterists? The ones who signed the Charter '77? You dare to call them thieves? They were the only ones in Czechoslovakia who stood for anything—don't you know how they were hounded? Thrown out of work, school, locked up, how the state made problems for their *children*, even kids in grade school. And you call them thieves?

—Well, apparently you are not a Charterist, inasmuch as you'd be sitting in your pretty little nest in Mother Vienna. So why do you defend them? Go to Vienna to see them for yourself. A gang of scum, they are, all of them.

—I think the ones who stayed are the real heroes.

—Well, the ones who stayed, maybe, but the ones who come here are a bunch of scum! They were cruel to them, you say? Bull! They sweated through a couple of interrogations, and when they applied to emigrate they let them go in a year.

—But that year—

—That year did them no harm. Do you think they didn't have it all planned out? And then they come here straight into the lap of luxury, a nice little apartment with all the conveniences, collecting all sorts of aid. How long are these Austrian bastards going to suck us dry before we get what their darling Charterists get right out of the gate? All I'd give them is a good flogging—

—And just what sort of dissident are *you*?

—Me, young man, me? I was *imprisoned* over there, I sat biting my nails for over five years in a criminal institution, wrongly convicted for political reasons! But when those chestnuts call me in for my interview, I'm going to tell them straight out: Sirs, I—

—Olda, you went to jail for that short delivery.

—Quiet, you! Stupid woman! You don't know what you're talking about! I was a political prisoner and no one can say otherwise!

I was a victim of the regime! And that's exactly what I'll tell them, too, I'll get it through their thick skulls . . .

●

Europe. Asia. America.

Africa. Australia. Antarctica.

My heart is an orphaned blue flake of ice. Is Antarctica still accepting émigrés from Czechoslovakia? Or are they trying to preserve the purity of the population? Sorry, they're only taking polar bears this year . . .

Africa. Asia. America.

Stick your head in a kangaroo's pouch and croak. Pink, white, blue meal tickets. A flood of new fugitives from somewhere, oh, they are all still so laughably foolish. A million languages. Exhausted Afghani eyes. The reproachful eyes of the couple with children in Tadek's room. The sole of a shoe instead of dinner, and cabbage salad. The color of tangerines. Europe. Asia. America. Do you have any relatives there, miss? Tadek and I are playing with dice made from bread. He wants me to go with him to Canada. He's in love with me, he says. Idiot.

●

Marks on the body. Scars. Burns.

Why do you want to be here? Why don't you want to be there? Why don't you just go someplace else?

10

Almost every day for the last couple of years I had awakened this way: frightened out of sleep by an inner distress that is actually always with us in one form or another, but usually doesn't bother us except when in the morning, half asleep, we forget to control it. It is almost as if somewhere inside, in your stomach or in your soul, fifty or so clanging alarm clocks go off without warning. It seems as if something inside you has shattered, burst, that the splintered shards of your soul are stabbing you from within and can't find a way out.

So that everything around your heart is constricted by a strange sorrow. For a moment you almost long to die, to bury your head beneath the covers and forcibly disappear into sleep, into *nothingness*. But a moment later you know it's all right, that you always feel this way, that all you have to do is take a couple of deep breaths, gasping like a boated pike—and in ten minutes, in a quarter of an hour, the fist of terror will release its grip on your heart. It is best to do something. Go for a walk. Run. Shower. But I knew that this time I had to be quiet. Otherwise there would be hell to pay.

Room 7 of the Henhouse was still snoring happily. But outside there was already light, that tart morning light that lifts wisps of steam from the dewy grass, that lingers around the camp from end to end and throws flickering flecks from the acacia foliage high onto our wall.

I was wrapped in my army blanket, because I had of course long since kicked the sheet down around my ankles. I enjoyed the warmth, its embrace; the blanket's coarseness didn't bother me at all. After all, it belonged to the Traiskirchen topography.

I no longer woke up asking myself where I was. I no longer wondered desperately where my legs were, which way my head was pointed, where the door was, the window, the wall, just what ceiling was hanging over me. The coarse touch of the military blanket immediately brought me to reality: I was in the camp at Traiskirchen.

I stretched out my hand to find my watch on the windowsill. In less than a month of residence in Room 7 I had managed to take over the bed by the window. The window let in a draft, true. But at the same time it provided me with the smells of night, and through it I could see the light of the stars and the depths of the universe. Through it I could sense the distant worlds beyond . . . the roundness of the globe that I would one day circumnavigate.

I stretched out my hand to grope for my watch on the broad sill of my own personal window. That warped and cracked wooden board, painted with grayish green lacquer that had of course started to peel long ago, served me as a shelf and occasionally as a table, and I already knew this green paint that rubbed off beneath my fingers and showered all around as perfectly and intimately as if I had never lived anywhere else. I extended my hand carefully, so as not to crumble the paint. The first thing I came upon was an apple core (it was the apple from the previous evening, green and fragrant, the one you had to gobble down in a hurry, otherwise someone else would eat it for you); I brushed across some rustling writing paper, on which for a good week or more I had been trying to compose a letter to my parents; I passed over a couple of barrettes and some rubber bands tangled up with a few hairs from my scalp; I nearly knocked my ballpoint pen down to the floor—and as I barely caught it with a pinch of my fingers I was momentarily horrified by the thought of the sound of the falling pen, a couple of creaks from Marta's bed, and her sleepy, hostile soprano: "So, what is it this time? Can't you let me sleep in peace just *once*?" I couldn't have cared less about Marta's sleep, of course, but who needed to hear her bitching?

Finally I found my watch. I brought it before my eyes silently, so that not even the blanket would rustle, so that the worn, used springs of my bed (underlaid with the doors from the cabinet, which one of my predecessors had torn off, because otherwise it was like sleeping in a sinkhole) wouldn't even consider creaking and disturbing Marta's morning dreams of lovesick Austrian millionaires. It wasn't five-thirty yet, which meant that I would have to lie here on my back, arms at my sides, at least three more hours so as not to antagonize my roommates. My bladder was pressing on me. If I got up then and walked across the room, first my bed would give a loud complaint, then all the half-rotted, creaky floorboards would strike up a concert like five feral cats, the key in the lock would give a loud clack, and the door, of course, would scrape no less loudly. The hinges needed oil.

So I lay on my back, feeling sorry for myself. Like almost every other morning. I knew I wouldn't get back to sleep now, and even if I did, that dream of mine lay waiting for me. It would have given me a headache for half the day. I gently extracted myself from under the itchy blanket and tried to think constructive thoughts. After a while that boulder, whose insufferable weight made it so difficult to breathe, began to dissolve: it was ground into pebbles by a reality that was not so terrible after all. It was not easy, but it was nevertheless constructive. Like digging a well.

I lay on my back and listened to the sounds that interlarded the atmosphere of our room. Some of them came from outside, others had their origin right on the spot. The latter were the hostile, nearby sounds, not necessarily louder or less pleasant than those from outside, but much more annoying because in your naïveté you thought you could do something about them. But of course you couldn't. The sound of Marta's radio, now, at night, relatively quiet: twenty-four hours a day it played sappy Austrian pop that drove me nearly to despair, but Marta needed it in order to live. Now I heard the sighs of sleep, breathing, the soft whistle by which Marta indicated that she was momentarily unaware of the world. Thank God. From the bed by the door, hidden from my sight by a curtain and cabinets, there flowed a series of the gentlest scrapings followed by a throaty rattle that grew louder with each breath. Marta clicked her tongue. And Hanka, by now most likely half-smothered by her Zděneček, tried to turn him over again from his back onto his side. Her whispering voice begged him: "Zděneček, quit snoring! They'll throw you out on me—and what will I do here without you? Zděneček, quit snoring! Please!"

The camp was awakening. From the Albanian women next door could be heard the clanging of alarm clocks, the creaking of beds—then doors banging open and a mob of quarrelsome male and female voices flowing out into the corridor. Or maybe that was just the way they talked. The streaming of water in the washroom could be heard, splashing, quacking, and an argument in Polish. Or maybe that was just the way *they* talked, too. The banging of the restroom doors, two seconds of silence—and then, all the way through two walls, could be heard agonized, heavy sighs, accompanied by the splashing of watery stool. I listened for a moment longer. No one ever flushes. Pigs! Zděneček started snoring in his sleep again. Softly for the time being. Hanka pleaded with him. From Marta's radio the announcer with badly acted enthusiasm wished everyone a good morning and in his somewhat smug Viennese accent announced the songs that were to torment my poor ears. And below my window, a gang of early breakfasters rushed across the camp yard: for weak coffee and a couple of rolls.

Two cops walked along the path beneath my window. I heard the muffled sounds of German and loud, self-satisfied laughter. I figured they had just come from the Hungarian girls. I grimaced mentally. Not that it was any of my business, but the camp was our private little town—and even my mind was beginning to record gossip.

The clatter of mess tins below the window intensified. The rooms of the Henhouse were sending swift envoys in the direction of the Hilton. I heard Hungarian by the front gate, and I knew that the two Hungarian lesbians who had roomed with me in isolation were rushing to breakfast with a big bag for rolls and a plastic pail, arms linked.

I knew that the morning rush to the mess hall resembled a running race combined with a wrestling match. They unlocked the kitchen gate at five-thirty, by which time the Albanians and the Romanians would have been rattling the bars for a good half hour, sleepily ribbing one another, sluggishly fighting among themselves, so that they would be the first to breakfast, after which they could rush off to stand outside the camp gate in the hope of getting picked up for day labor. Then heaps of others fell drowsily out of their dens, gaining speed on the run across the yard—and finally pushing, shoving, and haggling before the kitchen gate, apparently every man for himself, only forming short-lived treaties, clans, and alliances against the others so that each and every single one of them might be the very first one into the kitchen. So if you didn't know your way around these politics, you might as well linger peacefully in bed and go for the remains of the coffee around seven. Down there you would just end up standing stock-still in that line an hour, for some mysterious reason always remaining at its end.

Zděneček started snoring again, followed by Marta's clucking and Hanka's pleas. I listened to the buzzing from the washroom. It was getting louder now. Another pig that didn't know how to flush after himself. And I knew that in twenty minutes or half an hour all these sounds would again cease, that the early birds would go skipping off to their *Plätze*: to clean, cook, sweep, make beds, wash dishes, or serve guests. I knew that from now on only the occasional alarm clock would ring, that everyone who had somewhere to go would stagger out of the camp—and the rest of us, who didn't have to get up, who had no *Arbeit*, would keep right on snoring here until nine or ten or noon and then rise to the lazy life of the do-nothings. Breakfast, lunch, dinner, and a couple of unfinished conversations. Gossip and washing dirty laundry. Letter writing, the eternal radio, getting tan in the tall grass. Hurriedly constructed quasi friendships, intolerance, ar-

guments with whoever happened to be there at the moment—
and whispered slander about those who had just dashed off somewhere. But I guess that's just about normal when seven assorted
women try to endure one another's company in one tiny room.

●

This particular morning really wasn't so bad. Baška, the Polish
woman (who usually crashed into everything within reach at
about five in the morning, loudly cursing on top of it), had flitted
off to Vienna for the weekend with her husband-to-be, Madam
Anežka had flown with her daughter to Canada—and Mira was
sleeping around somewhere at the Hilton again.

So four of us remained. Martička who, having been abandoned
by her 147th camp Tomcat, required for her happiness the sound
of the radio all night but nevertheless clicked her tongue peevishly
at any loud breath drawn by any of the rest of us. Hanka and
her beloved Zdeněk. And, of course, my humble self.

Not that we liked each other, but at the time the conditions
under which we existed were fairly important to us. There were
seven rooms in the Henhouse, and ours stank least of all. We
washed our floors. We washed ourselves. We periodically threw
our moldy dinner leftovers into the refrigerator. We communi-
cated, did not resort to physical violence, and stole from one
another only in moderation. We slept tolerably well at night,
because no one dared make a sound. Before she left for Canada,
Madam Anežka had put everything in the room in its place. She
had also put her daughter in her place: she forbade her to work
at all, since it would have ruined her nails. Strained her angelic
face. Washing dishes or cleaning would have parched her lily-
white hands. Not to mention that physical labor would have
spoiled the perfect proportions of her figure. Madam Anežka
silenced us at night, partly out of fear for her daughter's morals
and partly because, if Marunka didn't get her beauty sleep, bags
would form under her eyes! Madam Anežka intended to deliver
her daughter to Canada in mint condition. Fresh as a rose. Like

parsley from the garden. Her Marunka was such a beauty! Look at those ankles! Those wrists! Those alabaster hands! Just look at those cheeks, like peaches, and her almond-shaped eyes! Marunka didn't even blink at her dear mother's praises. She sat in a chair with her hands in her lap, her almond-shaped eyes staring dully into the distance. She was waiting for her mother to shut up. Madam Anežka would work her fingers to the bone, wash dishes, cook, and iron, in order to buy Maruška something pretty. Madam Anežka was looking out for her daughter. She wanted her to be a model in Canada: everyone would be running after Maruška over there!

This we could believe. Everyone was already running after her right here in the camp. We compassionately managed not to let it slip to Anežka that, while she was serving meals for a miserable couple of schillings in Baden, her darling daughter had for some time already been wrestling with a certain Persian in the tall grass in the corner of the camp wall.

Besides, none of this really piqued anyone's interest. There was much better dirt making the rounds of the camp.

Baška the Pole had always been pretty virtuous—for a Polish girl, the Czech girls asserted. She just made a little racket in the morning, then disappeared for work, and we didn't see much of her. For chitchat she visited the Polish girls' room, for sex she went to Vienna. When Baška spoke, she spoke about *pieniądze*: money. Like that tidal-wave majority of other Poles, she had come to Austria to rake in some cash, and she made no secret of it: she caressed her savings account passbook, showed us the numbers in it. She had applied for Austrian asylum, true, she had to, but she had no use for it. This would only make it harder for her to return home to Poland. She had applied for asylum only in order to remain in the camp: she lived there for free, ate for free, drank for free. Her clothes—stolen—she bought for next to nothing from the Romanians, and at the moment she was working as a chambermaid in a pretty little pension—for thirty schillings an hour, imagine! She counted her little schillings and carried them to the bank. She followed the international currency exchange and every day without fail recalculated her nest egg in zloty. She cried when the rate of exchange appeared disadvantageous to her. She beamed when accelerating inflation in Poland sucked more and more zloty out of each schilling. Just hold out another two or three years—and upon her return she would be a millionaire in Poland! It was only we Czechs who could not return to our homeland; more likely than not the police would have just locked us up and taken the whole bundle for themselves. But not Baška the Pole, oh no! She was going to return to Gniezno, pay her taxes like a good citizen—and she would still be a millionaire until the day she died! Just hold out another two or three years in Austria!

Mira was a unique case, actually a rather sad case—so sad that constantly telling stories about her soon ceased to amuse us. She was always over at the Hilton anyway, and none of us could have cared less whose bedsprings were creaking over there. As long as it wasn't in Room 7. And so our little room was quite peaceful.

Although it happened that way primarily thanks to Anežka. Anežka had lived here since time immemorial: a good eight months, at least. She'd had Room 7 so completely under her control that her influence had created an entirely different environment. With her schoolteacherly diction Madam Anežka announced to Mira that it was simply unheard of to parade two or three of her "friends" before our very eyes every week: if things continued like this, Anežka would have to have a talk with the camp commandant. Not that she wished to meddle in Miss Mira's personal affairs, but it was *such* an ill-mannered example for her daughter Maruška! And you, miss, will certainly understand a *mother's* responsibility! (Behind her mother's back Maruška raised a pair of almond-shaped eyes to heaven, thus making herself more tolerable to us.) Madam Anežka put Zděnek and Hanka off screwing altogether, issued directives to Baška as to when she was allowed to get up in the morning, told me that by ten-thirty there had to be absolute dark in the room—and turned off our dear Miss Marta's radio. This last deed earned her my eternal gratitude.

Madam Anežka wrote out weekly schedules for bringing food from the mess hall and stuck them up on the door frame. She also wrote out schedules for sweeping, mopping, and washing. We mocked her for this, but in the end we submitted, every last one of us. To pour water on the wood floors and wipe it up with a rag and some suds was decidedly more pleasant than Anežka's upbraidings. She also divided our refrigerator into compartments, supposedly so that none of us might mistakenly take someone else's provisions. Madam Anežka's provisions in particular. At that moment, in each of seven individual compartments in the refrigerator were ensconced a slice of salami from dinner, some leftover camp cuisine in a pan, and a stick of butter or margarine. It was a bit like a madhouse. But it worked.

Not to mention that Madam Anežka had gone to a store and bought a toilet seat, nice and white and padded, so that neither she nor Marunka might get an infection "down there" from all those "unhygienic people." In fact, Marunka did get an infection down there, and she bragged about it to us all—some kind of crotch itch, which the Persian claimed couldn't possibly be the clap and which, in any case, she couldn't have gotten from him. As a result Marunka, who didn't dare see the doctor about her condition, acquired the habit of sitting uneasily on a chair while inconspicuously rubbing one alabaster thigh against the other. Marunka was really quite simple. Her mother, who could not for the love of God break her of this rubbing habit, insisted that Marunka was so, so anxious because she just couldn't wait to get to Canada.

That toilet seat had stuck with us, hanging right next to the door. Originally, of course, we had not been permitted to use it, especially since the time Anežka had scraped an inexplicable brownish ring off it. Immediately before her departure Madam Anežka decided to sell the seat to us at a discount, but we didn't want to buy it. Then she tried to pack it into her suitcase, but it was not very portable and so Anežka stood over her incompletely closed zipper, meditating under her breath: "Well, it's a shame to leave it here, it's served us well, it would make a good souvenir. But still, we probably won't need it, they probably have different toilets in Canada anyway. And my Marunka . . . my Marunka will make enough money for a new one with her modeling." And with a sigh she hoisted it back onto its nail.

That toilet seat now served us all. We also had a communal rubber hose, about a meter long, with a cut in one end so that it fit easily over the washroom tap. There were no showers in the washroom.

And that's how we lived there: seven women and girls and our lovers. And in these most forced conditions of intimacy we all shared our fears of the unknown, our secret dreams, our lovers, our distant pasts and longings for the future. But above all we shared that one padded toilet seat, which each of us placed every day over the naked porcelain, and that rubber hose with one end cut, with which each of us washed her body, cleansing herself of the dirt, the dust, the sedimentations, before nights of screwing before one another. We cleansed ourselves before fulfilling the longings of our far too lonely nights—and we shared that hose with one another just as we shared that boulder on our chests each morning, that dream about which we spoke little, but which each of us alike tried as often as possible to chase away.

11

"And most of all, you shouldn't talk to anyone here," Nad'a
had said to me the moment the Austrian cop led me in that
morning from isolation. (Nad'a, who just a month earlier had
been staying in Room 7, in this very bunk in which I now slept.)
"You're new, you don't know anything. So don't talk to anyone
here."

I closed the door behind me with my knee and threw an armful
of clothes on the bed, apparently the only one that was still free.
It was right beside the door, bare, worn through, and not particularly clean. "I'm Jitka," I said tentatively.

"Call me Nad'a," she said. "There's a bunch of other girls
here, but they're not around today, they all went off to their
sweatshops, you know? If you want, I'll help you get work, it's
not hard, you just got to know how to go about it. I'll be needing
some kind of new grind myself, now that my rupees have run
out. Not that I'm in hock yet, but I've got about nine schillings
left to burn, and you can't even get a pack of cigs for that." She
gave her empty wallet a demonstrative bend and stuffed it back
into her cleavage. "You're still pretty dazed by all this, aren't
you? But you'll catch on, the main thing is to give up lying around,
or you'll get lazy. Almost everybody's got to work here, really
work their asses off, see, because these Austrians in the camp
don't give you much. Some toothpaste that eats away at your
gums. That bar of soap you're holding, don't even unwrap it,
just throw it away. Most of all, please, don't wash with it, you'll
stink like those Albanian shrews, and who needs that. I'll tell
you what kind of laundry detergent to buy, once you've got a

few shingles—that's what we call schillings around here, see. Your
head'll still be swimming from all this. Speak any German?
Where're you headed? That is, where do you *want* to be headed,
I should ask, because no one's guaranteeing you'll get there, as
you probably know . . . I wanted to go to Canada, then to the
U.S. They turned me away everywhere, they made me fill out
applications, wait around, file appeals, and they still didn't take
me. Almost two years I've been sitting on my butt here, and now,
finally, Australia came through, so I'm flying in a couple of weeks
. . . Have you registered with one of the organizations? Sure, you
don't even know a thing about that yet. Wait, I'll show you.
Where is it that you want to go? And before you do it, think
damned well about which refugee organization you want to go to.
There's the Charity, IRC, AFCR, that's the American Fund for
Czechoslovak Refugees; there's a really nice girl in their office,
but they're the slowest of them all, if you're trying to get somewhere. They're so slow that the geniuses who want to stay in the
camp apply to them just to keep up appearances. Yeah, and over
at the Charity, they pretend to be all religious, and the IRC deals
mostly with Jews. Make the rounds, have a good look at them all
until you get the picture. Don't be as stupid as I was. On account
of Míša—she's that girl I told you about in their office—I let
myself get signed up with that AFCR, yeah, and it took them two
years before they got me anywhere. And two years in this camp,
girl, that can make anybody nuts . . . And there's a whole lot of
things here you don't even know you can take advantage of, since
no one ever tells you about them. You can get sanitary napkins
for free, for example, up there at the infirmary, in the medical
building. At least they *call* it an infirmary, but there's just one
nurse on duty and there's no one there except a couple of stitched-
up wounded guys they're too cheap to send to a real hospital.
But never mind, you'll see. Throw your stuff into the wardrobe
and as soon as you get some schillings, buy yourself a lock. But
don't waste your money on one of these little baby ones." She
shook the doors of one of the wardrobes. "Get yourself a decent

one, a good hard one, so the stealing bitches around here can't open it with a pair of nail scissors. These locks are symbolic, anyway. Since there're pros in this camp who'll pinch the butt you're sitting on before you know what's happened. Get used to the idea that people steal from you here. They'll steal everything you've got. It's a criminal tribe, a shameless lot, every one of them. You'll get used to it. Know anyone here?"

"Five minutes ago I—"

"I'm not asking about that. I'm thinking relatives. An aunt. An uncle. Ex-lovers. No one here? In Vienna? No one at all?"

I shook my head.

"Well, then, you're kind of screwed, because you've got no one to take care of things for you. And nowhere to go to relax when you've had it up to here with the camp. But at least no one's going to drag you around Vienna, like my aunt did to me, making you look like a fool; that's an up side, girl. These Czechs who've been here awhile, they're already so sick of us they don't even give you advice, they just make fun of you. I found everything out for myself, so you'll find out for *your*self. But I'm telling you: don't trust anyone trying to pull the wool over your eyes; you've got ears, you've got eyes, look around yourself. Main thing is that you're healthy—are you healthy? Then make sure you don't get sick, because no one wants to sit in that waiting room at the doctor's with all those creatures with their ears lopped off and crying babies and those poor slobs who come in carrying their oozing peckers in their hands. The doctor, he's here every day from one to three, in the medical building; it's such a bloody morgue, I'll show you later. But if you've really got something, they'll take care of you, there're international inspections, and they can't afford to let anyone drop dead on them. The doctor, he's always in rut, and if you've got a splinter in your heel, it's 'Take off your bra, please, miss'—but you can at least go to him for vitamins, although even that sometimes requires a striptease. I had my teeth fixed by that butcher of a dentist, he's over there too, in the medical building, in the other wing. This I don't recommend, girl, he screwed it up good, and now all my fillings are falling out." She gave a tug at her upper jaw. "Main thing is, make sure you don't let the local male population get under your skirt. Then you're in for it! But you saw that in isolation, or didn't you?"

It wasn't completely clear what I was supposed to have seen in isolation, but I figured that I had seen it. Or felt it. Beneath the army blanket.

I nodded eagerly.

"You see!" Nad'a said, beaming. "You saw it in isolation, the whole stinking mess. As soon as a girl's on her own, they're all trying to paw her. And you're not ugly either, so these gentlemen will give you hell. Wear a burlap sack, tie your hair back with a stupid band, just like you've got it now, because it doesn't flatter you at all. And most of all: *don't talk to anyone!* Otherwise they'll eat you alive."

"What about you? Didn't they eat you alive? I don't see you dressed in a burlap sack. Or—"

Nad'a guffawed and clapped me across the back with her massive hand. "The main thing is don't talk to anyone here, that's what I mean. Parties, good times—see that you don't get too hammered, 'cause no one here's going to take care of you. Things happen here, girl! Don't even think about dropping by the Hilton—that's that big building over there, that's where all the single guys live. You go to have a nice chat with a friend, but before you make it out to the front steps, a band of Albanians or Romanians or godknowswhat shoves your head under a sheet and rapes you."

"Does that really happen here?"

"You bet your ass it does, did you just fall from the moon or something? Things happen here, girl! Legionnaires and murderers and cutthroats, and you can't always tell by looking at them. If anyone asks you anything, just say 'I don't know, never heard of it, I don't understand, I am a total idiot!'—Hold on, I'll help you put those things of yours in the wardrobe!" Nad'a headed across the room with a full armload of my stuff. "But wipe it out first. It's dusty, it stinks in here. And most of all don't trust anybody. Don't leave anything in the cabinet of any value at all. They'll steal anything here, even your pants from the line right in front of the building." She pointed out the window toward a cord stretched between two acacias. "I had a pair of freshly washed jeans disappear from right over there just last week, and I was checking on them every three minutes from the window. If you've got any money—"

"I don't."

"But if you do, just keep your mouth shut about it. Keep it nice and warm in your bra. Take it to the bank, there's a good bank here in Traiskirchen; the people who come crying to you about how they have absolutely nothing, they have thousands there. Don't lend anyone anything! If it isn't cemented in or chained down, it'll be gone by the day after tomorrow. And try not to walk around the camp alone. At least while you're still new. The esteemed gentlemen from the Hilton have got us all sussed out, and when a new girl turns up, they try to find out what you're made of right away. If you don't talk to anyone here they'll all leave you alone eventually."

Nad'a bent over my new bed, lifted the mattress with both hands, leaned it against her knee, and skillfully tucked the sheet under. "Of course, as the newcomer you've got the worst sack, but you'll move as soon as someone leaves. To a better bed. This one hasn't got any support and the springs are all *ausgeleiert*, from everybody screwing around on it. It's like a hammock." She sat down in the middle of it and demonstrated for me. "If you see a cabinet door you can rip off, rip it off and put it under the mattress for support . . . All the others already have supports. And watch out you don't catch something off this bed. I've pulled shards of glass out of mattresses before; they're all pissed on, barfed on, and ten thousand fuckers have made birthday presents to each other of four generations of clap on them. These spots aren't from blood, don't worry about them, they're actually from red wine; when Božena left the day before yesterday we gave her a farewell party. In a couple of weeks I'm flying off to Sydney, so you can get my bed, if you keep your wits about you. But the main thing is, don't talk to anyone!"

Nad'a finished making my camp bunk. "Want to go for a walk? I've got nothing to do right now anyway. I'll show you around the camp. And outside the camp too—because remember, you shouldn't stay between these four walls too long, a girl can go nuts in no time in here. Go out a lot, work, go to Vienna. Or else you'll crack, like so many before you. Here's a key to the room, hold on to it, Božena left it, wear it around your neck or something, and don't give it to anyone. The door has to be locked at all times, otherwise they'll steal the furniture and everything. Don't tell anyone you live in *Zimmer Nummer sieben*, they'll sniff you out anyway.

Nad'a led me through the camp as far as the gate with its striped barrier and cop on duty, and in her lively presence those rain-streaked buildings—the Henhouse, where I lived; the Hilton, where I should never, ever go—no longer seemed threatening. Not in the least. Instead, they seemed secretive, mysterious, like a wizard's castle, like an ancient book bound in leather that I longed to leaf through before it was destroyed by gnawing mice. As if the camp were a decrepit, rotting chest left by my great-grandmother, possibly containing treasure. The camp lay before me, mysterious, unprobed, and slightly dangerous, dangerous in the way of old mine shafts, which one was also not supposed to enter. The camp lay in the summer sun like a challenge, a gift, an invitation, like a machine designed to round off the edges of those worlds which we all would one day reach. Everything inside me tingled with happiness (or was it sadness?), delight (or was it fear?): the camp was right here, and I had the possibility of knowing it, of living in it.

(I *had* to live in it. I had no choice.)

Nad'a, incomprehensibly friendly after all the horrors she had survived here, led me by the elbow out through the camp gate. Past the dully staring cop in his lookout, at whom she nodded. Past the striped barrier that looked like the door to the world. Past men of every possible nationality who, in jeans, shorts, lousy suits, or Turkish trousers, waited along the camp fence, leaning against it and talking, squatting or sitting cross-legged, and devoured the passing women with their eyes. But Nad'a did not turn her head at their *Entschuldigen*s or *Bitte*s, their whistles or tongue clicks. She stared rigidly ahead and led me away with rapid steps. "Come on, come on, hurry, we'll go around here, to the left, there, by that high wall. We can walk all the way around, so you can see how big the camp is. Don't pay any attention to those guys, they're here for day labor, waiting for work. The Austrians drive by here every morning looking for workers. So every morning, starting at five, the guys are standing out there. Girls too, sometimes, but I don't recommend it. Otherwise your gentlemen colleagues will whistle at you non-stop, until your ears fall off—and then, these Austrians think we're all just pretty little whores, you'll see what I mean. I hitch-hiked back from Vienna a couple of times, and you should have seen it, girl. *Ich fahre nach Baden*—now it's okay if you say that, that's about four kilometers up the road. Then they still think you're a tourist. But as soon as you say Traiskirchen, before you finish saying the 'kirchen' part, they're feeling you up on a dirt road, thinking you'll do it with them for cigarettes or twenty shingles."

We hooked around to the left down a chestnut-lined alley, accompanied by the obligatory male sounds. When we had rounded a bend in the wall Nad'a took a breather. "Finally, we don't have to look at their ugly mugs, we can take in the ripening grapevines. Once they're ripe you can get some *Arbeit*. The harvest time is still the best, they don't pay much, but you get to stuff your face with grapes and you can work every day, so you come out on top after all. At grape-picking time not even the darkest ones get left standing out there. It's natural selection, you'll get a chance to see it for yourself. Early in the morning, if you look sometime, you'll see how many guys there are out here. The Austrians drive up: *Deutsch sprechen? Nichts?*—and the ones who can't say a peep just go *JaJaJa*. And the Austrians stop, look around; guys in T-shirts make a point of showing off their muscles, and the Austrians look them over. I'm surprised they don't pull their lips apart to check their teeth. First they take muscular blonds. Poles, Czechs too, then the lighter types —and those Albanians, Persians, half-Turks, they get left to hang around. —But hold on, Jituš, I've been blabbing so long your head must be spinning. At least I should describe the people you'll be living with in the *Zimmer*, so you can prepare yourself mentally. You look like a pretty decent girl, so they'll be sure to walk all over you. Me you already know, and I can be a real shrew, too, sometimes. Mostly when you don't lock up or don't wash yourself and things like that. Otherwise, it's a regular cavalcade of morons, prepare yourself for that, and the minute you turn your back they'll stick a knife in it. There are seven of us now, counting you. The hardest one to deal with is probably Miss Marta, she . . ."

We sauntered along around the camp wall. Nad'a, the garrulous veteran, and I: taciturn, fresh-off-the-boat, inexperienced I. I, who still needed a chance to check everything out. The sun, which in the meantime had climbed up higher in the sky, beat down on us with Austrian moderation. And Nad'a looked forward to Australia, where she would arrive in the middle of spring, so she could stay tan for an entire year. It smelled of fresh vineyards here; the clusters, which in no time the camp residents would be plucking for next to nothing an hour, were now covered in hoarfrost and gradually approaching ripeness. We walked slowly along the path of fertile brownish red clay, the wild roses blossomed by the camp wall, the Wienerwald loomed green in the distance. (The forest in whose cozy corners I was not to take up with anyone, for they were nothing but a gang of thugs.) Nad'a pointed out the neat Austrian villages laid out to the sides and in the valleys, she estimated how far away they were and recalled their names. "Discover Austria for yourself. Everyone makes fun of it, but it's not bad at all. Look at those sunflowers. See the forests, see the nature, do it while it's summer, while you still can. That's what I did all the time. But most of all, don't talk to anyone here."

Here was Austria, unknown, sunny, and laughing. And here was the wall. High, made of baked red bricks. Behind the wall the camp was almost unknown to us. It reminded me of Berlin. And as Nad'a spoke I turned toward this wall and gently stroked it. It was as real as real could be.

•

Three weeks later we threw a flying-away party for Nad'a. About thirty of us got together. And probably since my bed was the closest to the door and to the table, almost everybody sat on it. Madam Anežka barricaded herself and her daughter in the back corner with three cabinets, lest anyone lay eyes on her Maruška; Martička made a big show of leaving for Vienna, since she and Nad'a did not get along. Nad'a carefully packed her belongings in two suitcases, said goodbye to her aunt in Vienna, then brought us five bottles of white wine and got so hammered she couldn't speak. While she could still control herself, at least a little bit, she performed a striptease on the table, throwing her panties behind a cabinet and her bra onto the chandelier—which was a bare bulb hanging from the ceiling—where it caught on fire. She enlightened us as to how disgusting the camp was. She successfully aimed our Sunday-best wineglasses at the wardrobes and refrigerator. Then she collapsed on the floor, waving her arms in the air, saying that she would miss Traiskirchen, after all, dammit, it was two years of her life. "I'll be homesick, I'm telling you, in Australia. And you guys, I want you, guys, as a farewell, and all of you at once!" And while a couple of volunteers fulfilled her final wish on her bed by the window, Anežka fumed viciously from behind her cabinets, Hanka went with Zděnek into the washroom to screw, and Mira was nodding with someone in the corner by the hot plate to the rhythm of a song screaming from the radio. And in the fumes of wine and booze, in the cigarette smoke, in the stench of love, vomit, and Nad'a's burning bra, a strange individual crawled into my sagging bed, an individual who enthusiastically, if impotently, groped me and called me 'Marcelka' until the very light of morning.

Only when I had gotten up in the morning onto my wobbly hung-over legs, helped Nad'a get her luggage together, and, along with three strong men, more carried than escorted her to her bus, only when—still in the glow of daybreak—I had stripped Nad'a's bed of the sheets stained by the multiple fulfillment of her nocturnal parting wish and, wading through the shards of broken glasses on the floor, transferred my *own* bed linens to the longed-for bed by the window, wasting no time, before anyone could snatch it out from under me—only then did I understand just what Nad'a had been trying to tell me about the camp on that very first day.

12

The camp seemed like some kind of nightmare, a monster, a nine-headed dragon that with its incandescent breath slowly but irrevocably transformed industrious people into lazy ones, thinkers into madmen, neat people into slobs, healthy people into cripples, virgins into whores, and clever people into idiots.

And the worst of it was that we had only ourselves to blame: we who, God knows why, couldn't shift for ourselves.

The ones who had placed us in the camp wished us no harm. Actually they were trying to do us good—or else perhaps they simply didn't care. We had come there ourselves, voluntarily; no one kept us in the camp. No one from the outside tried to give us advice or tell us what to do, no one scolded us for anything —and that handful of cops with billy clubs clattering at their belts, they were there only in order to protect us from one another. It had the same effect on a person as a home for juvenile delinquents.

All in all, we had no reason to complain. The food wasn't bad: they thought to include meat and vitamins, to provide good nutrition, and if it wasn't quite edible at times, it was probably because some of us refugees who worked in the kitchen didn't know how to cook. Or didn't feel like it.

We were each allocated a bed with a blanket and pillow and two sheets, which we could exchange twice a month for a freshly laundered and ironed set. Each of us—almost—got a wardrobe. We were issued menthol-flavored toothpaste, a toothbrush, and some coarse camp soap. At one time everyone had even gotten a couple of hundred schillings a month; but that had been discontinued, and now there were dozens of stories circulating around the camp purporting to explain this fact. One of the stories claimed that our brother Poles had used the money to get drunk every day and create chaos; other stories named the Romanians as the drunkards, or the Albanians, or the Czechs, or more or less any other nationality; another rumor asserted that too many men had spent their easily gotten gains in a manner that had cost the Austrian government thousands of schillings in antibiotics for the treatment of certain types of illnesses. And then there were plenty of other stories: that on paydays, thieves from Romania, Poland, Hungary, or Iran (or any other country) had ambushed the new donees, attacked them, beaten them, and stolen their money. The simple fact was, we no longer received this support. The most natural explanation was that giving alms month after month to refugees, of whom there seemed to be more and more each year, was simply too expensive. After all, they would find a way to make a living. They were just a gang of demanding swindlers anyway . . .

We weren't badly taken care of: we had a place to wash ourselves at the Henhouse and hot water in the baths in the courtyard twice a week. We had the little wooden buildings of the YMCA and YWCA in the yard beneath the chestnuts—buildings in which the children could play and where once every two or three weeks someone brought old clothing from the Charity shipment, over which we could all haggle. We had the guard in his little house by the gate, the striped barrier, which he raised for us when we showed him our *Lagerkarte*. We had chestnut trees and a couple of telephone booths out by the gate. Also outside maintenance services, paid by the camp, so that we of the Henhouse and the Hilton would not be buried in our own filth. We had the tall uncut grass and a couple of rose bushes out back by the camp wall, and the acacias, between which we could hang out laundry to dry, so long as we guarded it from the window so that the bastards wouldn't steal it. We also had the medical building, a dentist, and an entire infirmary floor, where at any given time there lay a few wounded and incapacitated . . . a few fighters or innocent victims with knife wounds, or bandaged heads from blows inflicted by the leg from a bed . . . where people with broken jaws or limbs regained consciousness after arguments.

We were decently taken care of—no sane person could deny it. People claimed that the Austrians couldn't have cared less whether we *Flüchtlinge* lived or died. They probably would have liked us to die, but they had to take care of us because of the UN. The UN supposedly supported the camp to a considerable extent, and if it hadn't been for the UN, who knows how Austria would have managed all these immigrants. As a matter of fact, God only knew how it all really was. We never found out on whose accounts we lived. It was a fact that when a two-year-old Afghan girl fell on her head from the third story of the *Familienhaus* (more likely someone had thrown her out during a family quarrel, but that was never verified), a helicopter flew in for her from Vienna. And it was also a fact that every once in a while an ambulance came roaring up to the front of the Hilton and two strong men carried off the stabbed, sliced, or pummeled men who had been left lying in the corridors, the wailing remains of an Albanian-Romanian, Polish-Hungarian, Czech-Albanian, or who knows what sort of dispute. They were taken off somewhere, sewn up, patched up, cleaned out, or buried at the expense of the government. And investigations were conducted only rarely.

The camp was generally swimming with violence. And riddles. The mysterious recesses of corridors, rooms, and jungles, the recesses of people's minds, whenever they came to the surface. And they came to the surface plenty.

Except for minute bursts, such as the influx of Poles in 1982, the structure of the camp inhabitants did not reflect the structure of the population that fled from every possible nation. In isolation, yes, there we had all been locked up together nicely, just as we had arrived—families with children, couples, singles—but before long the Austrians had redistributed us. Most of the families had been taken off to pensions, smaller and larger hotels, where each family had its own little room and life was pretty as a picture, like in a peaceful small town, where no one stabbed anyone in the back, no one murdered or stole. Many a person in the camp longed to dash off into the dubious privacy of such pensions, but in prudish Austria people had to be legally married for that. And so couples hurriedly slapped together at home— or else even more hurriedly slapped together here—subjected themselves to the somewhat old-fashioned matrimonial rites in the perpetually besieged town hall in Traiskirchen, without rings, without flowers, without relatives or ringing congratulations— and often, in the case of those who had fled their spouses, without a prior divorce, a decision which in time usually proved itself quite unwise. Equipped with this scrap of paper stating that they were now husband and wife, He and She applied immediately to be housed in a pension and were later taken by special transport to some village or other, to some microroomlet, where at least they could screw in privacy. Granted, in this respect we in the camp were worse off.

Who remained in the camp? Well, those of us who were single; a few couples of the Hanka-Zděneček type, who were both married, but whose spouses had remained behind; and here and there a family that had explicitly expressed the desire to stay, or one that had been kicked out of a pension after two years because of local politics. You could stay in the camp as long as you wanted.

Or, rather, as long as you didn't want.

Because the camp was an institution of waiting. A place where nothing that happened at the moment held any meaning unless it directly influenced what would (hopefully) happen at some point in the future. The camp was as alive, agitated, and unpleasant as a train station waiting room where the delays of express trains posted on the board were growing by months and years. The camp was an institution from which we would all disperse to separate points . . . someday, as soon as our train arrived. So that here, now, we were nervously shifting from one foot to the other and sharpening our elbows for the upcoming battle for a seat. Someday our train would arrive. Or maybe it wouldn't. But it was better not to think about that possibility. This camp existed so that we *Flüchtlinge* had a place to wait, protected from the wind and the rain. For America, Canada, Australia. For asylum. For a decent job. For an apartment that we would find someday in Vienna. To earn enough shingles to return to Gniezno with a million zloty. For a better love than the shallow kind that was available in the camp in surplus quantities. For longings. For someone at home in Uganda to shoot the ruling authorities—for this the African called Good Morning had been waiting a good fourteen years. There were a lot of things we could wait for in the camp. For a rich Austrian who would take us away from it all. For someone who was still sitting in Czechoslovakia or Poland or Hungary—but who was also the one and only person with whom we had ever wanted to take off into the distance. We could wait here for our futures. For hope. For the fulfillment of our dreams. Or for death.

The camp was a brownish itchy spot on the face of Austria . . . a gullet, a pharynx into which we had all been thrown by fate, but not all of us crawled back out of it. Thus the camp became the last refuge of the bankrupt—who had been unable to dig their way out for years and now would have great difficulty doing so—the last stop for a lot of people whose aimless voyage across Europe no longer offered any refuge. And so the camp grew thick with these incompetent, unsuccessful losers, like the grounds slowly settling to the bottom of a cup of Turkish coffee. Those to whom the world had shown a little kindness had already flown off to Canada, America, Australia. They had not spent much time here, they had taken off in a hurry, and they sometimes wrote to us about whether they liked it there. So that life in the camp became eternal waiting, an eternal rush between shipments of new refugees, the influx of frightened newcomers from isolation; between applications for acceptance in one place or another; between filling out forms, hoping for invitations to interviews, and waiting for the doctor and for a visa when we were accepted—or writing beseeching letters of appeal when we weren't. The camp was a lazy rush between breakfast, lunch, dinner, writing letters to send beyond the Curtain, and daily trips to the camp post office; life was lines in the *Lagerleitung* building, where every Tuesday we had to register and every Friday receive our meal tickets. A shipment of clothing to the YMCA and haggling with Romanian women over two faded blouses. Doing the wash in a bucket below the bed. And waiting. And hoping. And longing, longing for the distances. The most enormous distances. And also longing for what was close. What was closest of all, what chased away the dream.

The camp was small loves and passions, and hatred, and an incredible amount of time that needed to be killed. Learning the languages of lands to which we might or might not make it. *Ich bin, du bist, I am, you are.* Eighteen hundred refugees from twenty-eight countries, they said. A few aspirations, a lot of waiting, and cheap new clothes. Bought from the Romanians. Stolen clothes.

The camp was simply an international small town. Lousy food, disgust, and hope. And a ceaselessly festering sore on the face of dear old Austria.

13

Stinking Jezebel stood in the doorway of the Henhouse bathroom and stank. Her stench poured through the corridors all the way to the exit and out the door; it crawled out the open bathroom, crossed the yard, and drowned out the scent of the freshly washed laundry hung out to dry between the two acacias. Her stench seeped under the door of Room 7, crept across the floor and under the beds—rising toward our noses in almost visible cloudlets—and managed to change the topic of our conversation.

"I can't believe it," said Martička, starting in on one of her favorite topics. "She does nothing but wash. She bathes three times a day, and she still stinks like a skunk. She hasn't even washed the soap suds off—and already she smells, even through the soap she manages to stink like a filthy Great Dane. It must be some kind of illness, because no healthy person . . . Unless all Arabs—"

"But she's Persian."

"Oh God, does it really matter whether I've got to smell an *Arab* stench or a *Persian* one? They ought to quarantine her in some far-off corner of her own somewhere, or just throw her right out of the camp."

"Well, Marta, not that I want to complain or anything, but now and then I get a little asthmatic from all your deodorants and perfumes . . ."

"I beg your pardon! I use only the best, name-brand cologne!"

"Name brand or not, fact is, it smells like piss, and if you plan to catch a millionaire with that, you might do just as well rolling around in horse manure. I'm just saying that . . ."

Martička slowly puffed out her chest.

Zděneček scanned the room, looking for signs of support, then sniffed provocatively. "That it lingers around here in every nook and cranny, and that Persian—at least she washes."

"I beg your pardon! Are you trying to say . . ."

"Zděneček, stop it, they'll throw you out on me," Hanka said.

Zděneček waved his hand in annoyance. And as if in continuation of that motion, he reached for the toilet seat bequeathed to us by Anežka. He opened the squeaking door, through which immediately gushed a whiff of the Persian (or perhaps Arab) woman nicknamed Jezebel.

"You put that back!" screeched Martička, who was, as usual, beautifying herself in front of the mirror, turning away only for the purpose of displaying her rage or upbraiding someone. "Put that right back where you found it this instant. It isn't enough that you use the ladies' room, and that we put up with you here, you've got to take our toilet seat, too. Hang it back up! This very second!"

Zděnek hung the seat on its nail in embarrassment. "Aren't we the perfect lady today," he mumbled and took off in the direction of the bare porcelain bowl.

Hanka maintained a surly silence. She didn't dare object, for fear that they would throw Zděneček out on her—but, on the other hand, Zděneček belonged there. Who was it who had fixed the handle on the window when we feeble women couldn't manage it? Who had declared war on the cockroaches and then slain every one that dared poke so much as an antenna out from behind the refrigerator? Who had nailed down the rotten floorboard and propped up the wobbly table with matchbooks? Who was it who had taken the doors from the cabinet and used them to prop up Hanka's bed? True, sharp tongues claimed that he did this only for the sake of better sex with Hanka, but then sharp tongues will claim almost anything.

For example, that Miss Martička had a crush on him and was jealous of Hanka. After all, Zděneček was a real man—he even had hair on his chest. Meanwhile Hanka, according to Marta, wasn't the slightest bit pretty. Tall and slim, for sure, but stoop-shouldered, with a back like a bow and a hole between her thighs ("But you've all got that," quipped Zděneček at the time), and she didn't even brush her hair out properly. She looked like a hag. By contrast just look at Martička! She may be thirty-four, but take a look at that fine body! Those beautiful legs! What a looker! And over those legs—stockings; and over those stockings—pumps; and not just any old kind: these pumps were good enough to kiss. "Every man has to start kissing me from the bottom up," she let it be known. Once, the story went, Zděneček had walked into the room when Marta was the only one there. "Men have to kiss me from the bottom up," she said and stretched out her leg toward him. Zděnek did not kiss her leg, needless to say. From that day on, she carried a grudge.

We sat in the Henhouse, mildly irritated, and the breeze brought to us the scents of Indian summer. At the moment, unfortunately, dominant among them was Jezebel's stench. She had now, thank God, shut herself in with—probably with the Albanian girls, since she had long since been thrown out of the room next door because of the stench. After that she had slept outside, wrapped up in a blanket, but when it began to rain hard she could think of nothing better than to crawl tearfully into the camp guard's booth. The booth was cramped; the guard couldn't stand having her there for long and brought her back to the Henhouse—using his power of office to stick her in with the Albanians, who didn't speak German well enough to defend themselves. Jezebel was good-hearted, hospitable, and kind: she never got in anyone's way; she just went on quietly stinking all by herself. The Albanian girls built a kind of wall for her out of plastic bags that reached from the floor to the ceiling. They pinned up colorful bags they had brought back from a Billa supermarket, and Jezebel had to stay on her side of this wall. She didn't complain. She existed peacefully in exile behind the red-and-yellow screen of sacks, each bearing the inscription BILLA HEUTE

FREUT EUCH LEUTE, went to breakfast, lunch, and dinner, and occasionally could be heard humming an Arab, or perhaps Persian, melody.

All told, she had an open heart, and probably would have had an open bed, too, if it hadn't been for that stench. It was rumored that some Albanians had once kidnapped her from the camp yard, taken her off to the Hilton, and screwed her there while holding their noses. Jezebel had supposedly seemed quite content, making no effort to resist.

In any case, Jezebel had been exorcised for the day, off behind that hanging wall of bags, so that now the air brought us only the legitimate scents of summer. The scent of the uncut grass, left standing to wilt out back by the camp wall, where we sometimes went to lie in the sun. The scent of vineyards. The odor of the leaves on the trees, in whose veins the autumn rot was already gathering. The breeze bore the faint scent of dust from the yard and also a few snatches of melodies, mostly Arabic. These chords also had scents; for me, at least, they smelled like the distant expanses I would someday visit. At times they even tempted me to go down to the yard to listen up close—even though I knew that it was dangerous, that I might suddenly find myself against my will somewhere in the Hilton . . . Such cases were not at all infrequent. Nevertheless, now and then I stuck my head out the window and soaked up the distant melodies, imagining myself reproaching Martička for not finding them fragrant. She isolated herself from them with the wall of sound erected by her radio. Marta thought in terms of Europeans. More precisely, in terms of the millionaires who would fall in love with her and transform her life into heaven on earth. ("And why shouldn't one of them fall in love with me?" she would say, bristling, and when we said nothing, she would hoist her breasts on her palms or stroke her graceful legs. "Look at this body, how beautiful I make myself! If you all only paid a little more attention to the way you look . . .") So far only one Austrian millionaire had fallen in love with her, and that turned out badly. As a matter of fact, he wasn't an Austrian, but a Bulgarian, and he wasn't a millionaire either, but a bricklayer. Nevertheless, Martička disappeared from the camp and went to live with him in a trailer somewhere near Baden, in the hope that he would marry her. As the story goes, the bricklayer, upon coming home from the job each day, would stretch out on the bed in his filthy knee-high boots and say only: "Take off my boots! *Schuhe abmachen!*" Upon which Miss Martička would devotedly remove one boot, then the other, pull off his socks, and, just as she had always talked about it, from the bottom up begin to kiss him. She gnawed away at his soles, his ankles, his calves, while he lay there like a Turkish pasha, and by the time she reached his cock, it was already hard. In the end he kicked her out of the trailer, saying he wasn't interested in cutting himself on her bones anymore.

The waning moon was about to emerge over the horizon. The breeze brought us scents, odors, wafts of the evening; it brought us the scent of music from the camp yard. It brought us the distillation of every sort of masculine longing. There were seventeen supposedly available women here, and nearly eighteen hundred men at the Hilton who, as Zděnek put it, had no place to slip it in—and would have liked to. That meant more than ten guys for each finger—right? Hanka wasn't interested, she had her Zděnek. Baška had her honey in Mother Vienna, and she always returned from him in the brightest of moods. Mira, who had shown up after dinner, couldn't have cared less about this topic either. She had only come by for her portion of sausage with rotten salad and potato mush, which we had managed not to eat today. In any case (Zděnek observed indecently), it was inspiring to watch that sausage disappear into her; he wouldn't mind the same fate himself. Hanka gave him a slap, Marta clucked—and Mira the exhibitionist loaded the sausage into her mouth as inspirationally as possible. She threw the end of the sausage into the mush, and Zděneček swiftly nabbed it. Mira was gone in a flash. She disappeared into the Hilton as if beneath the surface of the sea, incalculable and refractive, yet hospitable and enveloping. Mira may only have been nineteen, but there were certain things she understood.

●

And so I stretched out on my back on my well-supported camp cot (the one that had originally belonged to Nad'a, on which all the guys had exchanged their goodbyes with her) and covered my head with a handkerchief. "Our Jitka is meditating again," Marta remarked tartly. But I was already observing all this from far away. As if the snot-rag over my eyes were a space suit, effectively shielding me from the atmosphere of an alien planet. Only the bare bulb near the ceiling shone yellow through my space suit, lighting it up like an electrified pear.

I dozed off a bit behind the curtain of my handkerchief and thought about those ten men for each finger, about the exciting but dangerous Eastern music, about the camp, about work, about not having enough money to buy stamps to send a letter home, about Standa, and about life, but mainly, mainly about those ten men for each finger, about the moon that would soon rise, and about how today, precisely today, I didn't have a damned soul to make love to.

●

Whatever had happened to the Pole Tadeusz, and whatever had happened to the few people I had talked to back on the isolation floor? They were all either in pensions or up shit creek. The religious family had decamped to Germany. And Tadeusz had been absorbed into the entrails of the Hilton. True, he had searched me out a couple of times at the beginning, we had screwed out back by the wall, undressed only partially, because he was extremely shy about it, and standing up, because the grass was cold. Our relationship had run down like a battery, been sucked clean like a tea bag—not even the bitter aftertaste of tannic acid remained. Our inexplicable passion was still locked behind the doors of the isolation block—lying in wait, perhaps, for others, the next ones—so that now I couldn't even remember the Polish verb for "screw." Those two Hungarian girls who, according to Oldřich, had always been blabbering now lived in the room below me—and, perhaps because they were so tenderly accustomed to one another, they had no trouble keeping company with the camp police for money. Presumably for money. The other girls from their room claimed that they laughed during the act.

Whatever had happened to fat Oldřich, who had so enlightened us in isolation? We heard that he and Božena had gone off to some pension in the foothills of the Alps, where he had nothing to do and so spent his days entertaining the whole pension with his speeches. It was said that this sufficed even to keep him in booze. Only dead drunkenness could silence him.

·

Where was the Pole Tadeusz now? My little blond-haired seal, who had been so good at chasing away the dream? I longed for him, but not for him at that moment: for him as he had been before, on the isolation floor. Because everything there—my intoxication with the great world, the confusion of tongues, Wodka Wyborowa—everything had been clear, visible, and necessary. In isolation it had been okay to make love with Tadek simply because he had a well-groomed blond mustache (altogether different from Standa's prickly whiskers), because he poured me Wodka Wyborowa, because he knew how to make dice by drying molded pieces of white bread on the windowsill. Nothing had been more pleasant back then than snuggling up, in the tobacco aroma of a Polish *papierosa*, against someone else's body beneath that rough military blanket. Back then, nothing had been more splendid than to count up my continents. But all that was over now.

The continents were no longer a game played with the brownish gold spots on the ceiling. They had begun to acquire precise, unpleasantly concrete outlines. They had become the lands in which we would have to make a living, if we ever made it to them in the first place. The continents had taken material form and had ceased to tantalize us. No, that would be a lie: they tantalized us, mostly in savage dreams just before morning, or when I (not too often) lay on my back in the grass by the wall of the camp and looked up at the airplanes. At the silvery vapor trails they left across the sky.

●

The camp accelerated the processes of life and maturation. At the very least, it accelerated the loss of illusions. From the continents arrived postcards from people who had been here with us before—and whom one of the planes had taken *there*. We received all sorts of reports: naïve and informative, bitter and euphoric. A card arrived from Australia, from the veteran Nad'a. It consisted of only a few lines, written in quite formal language. Each line immediately (even as I was carrying it from the camp mail room back to the Henhouse) translated itself for me into Nad'a's picturesque slang, swelling with potency: "Jituš!!! Everything is screwed down under, stay up top! Everything here is upside down. Half the time I don't even know which end of me is up (I know what you're thinking!). It's summer, winter I mean, and the heat is stifling. There are four koalas in every eucalyptus tree trying to shit on you. There are ten-foot lizards running down the streets of the suburbs without any supervision, no joke. I'm sitting here sweating like a pig. The ocean is a beautiful tropical blue, but before you even get your foot in the water, a shark has bitten it off. Everyone drives on the left!!! And you know I was trained as a goldsmith, and just how was I supposed to get rich at that when everyone here walks around in T-shirts and boxer shorts? I haven't even seen Sydney yet, welfare comes to twenty-eight dollars a week, so I work like a slave at a bakery for a couple of lousy, bloodsucking half-Czechs. I hit the sack at about one in the morning and at four they start shaking me, yelling that the dough has risen. My best advice is: don't come here. I'm making for Borneo."

I read Nad'a's postcard and I felt like screaming. Not because of those ten-foot lizards running through the streets of Sydney. I knew she'd be sober in the morning. I felt like screaming because Nad'a wasn't around anymore.

•

The concretization of the continents was proceeding on other levels as well.

From America, for instance, a Slovak businessman arrived to pick himself out a wife from among the camp women. Thirty-two years old, time to get "hi-i-itched," as he put it in the drawl of the east. "After all, a man with a business needs a wi-i-ife." And here we were . . . not as "fre-e-esh" as the girls in Bratislava, but then a body couldn't get to Bratislava these "da-a-ays." And "after a-a-all," we were all "we-e-ell-brought-up, unspoiled ga-a-als." So he said, but when he walked through the door of *Zimmer Nummer sieben*, he just said "Fuck i-i-it!" and polished off with us the bottle of Johnnie Walker he'd brought to celebrate his engagement. Under its influence he made an attempt to grope Mira under her skirt, " 'cause we Slova-a-aks have to look out for one ano-o-other"; but when she recoiled he went sprawling across the wooden floorboards with his horny hand still stretched out in front of him, said "Fuck i-i-it!" once more, then got up and disappeared at a stumble, probably to find a wife through the personals.

From America some Baptists or others arrived, set themselves up under a linden tree, and started sermonizing at us through a loudspeaker. About what, nobody knew, we didn't understand a word. But it was definitely sermonizing, roaring above our heads, so condescending, indulgent, and menacing that, like the archangel's resounding trumpets, it drowned out all the music. In this manner the proselytizers of the Christian faith managed to catch themselves a couple of sheep, although this fact probably owed more to the new Christians' hopes of reaching the States than to any religious sentiment. Supposedly, the missionaries wrapped the converted in white sheets and dunked them in the Danube, bestowing on them in this manner the Holy Sacrament of Baptism.

That's how we came to understand that America was the land of crazed Slovak businessmen, where people went jumping into rivers dressed in white bed linens. But everything else we'd heard seemed fairly encouraging.

●

I applied first to Australia. Perhaps thanks to Naďa's influence. Or maybe because it was the farthest place from Europe. If you're going, might as well go all the way. Not long after that I received notification that I was not a suitable candidate for them, and I was not exactly crushed by the news. I applied to the U.S.

By that time Hanka's Zděnek had it all divvied up. According to him, the ones who went rushing to America were the bold go-getters, thirsting for dollars. Canada was for the more timid, those with families, for instance: after all, in Canada they supposedly had good welfare. And Australia, that was left over for the adventurers, the ones who didn't mind a few ten-foot lizards.

We applied for our continents, filled out forms, and by the very act of signing them we became—albeit only in our own eyes—Americans, Canadians, or Australians. We still had never set foot there—it still wasn't clear that we would ever be permitted to—but we were already getting used to our continents by means of the silvery trails of the airplanes high above our heads. Zděnek, who along with Hanka had also applied for the States, was already practicing to be a Yank: he would chew three pieces of gum every day until his jaw ached. And to Marta's great delight, he took to sitting with his feet up on the table.

●

I lay on my back on the bunk, my eyes covered with that snot-rag, doing my best to be as far away from here as possible. That had been my typical evening pastime in recent days. Not unusual in the camp, they said. I didn't feel like walking through the little town of Traiskirchen, I didn't feel like shooting the shit with anyone, I didn't feel like doing anything. I no longer had even twenty schillings to buy cigarettes. Even though I hardly ever smoked, the mere knowledge that I couldn't afford cigarettes depressed me. And I had no money for stamps, so why write letters? Not to mention that writing letters home in this state of mind would only alarm my family. I was totally, tragically alone. As if all around the Henhouse, all around Room 7, closing in around my very bed, a jungle had sprung up, complete with pythons and boa constrictors, my own, true, personal jungle, where I would be lost as soon as I stretched one leg down off the mattress. Only the bed was private (since even your wardrobe could be opened with a pair of nail scissors)—two square yards where no one but me had any business being—and no one invaded it.

No one? I remembered the night when, behind the two wardrobes and the divider, the eager young men had said their good-byes to the sobbing Nad'a on the eve of her departure; the stench of something burning; the wardrobes swaying drunkenly; and I also remember the drunk who climbed into my bed uninvited. He greeted me as "Marcelka." At the time, I registered with the skin of my whole body that, perhaps like every Czech man, he had sweaty hands; and when he came by the room afterward (he had the slightly annoying habit of scratching on the door like a little shrew), I learned that he answered to the name of Mirek. Or was it Miloš? Anyway, this Mirek (or Miloš) had totally destroyed the sense of inviolability I'd had about my own bed. That meant that the jungle could get at me.

Or perhaps I didn't want my bed to be private, maybe I even longed for it to be populated. I wanted to populate it with the Hilton: with the male essence that had no name and every name, that would drive the dream away. The dream was back again. And it was more intrusive than ever. But I couldn't bring myself to consider one, or perhaps several, of the Hilton guys who periodically came by to try to pick us up with the help of a bottle of Ballantine's whisky. That was the brand you could put away until all hours—and then trot off for the day-labor pickup by the gate before five in the morning, ready to earn enough for another bottle. With the whisky's help the boys sometimes made passes at some girl down in Room 3 or in our own Room 7—and the rest of us would listen to the guys' cheerful screwing. But I required the male essence, a perfectly dreamlike chaser of dreams. And the fact that the Hilton was roaring, rumbling, howling with dozens of horny lechers didn't really have much to do with it. I couldn't bring myself to consider the men in the Hilton, but the Hilton itself, yes, the Hilton . . . the dangerous, mysterious Hilton that could envelop you like an octopus with its dozens of suckers and tentacles, smother you with its aroma of various tobaccos, bring you to absolute nirvana with its throbbing pulse. The Hilton was the most complete, perfect lover. And I began to tune myself to its wavelength.

●

There was a scratching at the door. It sounded like a shrew digging behind the wall. "Door!" yelled Zděneček, and by the sound of his voice it was clear that he was lurking in ambush for cockroaches behind the refrigerator. "*Herein!*" said Martička in a bureaucratic voice that succeeded in transmitting the disparaging look she must have been giving Zděnek. Hanka giggled. And through the door stepped—well, judging by that "Hi, gang!", one of them had to be Mirek (or was it Miloš?).

"We brought you a li-i-ittle booze, i-i-if the ladies don't object," chimed in the second Slovak voice, oozing with sperm. It was obvious that at least one of them was determined to end the day in Marta's bed. And so I was careful to be *very* far away from here.

"She sleeping?" Mirek asked in disappointment, apparently pointing in my direction. Of course, my handkerchief protected me as a sarcophogus protects a mummy.

"Jituška is meditating," Marta replied matter-of-factly. "But tell us what you've brought. Just don't smoke in here. She's sleeping—but at least that way there's more for us, like I always say—"

"The-e-ere'll be enough for e-e-everybody," boomed the Slovak voice, sounding somewhat drunken. "The-e-ere'll be enough for the sleepers, the-e-ere'll be enough for the dead. Like the Communi-i-ists always said, No one eats who doesn't put in an honest da-a-ay's drinki-i-ing. Do you know what comra-a-ade Lenin said? You must learn how to dri-i-ink, comra-a-ades, before you can learn how to li-i-ive!"

"Don't go attacking us with that Soviet crap," Zděnek yelled from the floor where—judging by the sound of his shoe slapping —he was knocking off roaches.

"Don't be so serious! Have a drink with us! Jituš . . ." Mirek seemed to have caught on that I wasn't Marcelka. As if it made a difference.

"Let her be," said Zděneček, defender of the downtrodden. "Maybe she's having a bad day. Just pour it."

"You know, we really brought this bottle more for the ladies. If they don't drink, they won't be so cooperative."

"Come on, come on. I'll be cooperative."

"Oh sure, you don't have to get anyone drunk. You've got that in-tellek-shual beauty of yours, with beautiful hair and beautiful eyes and a nice, uh, soul . . ."

"He-e-ey, Mirek, quit messing with my Hanka."

Hanka let out a satisfied laugh.

"I'm not messing with her," Mirek fawned in a honeyed voice. "I just want you to know, Hanička, if this hick ever dumps you, I'm in *Zimmer zweiunddreissig*, the cubbyhole right below the window. But be careful you don't fall into the first bed by the door, there's a legionnaire in there and he's got the clap. Mira told me. Under an oath of secrecy."

"That means she's got it too," said Zděnek the realist.

"Well! Who needs to live this way, in this . . . ! Now it's venereal diseases. Godknowshowmany times she's drunk from my mug! And you can catch it off a toilet seat before you can say—"

"Calm down, Marta, calm down."

"It's like I always say: you never know when or how—"

"Hold on, the story is a little more complicated than that."

"One fine day a person sits innocently down on *her own* toilet seat that she washes every day with her own two hands—"

"*Your* own?"

"—then all of a sudden she finds out that . . . How could she be so inconsiderate of us. It's just like I always say—"

"But she doesn't have it anymore. Ládík dug her up some penicillin, so she wouldn't have to go to the doctor. Actually she gave it to the guy for slapping her once. Mira's not a bad girl, but there are certain things she . . ."

"Tell me about it, but how—"

"I'm telling you, he's got the clap because once when Mira was drunk, instead of going across the room to Ládík, who she's sleeping with, she tumbled into that guy's bed. He was just then engaged in onanism, to put it politely, and he wasn't in the mood for a woman, so he slapped her with his free hand and kicked her out. Mira burst into tears, and, as you know, women are vengeful creatures, and so when she caught the clap from that Hungarian Gábo, she simply fell into the Legionnaire's bunk again. At the time he had a bad case of the run-and-hurries, as the Slovaks call it, as a consequence of the night before. This one guy had some plum brandy his mom sent him from Moravia, and the Legionnaire, when he catches sight of it, puts a big old switchblade on the table and tells him, 'I was in the Green Berets.' So what was the kid supposed to do? The Legionnaire grabs the bottle, rips the cork out with his teeth, and tosses it back, almost to the bottom, but it was home brew, a good hundred and fifty proof, and so the Legionnaire puked his guts out and got the runs and the whole next day he was running to the can to shit." (Marta sighed theatrically.) "And so one time when he gets back from there, all shat out of shape, if you'll pardon the expression, he finds Mira all undressed and spread-eagled on his bunk. So he jumps on her, she gives it to him once, then one more time for good measure, to make sure he's got it good, then she laughs right in his face, says it was like fucking a rabbit, small and quick, that she'd rather get it from Ládík, who's already waiting for her in his own cubbyhole. The Legionnaire turned purple with rage, but a lot of good that did him. And Lád'a—he doesn't care who Mira's sleeping with, he's even lent her to us before . . ." (Marta voiced her alarm, expressed as a hissing sound.) "That is, he would have lent her to us," Mirek corrected himself. "But I didn't even want to. She's a fine-looking girl and all, and not even twenty yet, but after all those . . . Well, I like a different kind of girl, the nice, fresh, innocent kind, the kind that just wraps her head up with a snot-rag and meditates . . ."

"The innocent kind!" Hanka laughed.

"We-e-ell, at least we can dri-i-ink to that!" To my perceptions were added the smell of Ballantine's, the clinking of glasses, and a familiar gurgling sound.

"Well, I'll tell you something." Marta. "I may be thirty-four, but you should see the guys go after me. But I'm not going for anyone from here. Except maybe an educated, respectable man who knows how to take care of his wife. I can take my pick. It all depends on how you take care of yourself, just look at these legs . . ."

Although all I could see was that yellow bulb up there by the ceiling, I could imagine in the most painful detail the gesture with which Marta stretched out her legs. I quickly closed my inner eyes and the image dissolved into red, green, and blue disks.

"How many more times is she going to stick her damned shanks in my face!"

Hanka: "Zděneček . . ."

"And what about our Sleeping Beauty? Isn't it time we woke her up with a kiss?"

"Then you'd be in for it, my Prince!"

"Oh no. Jituška's a nice girl." Mirek crossed the room to my bed, accompanied by the creaking of floorboards. He leaned over me and lowered his voice. "Jituška didn't throw me out that time I wanted to be nice to her, it was just that I'd had a few too many drinkies and my thingy wasn't working. But next time, see . . ."

"Would you all just leave me alone!" I heard myself say, and I turned my face away from them. Away from the jungle. Away from the boa constrictors.

"And what, no striptease today? Ladies, it's almost time for it . . ." Zděnek. The crack of his shoe on the floor.

"I wish you wouldn't all say such vulgar things." Little Miss Marta in a weary voice. "And that Jituš is just ignoring us. As if we didn't exist."

●

But how was I to explain it to them? If they couldn't understand that . . . ? That the yellow light bulb shining through my hand-kerchief was sometimes better than their faces. That I sometimes longed to be alone. That I wanted to survey my country's land-scape, which I had made a copy of in my head.

It was that flowered, bewitching landscape that had been left in the wake of the semi as it moved forward like an opening zipper. The landscape in which Standa waited for me. The land-scape to which I would never be allowed to return.

I walked through my recollected landscape hoping to resusci-tate it, and afterward I was struck by homesickness. Because my long-ago landscape was fading away within me, getting pale and oxidized like an old photograph in a family album; it was becom-ing scratched and clouded over by dust like a silent film. But how happy I would have been to throw myself down on the grass in that film!

●

I tore the handkerchief from my face, blinking into the pro-fusion of light. "I know you're out there. It's just that I . . ."

"So come have some Ballantine's with us."

"But," I blurted out guiltily. "But I don't feel like drinking today."

"She never feels like drinking," Zdeněk said reproachfully.

"With *us*!" Mirek said even more reproachfully.

"Because none of you ever care about anything except getting laid and using a woman, you're all a bunch of pigs," Hanka concluded resentfully.

"But, my little bedbug, it's so lovely sleeping with you when you're drunk . . ."

"Sure, you got me plenty drunk that first time, when I was still with Pepík . . ."

"But, bedbug, you made such good use of me, too, that time, it was so sore the next day I couldn't stand up, and how your eyes were shining after that!"

"Because I had a fever thanks to you, smarty-pants, from the bladder infection I got from you screwing me on the linoleum in the kitchen, every three minutes I had to march off to pee, I was taking pills for it and everything . . ."

"It is so beautiful to suffer for love . . ."

"But I was suffering for *you*, you beast. As if you couldn't have waited until we made it to the bed, but not him, no, he has to tackle me by the leg . . ."

"I don't know how I *stand* it here in this room. As if it would do you any harm not to constantly speak of such things. How can you be so *primitive*! It's like I always say—"

"You're always saying bullshit!" Zděneček.

Marta: "*What* did you say?"

"I just wanted to point out that there are people in this room who cannot bear to *talk* about it, but as soon as the lights go out they're the first ones to spread their legs. Have you forgotten your Tomcat?"

Marta turned red. "That . . . don't remind me of that. I can't even describe that, that was . . ."

"He was the most handsome Tomcat you ever screwed in front of us here, Marta, with the most handsome hairy chest . . ."

"Would you all just leave me alone!"

"I think we've already heard that line once today," Mirek deduced. "But then our Sleeping Beauty came around nicely. Would you like a shot, Jituš? Hold on, I'll get you a glass." And he reached toward the shelf.

"Not that one, not that one," shouted the ever frugal Hanka. "That's the one I am soaking tickets in." Hanka had invented a method of ridding train tickets of their imprints, so they could be reused.

"Aha, I see, help me find a glass, Josko, so Sleeping Beauty can have a drink with us. Even if I'm not the Wicked Witch, I'd love her to bite into my magic apple."

"Mirek, quit it." Tedious me.

"You're in kind of a bad mood today, Jituš. Not getting enough sex? I'd love to help cure you of that."

In the meantime they had scared up a glass. The smell of Ballantine's right below my nose. I took the whisky somewhat passively. "Guys, really, I am not worth shit today."

"Don't worry about it, Jitka, we'll cheer you up. Down the hatch."

"O-otherwise you won't be co-oh-operative . . ." Josko, who had by now managed to get quite tipsy.

"I won't be in any case."

Mirek enigmatically: "How do you know?"

Josko was now towering unstably atop the table and howling like an ox: "What kind of cunts have you got, girls? Li-i-ittle ones, big ones, or medium ones? I need to know which di-i-ick to screw on tonight." And he grabbed his crotch possessively.

Marta: "That's the last straw!"

Zdeněk inquisitively: "I imagine you as a racehorse, Marta. Judging by your sighing when your hairy Tomcat was doing you . . ."

Marta exhaled.

Hanka: "Zdeněk . . ."

From the radio, whose clamor we had ceased to notice long,

long ago, came a sound signal and an announcer gave notice that it was *Zehn Uhr.*

"He has no business being here, this is a ladies' room. We put up with him here, and he . . ."

"A ladies' room? Are there ladies present?"

"Hey, girls," Mirek shouts into the universal din. "Do any of you want some *Arbeit*? That Edita from Room 3 has a job in Vienna, washing dishes, for twenty-five an hour, not so bad, huh? But she can't do it for a couple of days, until . . ."

"She ge-e-ets an abortion," Josko gurgled from over his glass.

"Really? Whose is it?"

"Oh, girls, don't ask *us*. Because Edita—"

"The one they call Open House?" asked Zděnek learnedly.

"Su-u-ure, that's what they called her. Edita never wanted anything in return for it, she did it for pleasure. She went right around a room, from one cubbyhole to the next, no one bothered with her for more than two days, and when one guy had enough, he just kicked her out and she went flying across the floor, landed in the next cubbyhole, and when the next guy had enough, he kicked her out, she went flying . . . so she's got a dose of everyone's jism."

"Both of you included?"

"Yeah," Mirek said, looking embarrassed. "Well, she's got to go under the knife and it's going to take a couple of days before she's back on her hind legs, but she doesn't want to lose her *Platz*. Any one of you girls want to fill in? What about you, Jituš?"

"But it's in Vienna?"

"We'll explain it all to you. And you don't have to be there until eight in the morning, you'll be washing the *Geschirr* from *Frühstück*. Then you'll be there for lunch and dinner. Then you buzz off back to the camp and that's that. And I'll give you the *Geld*."

"You?"

"Yeah, they pay Edita every month, so I'll get it from her and we'll split it up."

"You seem to be taking pretty good care of Open House." Zděneček.

"So there's a whole pack of lucky fathers," Hanka added with a grin.

"Is it a deal, Jituš? For twelve hours you get three hundred . . ."

"Well, guys." Tedious, boring me, who didn't have the energy to think about this, or anything else that day. Maybe only about those ten theoretical men for each finger, who in practice, of course, were lacking. "But, guys, the train fare alone would cost me seventy schillings . . ."

"You can hitchhike. How do you think Edita was doing it? She hitchhiked, and because she was clever she always managed to make a little something extra that way. She would come to our place, waving a hundred-schilling bill, and say, 'Guys, look, it works.' "

Josko's neck had slammed against the table edge so hard that the folds of his skin spread out over the wooden boards like a Saint Bernard's chin. One eye was tightly shut, while the other languidly gazed at the last golden drop at the bottom of his glass. He sighed and observed in a deeply philosophical manner: "Oy, fucki-i-ing is a heavenly thi-i-ing!"

Marta said nothing. Her mouth was fully occupied with supporting her face, which looked as if someone had just taken her favorite toy away. Hanka was grinning over her Ballantine's. And in this unguarded moment Zděneček succeeded in tearing down from the wall the shiny white toilet seat and darting off with it victoriously to the women's bathroom.

●

Should I have been trying to impart some order to my recollections? The old ones hurt a bit, and the future ones frightened me. But just a little. I drank and the burning whisky flowed through me. From those couple of swallows I, too, had probably gotten a touch drunk. Mirek quickly refilled my glass. And behind the refractive, honey-gold surface of the alcohol, I felt invisible again.

I kept talking. To myself, of course; I began with Jiří, who not long ago bought me a draft beer in a pub in Traiskirchen and told me about how he longed for a woman, his wife, that is, whom he'd left behind with three kids (*three*, Jitka, can you even imagine it?)—and how he sometimes still, not to be crude, longed for a girl, not just any girl, you understand, but some sort of decent girl, see, one a person could trust not to give him something . . . and how he was a considerate guy, he knew perfectly well that here in Traiskirchen we had to be very careful about who we let in or kept out of that furry garden of ours, right, that since they didn't hire women like they did men for good-paying heavy labor we had to wash dishes or be chambermaids, if we were lucky. But I shouldn't get the idea that . . . Well, he, Jiří, was a considerate guy, he knew all about it, but those whores in Vienna, standing there in slit panties around the Gürtel and with numbers tattooed on their groins, those, not to be crude, only go with you with a rubber, and they want four hundred for half an hour . . . But me, I'm a considerate guy, I know that you girls have only got what you've got with you and nothing more. Nobody's going to hire you—like they hired me, a man—for example, for the kind of idiotic *Platz* like the one I have, namely digging a *Hausgrund*, standing every day in a stinking watery disgusting swamp up to my thighs, and the second you lean on your shovel, much less climb out of the hole, instantly the chestnuts are right on top of you yelling, *Gemma, gemma, schnell, schnell* . . . So a woman like you can't do that kind of slave labor, see, but I get eighty schillings an hour for it . . . So have another beer; after all, it doesn't cost so much for me, twenty schillings, I make that in fifteen minutes . . . So, yeah, see, money I've got, I work my ass off for it like a nigger, and a lot of it I send off home to my wife, 'cause . . . well, I miss her, I've got three kids by her, and suddenly something snaps in my head and I go running off. And on top of it, so my wife wouldn't find out, I arranged it all in secret, see, I had the passport and the visa to Yugoslavia hidden in the cellar under a pile of coal—so now, look, what if we helped each other out. I'll even give you, say, two hundred schillings—let's see, that's less than I make in three hours of work, not such a bad deal—what do you say? I'm making the money and you haven't got anything else, right?

And his moist Saint Bernard–like gaze fixed on me from beneath his matted, oily hair. Until everything clenched up inside me.

●

Or should I tell the story of Ekrem? The guy with the bewitching smile and the bullet hole through his shinbone? We first met when I saw him limping happily across the camp courtyard in the direction of the infirmary, an expression of divine bliss on his face. He spoke in broken Serbo-Croatian without declension and told me he was from Albania.

"Albania?" I asked suspiciously. "Or Kosovo?"

Since I had been in the camp more than a month, I already knew all about those two hundred or so Albanians who made a big show of wearing Turkish pants with knives in their belts (so that even the cops were scared of them) and who went around pestering the girls. (No one was safe from them; you should be reminded, my friends, of what happened just a couple of days ago to the one eternally drunk Polish girl, who made the rounds of the Hilton in her red overcoat, discolored by piss to dark brown.) I knew perfectly well that all these people were not real Albanians, but a bunch of shysters who had been born in the Kosovo region of Yugoslavia. But, since that would not have sufficed to gain them asylum, they thought up stories about how they had fled Albania across minefields, while in reality they had only crossed the well-trodden trail from Yugoslavia to Österreich, dumping their Yugoslavian passports along the way.

"Are you from Albania—or from Kosovo?" I asked Ekrem doubtfully; I didn't really feel much like talking to him anyway. After all, if a girl from the Henhouse were to get into a conversation with every guy she met limping across the camp yard, well, we all know where that could lead . . . But Ekrem fixed two deep black eyes on me and only said: "I'm from Albania." "That I'd like to see. Have you got an Albanian passport?" And Ekrem, with the most beautiful eyes I had ever seen in my life, laughed at me and said something like: "How could I have an Albanian passport when in Albania we have no passports? The only way to get out of Albania is to run for it—and in my case, I succeeded!"

The conversation was conducted on his part in broken Serbo-Croatian and on mine in a sort of universal Slavic language developed to fit the requirements of camp life. And I hardly would have been convinced if the beaming Ekrem had not pointed with the thumb of his left hand to his bandaged right leg held rigid by an aluminum splint: "Look! I had a bullet right here! I had a bullet in my leg. I got it fleeing Albania. Jesus Christ, how lucky I am! They shot at me, but they didn't kill me! They didn't hit me in the head or the heart or the stomach, they hit me in the leg. They broke the bone, but the doctors already fixed it, see . . . I'll just have a little limp. Aren't I lucky?"

That's what he told me the first day, and for many days afterward he would pull the bullet out of his pocket where he kept it as a good-luck charm, but he would not hand it to me at first, no: he held it carefully between two fingers and turned it around and around, so that I could at least appreciate its form with my eyes . . . And later, when he finally let me hold it, he just looked on piously as I touched it, as I held it up to the sun and allowed the ray of light reflected from it to enter my pupil. I rolled Ekrem's bullet between my fingers, feeling how it was cold all over except for the two points by which he had held it a second before. I knew that this little bullet, although it was scuffed and more elongated than spherical, held within it the roundness of Ekrem's world, the world that he would circumnavigate.

By that time we already knew each other a bit better and Ekrem was trying to convince me to go with him to Australia to stay with his brother, who had already been there eight years. Ekrem now knew this for certain. Before, he'd had no news of him, since letters never made it through to Albania, but now Ekrem had found his brother through a refugee organization: Let's go to him, to Australia. Ekrem was doubly lucky: he had gotten a bullet in the leg and he had found me. Ekrem's wound had suddenly given him a fever, and they put him in the camp infirmary for a couple of days. I can still see him reaching out for me from the bed, surprisingly dark among the white linens, puckering his lips and begging for a kiss; he would get it. Ekrem was twenty-four and had no wife; he had never thought of marrying, only of fleeing; as for the rest, he had been a student in Albania and that meant working eight hours a day—then going to school in the evening. He had also wanted to learn English, but how could he when there were no textbooks, no courses, nothing. If it hadn't been for the fact that a relative had smuggled a Serbo-Croatian dictionary across the border to him, he wouldn't have spoken even that language. But now he was lucky in every way: he had succeeded in escaping, he was madly in love with me, and he longed to be with me until death parted us.

He declared his love for me for so long that I finally had to do *something*; besides, there was that diamond spark in his dark, black-brown eyes. In those days he had no thoughts of work; he had a pretty bad limp, his leg was in pain—and so it happened that he led me to the end of the corridor on the first floor of the Hilton, to Room 44, where he lived with his Albanian friends—not the real kind, of course, but the ones from Kosovo. It was afternoon, his friends were off working somewhere, everything, he said, had been calculated so that they couldn't unexpectedly return; nevertheless, Ekrem warily looked up and down the corridor before quietly closing the door, and since it didn't lock from the inside he barricaded it with two wardrobes.

I sat on the bed, feeling pretty embarrassed; I watched Ekrem push the cabinets, the muscles standing out on his arms, his effort to overcome the pain in his wounded leg—until he was impatient and trembling from all that exertion . . . I observed him limping around the room, always with that happy, beaming smile. The moment when I would have to spread my legs for him was approaching, but there was no excitement on my part; I just had no choice, because he'd been talking my ear off too long, because they had just recently released him from the infirmary, because he had the most magnificent smile I'd ever seen in my life. And so there I was, on the first floor of the Hilton; the boy from whose shinbone the doctors had removed a bullet that opened the world for him was now dragging those wardrobes up against the door —and I was saying to myself: well, at least he's a real Albanian, that bullet proves it.

And I didn't know where to look when Ekrem clumsily tied a piece of sheet to a broomstick and hung it over the window to form a kind of curtain. I didn't know where to look, because through the dusty window and even through the sheet the bright yellow sun still penetrated the room. It illuminated the dust. And there was a smell, a smell here that forced you to remember what happened to that Polish girl in the coat red as a flower and all soaked with piss in the back. How could you not know about it, all of Traiskirchen is buzzing about it, the Albanians (or was it the Romanians?) got her—no, no, no, it was the Albanians, I know all about it. They dragged her off to their room, and not to rape her in a normal, humane way, so to speak, one, two, three, and it's over—sure, that happens—but not them, they stripped her completely from the waist down and banged her with her legs spread on the lower bunk, and to make it easier on themselves they tied her feet to the top bunk with belts . . . And they took turns on her, at least thirty of them, then they brought friends over to have a go too, and they were too lazy to go to the can for water, so they washed her underneath with beer . . . Well, you can imagine the stench, the whole mattress soaked with Kronenbier. How do I know? I just happen to know, and if you don't believe me, young lady, go on over there and ask them about it yourself, they'll explain it to you, dearie, and in graphic detail, I guarantee you that, just hope you don't have to get sewn back up like that drunken Polish girl, they say a doctor in Baden had her under the knife for two hours, just to put her piss-covered snatch back together again, so run along and ask them if I'm making it up . . .

It smelled here of beer slops, dozens of exotic smells from men's feet; it smelled here of sex, and even more so of the longing for it . . . Maybe we shouldn't close that window, since, uh, so much sun gets through anyway. It smelled of leftovers from dinners in filthy mess tins atop the wardrobes, and I thought about how it really must have been for that poor Polish girl; I knew her by sight, she was back in the camp and was making the rounds at the Hilton again, begging for beer . . .

I thought about the Polish girl, and Ekrem became suddenly nervous; he embraced me with the resolve of a grizzly bear, but he could not manage to lay me on the bed; all of a sudden, although he was older, he seemed so small in this way. Because I understood that he didn't know what to do with my body, it took him half an hour just to extract me from my T-shirt; he was afraid of me, because I was a woman and consequently on my body were located (and fairly well distributed) all the attributes of womanhood—and all of this was just too much for him, he simply couldn't take it, and I purposely didn't help him with anything; I just said to him—naïvely—that he should, for God's sake, be careful, but most probably Ekrem did not even hear me saying "*Pazi, pazi, molim, pazi*" in my newly learned Serbo-Croatian; I was suffocating under him in the bunk sealed off by a wall created with a military blanket, it was unbearably hot all of a sudden, the sun made the blanket glow brownly, but it didn't even have the time to move across it.

I got out of bed in a hurry; Ekrem tried to smile courageously and failed; I was pissed at him. I would have to go outside, into the camp yard, still so embarrassingly filled with brilliant sunlight. I needed to wipe myself with a handkerchief or something.

God, what a stench. Of course he hadn't been careful: he hadn't been capable of it, simply not capable. I was pissed. Ekrem, do you have any water here? He shrugs his shoulders and grins; I spot a can of Kronenbier on the windowsill. Say, Ekrem, would you mind if I used that beer to wash myself off?

After that, his apologies, declarations, entreaties, the trip across the camp yard. "Want to go to the pub, at least I can buy you a"—he thinks for a moment, then says—"coffee." But he really wasn't the type who could buy you a coffee, who knew how to take you out for a coffee; I guess there are no pubs in Albania . . . Thanks, but no thanks . . .

And afterward I made myself scarce when he came to look for me in *Nummer sieben*. Where's Jitka?—Jitka's not here . . . If only I'd been able to tell him *why* I didn't want to see him . . . that he'd almost reduced me to tears that time, that I couldn't stand him, that it was like he was from another planet.

Until one day he waited for me outside the Henhouse, and when I unsuspectingly came out, he rushed after me: "I want to talk to you!"—but I had no interest . . . And so Ekrem bounded after me, tackled me to the ground, and kicked me all over. "I lo-o-oved you, lo-o-oved you, *un-der-stand?*" and his foot struck my body with each syllable. But in the end none of it really mattered. I got my period on time, the bruises disappeared— and that was the end of Ekrem.

•

Or should I tell the story of Good Morning, who told everyone who wanted to hear it their fortunes, in English. No charge, of course; he would snatch your palm between his supple, caressing hands . . . and prophesy a brilliant, happy future for everyone except himself; he was from somewhere in Uganda (which had another name by now), and here, in the camp, in a tiny little room where he had no electricity, but where he lived alone and could make as big a mess as he wanted, he was in his fifteenth year, waiting for the situation in Uganda to change. He was called

Good Morning because he walked around the camp day after day, and when anyone greeted him in any language—whether it was *Grüss Gott*, Hello, *Nazdar*, or *Tschüs*—he raised his hand and answered, night or day: "Go-o-o-od Mo-o-orning! Go-o-o-od Mo-o-orning!" Good Morning interpreted my dream of embracing Earth: "When the time comes, you will become pregnant"— which made me nervous. But the most important part was the excitement I got from his velvety supple hands, whenever he held my palm and predicted by the lines what awaited me. And even though I knew he wouldn't do it, I hoped a little that he would slide that velvety hand up my wrist and forearm, higher, that he would pull me to him, but he never did.

●

Or should I tell myself the story of the Professor, how he set himself up in a little superapartment on the top bunk of a rather untamed room at the Hilton and how, ignoring the tremors caused by screwing, fights, and masturbation, he, by night-light, finally read Nietzsche in the original? At the age of sixty-five the Professor had decided to emigrate. For a long, long time he had believed that the situation in Czechoslovakia simply had to change—until one day he realized that he was too old to wait any longer.

●

What else came to mind? The savage fights at the Hilton, which came to us, the women of the Henhouse, only in the form of wild clamor and then afterward as stories, painted in vivid color by someone who, it would turn out, hadn't seen anything in the first place, because otherwise, instead of telling us the story, he'd have been getting sewn back together in the Baden hospital? Or should I have considered people's desires? *Zimmer Nummer sieben*, which was now our little world? Marta's Tomcats with hairy chests, with whom she always fell in love and who always screwed her over? Hanka and Zdeněk's sex life and Marta's clucking? Or

Mira and the Hilton? Sprawling Josko, in whom—to his satisfaction—a great, hairy, apish, drunken buzz was brewing at that
very moment? Or all of it, but in some kind of order? But that
wouldn't have worked, it couldn't be presented in any kind of
order, because there was no order of any kind here in the camp.
Every week or two weeks we created a minideluge for ourselves
in the room, wiped it around with a rag and some suds, and
pushed the dust off the window frames. Each of us here had dirty
laundry in a pail under her bed, and when in a couple of days
it began to stink, we washed it and then guarded it so the bastards
wouldn't swipe it from the line stretched between the two acacias.
So that was the only order there was in the camp, there was no
more and there never would be; for us the camp was a faceless
monster with no beginning and no end . . . two serpents devouring
each other by the tail.

•

Then there was a timid knock on the door.
"Come in!" Marta called out with bureaucratic mistrust.
Zděnek added: "Through the door!"
Whereupon the door swung open and through it stepped—
Wild Bára. I recognized her immediately, despite the fact that
we had never set eyes on one another. Bára had spent a considerable time, a good two months, living in Vienna with some guy.
Indeed, Bára's nickname fit: beneath her single, concrescent
eyebrow she had large dark eyes, the crooked nose of an eagle,
and a square chin. She wore a rumpled woolen dress in a blue-
and-green-checked pattern—and, underneath it, red patterned
stockings. Precisely the type of clothing that was left to lie in the
YMCA from the Charity shipments, since even the Romanians
wouldn't haggle over such things. It was apparent even from
Bára's manner of dress that she was of a gentle nature. And in
spite of the fact that the almost offensive red color of her stockings
disappeared into well-worn army boots, it was clear that Bára
would never have used those army boots to kick anyone's butt.
She was, in fact, the most unmilitary person imaginable. Given

her broad-shouldered Moravian frame, this seemed a miracle.

Behind Wild Bára entered her worn jute bag, already dragged a long way through the mud, and about two tons of embarrassment. It seeped into the room from all around her, from in front of her and in back of her. "Gi-i-irls," Bára forced the words out, "do you think I could live here again?"

"But, Bára, Bára, whatever happened to you?" Hanka chanted in a singsong voice.

"So you've come back to us," Marta mumbled from the mirror. I introduced myself to Bára and offered her some leftover potato porridge. It was Mira's, anyway.

Bára sat down at the table in a flash and started shoveling the oily porridge faster than she could fit it in her mouth. She had a certain . . . primal . . . primitive quality that immediately endeared her to me: that slightly hunchbacked figure, those curtains of rumpled black hair, that peasant movement, elbow extended, with which she brought the overflowing spoon to her lips. I registered Mirek's sideways glance; it seemed he too was thinking about Bára. And it began to bother me slightly that he looked at women the way that he did.

"So why are you here, Barunka?" Hanka asked straightaway in a honeyed voice. "After all, you announced to the whole world how you had this fantastic guy with an apartment in Vienna. Or was it a fantastic apartment with a guy, or . . ."

"Yes, you're right, Hanka," Bára said self-critically. "Except that it was a lousy apartment with a totally stupid guy. I knew from the start that it wasn't going to be ideal, but what happened after that, I never expected." Bára (once again with that country girl's gesture, elbow stuck out to the side) loaded up another spoonful of cold, oily camp porridge. She brought it to her mouth. And we were all waiting to hear what she would tell us once she'd emptied that spoon. It was silent in the room. Only Josko gurgled something, but we had not paid any attention to him for some time. Bára finished eating, loudly scraped out the bottom of the pot with her spoon, licked her chops—and began her story.

"So he was such a moron, I'd rather not even name him, just

in case you might happen to know him. Well, he let me live in one lousy closet in his place under the condition that my *room*" (Bára relied on sound painting to place quotation marks around this word) "had to look like no one lived there, so that the land-lord wouldn't come and raise the rent on account of me. So I lay a blanket out on the floor and I'm satisfied, it's comfortable and quiet. During the day I was going to work for this Slovak woman and, since my little place had no electricity, I studied German at night by candlelight. But I forgot about the guy, and after three days he comes to my bed. He says, 'You're living here for free —are you satisfied?' Sure . . . I'm satisfied. And so what am I going to give him in return? He wanted to screw, wonder of wonders. And I liked it in his place, better than being in the camp, right . . . ?" Bára's darkened gaze passed over her lis-teners. She met no dissension. She continued. "So, I say to myself, I'm no virgin anymore, I'll give him what he wants and that'll be that. 'Give me some *Geld* for rubbers,' I say to him, 'and we'll see what we can do.' And do you know what he did? He gave me *eleven* schillings, to buy a three-pack; that whoring bastard had it all figured out so that there wouldn't be so much as fifty groschen left over for me. So I bought the damned three rub-bers, and we went through them all that same day, and then he wanted to wash out the third one, said he wouldn't mind an-other go . . ."

Bára gave a small sigh and looked around the room. She ran her eyes over everyone there then lowered them to her lap, to her large, rough hands, in which she still fondled the pot smeared with potato porridge.

"So it was like that every day. He worked the night shift, as a bouncer in some bar, he would come home at five-thirty in the morning, start shaking me and . . . until one time he left me in peace for two days straight, so I say to myself, that's the end of it, maybe he's gotten sick of me now, but then he comes to my bed again, shakes me out of my blanket and says, 'He-e-ey.' "

In exaggerated Moravian fashion, Bára imitates the breathy, elongated endings of the Prague accent. " 'It's no fun screwing you anymo-o-ore, so you can scrub my floors inste-e-ead!' So fine, I'll scrub the floors and I won't even mind; after all, I've done more than my share of every kind of *spüling* and *putzing* in my day. But it was exactly the same way with that scrubbing as it was with screwing: not once or twice or three times a week but every day, two times a day! He would pull me out of bed in the morning: 'Fill the bucket with water!' Then he would stand over me and gape, or he'd lie under a quilt and beat off. Well, I could even have put up with that. But then he comes to my bed one morning, starts shaking me—it's a miracle I didn't give up the ghost right then and there—so I rub my eyes and head off to fill the bucket with water, but he says, 'I'm sick of screwing you, and you don't have to wash the floors anymore. You live here for free, sleep here for free. Do you want to suck my dick?' And at this point even I, and I'm a good-natured person, even I've had enough. No, I don't, I say, and I turn to the wall. So he leaves. But the next day, same thing: 'Do you want to suck my dick?' —'No, I don't!' And everything is quiet again. But he comes again on the third day. 'I'm asking you for the last time: Do you want to suck my dick?' And when I tell him for the third time that I don't, then he just says: 'Pack up your things and get the hell out of here!' —So here I am again."

Bára was done talking. And even on the face of the ever scornful Hanka there had settled a look of compassion. "And is that all, Bára?" she asked quietly as she gently pulled the emptied tin from Bára's hands. "Or what else did that moron do to you?"

"Well, nothing else, really," Bára said courageously. "He wasn't really that bad . . ." And we all watched as her face contorted, as her lower lip trembled.

"There's something else, isn't there?"

Sobbing. "And he also . . . he also said to me, Rhubarbara, go dig yourself a hole and plant yourself in it!"

And with this Bára threw herself headfirst into the covers on

Hanka's bed, huddled there like an ostrich, and started wailing like a newborn.

·

Before lights-out in the room that evening, a half moon managed to make its appearance. It filled the camp yard with such a bewitching blend of yellow and silver that the Hilton was transformed into the longed-for, ancient castle of a fairy tale. I wrapped myself tightly in my blanket, just so I wouldn't be lured out into the night. The room was quiet. Hanka and Zdeněk were not screwing today, they were just huddled together—and the sound of whispering could be heard, but not the actual words. Bára snored softly on Baška's untouched bed. She was sleeping like a baby, and the moon tinted her red stockings—which she hadn't gotten around to taking off—to the color of dull bronze. I had succeeded in humanely ejecting Mirek, and Josko, only half-naked but thoroughly piss-drunk, was sleeping in Marta's bed, without having fulfilled her expectations, and snoring directly into her ear. In other words: the nighttime quiet was disturbed only by the distant rhythms of the Hilton and the sound of Marta's radio. And the light of the waning moon now filled my camp bunk, my unassailable fortress, with a luminosity that was almost too silvery. So I couldn't really fall asleep. I snuggled deep down into my bed—and, perhaps in order to preempt the dream that lurked just inside of me, that lay in wait just beneath my eyelids, I decided to assert my claim to the dream that very instant. I forged it into an image of my own. I already knew that the dream was stirring inside me. And I decided that tonight it would be a dream of the sea.

Christopher, Chris Columbus! Can anyone today imagine what it was like for you the first time you headed for India—to the west? You set off with your flotilla from the shores of Spain; Santa Maria blazed a trail with her wooden bow, and the salty spray sparkled on her sides in the sunlight. And every night the sun sank into the waves of the Atlantic, turning its vastness into an orange desert. Didn't your heart shudder just a little bit? Didn't you fear that you wouldn't return but would fall off the edge of that small, flat earth?

The world *was* flat until you sailed around it.

"*Danke vielmals,*" I said as soon as I'd opened the door of the stopped Mercedes. "*Ich fahre nach . . .*" Suddenly I recalled the lessons of experienced Nad'a, but the word Baden did not come out of my mouth. It was more than just an issue of being hypocritical. I didn't look anything like a tourist. I had on a smelly kitchen T-shirt and hands parched red from washing dishes.

Despite Nad'a's warning, I actually did manage to finish saying the word *Traiskirchen* before the backroads part of the trip began. The detour among ripening sunflowers did not come until we reached Wiener Neudorf.

The only thing I could do was give him a little slap, not so hard that it hurt him, but hard enough that it did not seem like an erotic invitation. Nevertheless, I was struck by the pleasantness of the touch of caressing hands, I tried (in vain) to order my nipples not to get hard beneath his palm, I was suddenly ashamed of my sweaty, faded T-shirt, and I knew that he knew that underneath it my skin smelled better. He was supplicating, and not too pushy—and the measured signal given by that slap seemed only the defensive function of the rational mind. He was a bit older, potbellied, balding—in any case, he himself did not play any role in it. It was the warmth of the touch that excited me, the promise of the questionable security of those hands offering me a whole hundred schillings (four hours of dishwashing).

"You really don't want to make a little something extra?" he asked me sadly. "I'll be good to you. I'll be gentle. You don't have to do a thing."

I imagined it. Suddenly I felt an incredible urge to let him embrace me. But in the meantime he took out another hundred-shingle note.

Like many others I am enriched by the enviable talent of retrospective eloquence, even in languages I habitually mangle, like German. Not days or hours, but minutes after I should have said something funny, scathing, brilliant, or trenchant, the appropriate words come to me with the greatest of ease; but at the proper moment I clam up. Not long after this event the phrases came to me: *Was machen Sie? Du Trottel, ich bin keine Hure!* Even complex sentences on the theme of how I had spent the whole day working like a dog and couldn't he at least drive me to the damned camp in peace and quiet. But at the moment nothing of the kind occurred to me. Instead, I lay my head on the dashboard and broke out in sobs of despair.

●

For some time already I had been conducting a private study of the means by which rumors spread in the camp—and how it was possible that before a thing even finished happening, the sparrows on the roofs were already chirping about the very same trifle, faux pas, or sin. Indeed, having nothing better to do, I had occupied myself with the problems of camp informational dynamics, but in this case it proved a bit too much to be believed. Before I had managed to walk across the darkened camp yard, past the *Lagerleitung* and the "Gypsy building" right in the corner, past the medical building, which in the light of the moon (which was narrower by a sliver than it had been last night) loomed like a terrifying morgue behind its lawn of thoroughly choked grass; before I had managed to shuffle around Building 5 (in which were located the administrative offices) up to the gate of the Henhouse, accompanied as usual by whistling, clucking, finger snapping, and other greetings from my fellow camp inmates; before I had passed beneath the chestnuts and the linden, from which the leaves were beginning to fall; before I had a slight scare from several apparently Albanian characters who at one point—too close for my comfort—passed by in Turkish trousers and a cloud of danger; before I had managed to bulldoze my way headlong through the hordes of Turkish, Greek, Albanian, and Romanian men gushing out of the Hilton; before I warily deflected my gaze from a group of unfamiliar creatures spread out in strikingly un-European poses in front of the closed doors of the YMCA, chewing on blades of grass, letting off steam by scratching the more obscene parts of their bodies, digging shamelessly into their noses and yelling out at passersby in broken German; before I had managed to navigate all of this on the way from the camp gates to the Henhouse, the entire room already knew that our Jituška had bagged herself a totally new, totally bald boyfriend in Vienna, one who loved her so terribly much that he drove her right up to the camp gates in a white Mercedes.

·

"What are you talking about?" I protested immediately when Zdeněk peeped curiously out the door, requesting the details. "He just picked me up hitchhiking from Vienna."

"And how much did you make?"

"Mirek hasn't given it to me yet."

"But I mean extra."

"Oh, please . . ."

"Jituš," Hanka said with a worldly air. "Hold on to that one, that kind of guy can be damned helpful. A little older . . ."

"You might even be able to squeeze a little something out of a guy like that. If you took a little better care of yourself." Marta from in front of the mirror. Her usual location.

"Really, just hitchhiking? And he drove you all the way here? Boy, these women have it made. And they make an extra hundred on the trip. Now if I were a woman, then . . ." Zdeněk was squatting by the refrigerator again. With his body he had curtained off a square meter of the wooden floor into which he was luring cockroaches with a pan of dinner leftovers. Now he swung at a cockroach (more likely imaginary than real), whacking it with

his shoe to emphasize his words. "Now if I were a woman, then
. . . Aren't I right, my little bedbug? *I'd* like to give that a try,
a guy can fart farther than he'd get hitchhiking. Haven't you
heard about how Band'urka wanted to hitchhike from Vienna,
so he stood out by the ramp and stuck out his right hand, and
since no one was picking him up, he started getting bored and
started walking backward in the direction of the camp, and if he
hadn't hit his head on a sign saying BADEN—18 KILOMETERS and
rolled down into the ditch, I wager he'd have made it walking
backward all the way here without getting a lift. Yes, girls, you're
lucky . . ."

And another unfortunate, naïve, and trustful cockroach must
have stuck its antennae out from behind the refrigerator, because
Zdeněk crouched down like a prowling tiger, lifted his shoe, and
hit the wooden floor with such force that the glasses in the cupboard jumped.

●

But that evening I climbed into the bed, stretched out beneath
the military blanket—savoring its coarseness, letting myself be
embraced by it (since there was no one else at hand)—and prepared my dream beneath my eyelids. The last one, about Columbus, had succeeded very nicely, and, although I wasn't at all sure
of its historical accuracy, I would have been quite happy to repeat
it. It had been all azure blue and translucent, exactly as if my
camp bed were perched on some cliff over the sea. So much so
that it was not obvious whether the dream colored my mood or
my mood colored the dream. Today I was afraid that the sea I
was planning to dream would resemble dirty dishwater.

●

The silver-foamed crest of the wave changed into a crater in
the shape of a face without skin, in the nose cavity a heart was
aching, pulsating with gray-brown pain. I fell down into the abyss
of this face, and its gray nerves like veins reached out their

tentacles for me. Suddenly I realized that the face was *me*, that I was drowning in *me*, falling into *me*, and so I had no choice but to wake up.

Judging by Marta's sighs, Josko had screwed the right one on tonight. It seemed as if it was working surprisingly well for Hanka and Zdeněk, too. Hanka was purring, the springs were rustling. Even Wild Bára had found someone to gratify her, and, although he spoke only Hungarian, it must have been a nice change from scrubbing floors. Only the old stick-in-the-mud Miss Jituška was so disgustingly alone tonight that she even longed for that bald geezer in the Mercedes. And with gusto. Wrapped up in her blanket as if in a sarcophagus, she tried in vain to chase away today's dream.

·

And suddenly, out of the clear blue sky, for the first time since I had left home (since the body of the semi driven by Ramazan the Turk had relegated my homeland to the past), the question occurred to me. WHY?

WHY appeared to me printed on the ceiling in gigantic neon letters. It was the first internal WHY, the first *real* WHY with which I'd had to do battle. It was the first WHY that hurt. The earlier whys, the ones in isolation, the ones the Czech interpreter had translated for me from the Austrian's *Warum*—and afterward carefully recorded the answer—these had been important, of course: oppression in Communist Czechoslovakia, absolutely no access to higher education. Certainly, these were important whys, and I hadn't even needed to make anything up. Because of that winter evening, before I'd started seeing Standa, when I had stupidly gotten myself arrested at an illegal rock concert on that boat on the Vltava, and I wouldn't even have gotten mixed up in that if I hadn't been going out with that bassist, that was my big screwup. I should have taken up with the flute player instead, supposedly he'd also been interested in me. But there we were, dragging Franta's bass over the ice of that Vltava backwater. The ice began to crack, Franta panicked—and before we knew it we were at the police station getting a face full of it. He lost the bass anyway, because the neck got broken "in transit"; immediately after the hearing, in fact, poor Franta had been forced to watch the neck of the bass snap, with the assistance of two policemen—in transit. At first the bass had stubbornly refused to surrender, so, while one public servant sat on the body of the instrument, another, obese one had to jump on the neck with his entire weight several times. Here the interpreter chuckled, quickly explained to the Austrian, and said: "And what happened next?"

And, of course, there had been very little hope that I might go to university. Although they did allow me to graduate—just barely—there had been a ton of trouble for me at the high school, Franta the bassist dumped me anyway—and I ended up with Standa. Which was none of the Austrians' business.

In the end, my reasons for fleeing, one two three four, were not all that bad; better than I could have hoped for. Apparently, I made the impression that I was either genuinely political or a very good liar. The adventure on the boat and the ensuing sanctions looked great, even on an application for the States, but they still didn't give me an answer to the great question WHY.

In the light of the waning moon that silvered Room 7—more weakly by a sliver than yesterday—a great, violet, neon WHY blinked before my mind's eye with the impact of a Coca-Cola ad.

This was a WHY for which the story with the bass was no match. And if I managed to approach an answer, it seemed to have something to do with the roundness of the world.

It was the convexity of bluish spheres—and the hollow, melancholy, empty space within us. The roundness of the great world, into which I would make my way—and the roundness deep within me: the roundness of that dream in which, like a mother, you encompass the entire world.

•

In a state of therapeutic half-sleep, I reached down to the bottom of my soul, trying to revive my tiny little sufferings . . .

my longings, my recollections—hoping that through them I might come to some sort of understanding. I searched within myself for my small, sweet sufferings and instead of them I found only empty places. Monstrously vast empty places. So vast that I expected them to be projected in my dream.

Was that the way it really was? Did my dream close off these voids, did it—for a short time—simply fill in the empty spaces within me, only to leave them emptier and far more painful once the dream had passed?

During the day these emptinesses did not horrify me, because during the day a person cannot reach so deeply down inside herself. But at night, at night the emptiness knew no end, it was like falling into an abyss . . . The farther I fell, the more unfathomable the bottom. Thoughts bounced between the endless emptinesses like Ping-Pong balls between facing black mirrors. I leaned into the emptinesses, and their bottoms receded before me. And I was paralyzed by the suspicion that their bottoms did not exist.

·

All this absurd crap occurred to me as I dozed off, reaching out to touch my sufferings, my emptinesses, the black holes into which my whole world had disappeared. (That flowered landscape that I had left behind forever.) Back then, when Standa was embracing me, I had already known how the black hole left by his absence would appear, I had known its face with precision, and I expected it to be voracious.

So now everything was sinking into that black hole . . . everything I had taken for granted, everything that had protected me. My black hole devoured it all, devouring me from the inside like cancerous tissue, except that it didn't grow within me like a tumor, no, it grew tinier, but deeper and deeper: able to absorb more and more.

·

In the course of this meditation, even the understanding of what it was I had fled from in the first place disappeared into my black hole.

The boat story was now useless for me. The reasons for leaving, one two three four, were now not even remotely important, as I lay on my back and the nuclei of the black holes gobbled away at me from the inside. At such times it was necessary to turn to more lasting things, small, ordinary things, things that were the same here as they had been there.

The sparkling of water in a glass.

The scent of grass (which was now already withering).

The taste and aroma of coffee. Except that even that was a little different here; in Austria we couldn't seem to brew a good Czech-style cup of Turkish coffee. They ground the coffee differently here, or something, because the grounds kept floating to the top of the mug.

The crunch of the dirt and pebbles beneath your feet as you walked across the camp yard.

The phases of the moon.

The ripening grapes beyond the camp wall and the falling of yellow leaves from the chestnut trees. The pattern of their bark.

Fields of blooming sunflowers. These were almost like van Gogh's, except that afterward in that dream of mine they became poisonously yellow and were transformed into the blades of circular saws that cut your skull into slices, which then went spinning off into the vacuum. And as a result I was almost glad when at five-fifteen the alarm clock went off next to my ear, and I set out for Vienna to *spülen Geschirr.*

●

Physical labor, even when I hated it, was still without a doubt a breather from such dreams. Twelve hours of dishwashing, together with bending over the sink, red parched hands, the not very tasteful jokes of the proprietor, and the intrusive smell of detergent—and afterward hitchhiking from Vienna to Baden (on the second and third days I was wiser, I said Baden—and I have to admit that it worked, although the drivers were not at all surprised when I told them, "*Halt,*" in Traiskirchen)—this sort of work helped, although it was significantly better when Edita the Open House got back on her feet, so that I could lie on my back by the camp wall, getting a tan in the last rays of the sun in the Indian summer of that year—and watch the small airplanes that linked us with the world out there.

16

"You have gorgeous nipples. Just like rosy little mountains. If you let me, I would caress them right now. But I guess this is not the time . . ."

It was better to go lie in the sun with two or three companions, and to take some guy along with you for protection. Then we could safely trample down a comfy little lair in the corner beneath the brick wall—and bare ourselves without fear, guarded by the tall stalks of grass. Marta left her blouse on, just giving it a good loosening around the collar—but I intended to feel free today. Maybe that was the most important thing. It was bewitching to let the sun envelop you, to be aware of the darkish, striped shadows of the grass stalks on your body, to merge your back with the moist earth and your eyelids with the sky. At times it seemed to me that this was the only freedom we had here. The grass was redolent. The air was translucently blue and glowing with sunlight. No black holes in sight. From time to time a plane crossed the sky, the plane that one day, glinting silver, would carry us into the distance. The rumble, buzz, and shouting of the camp were now somewhere far away, dampened by the tall grass as if by a scorched pampa. And when a brown grasshopper jumped up and landed with a little thump on the sensitive skin between your breasts, the world was absolutely beautiful. Peace and quiet. Yes, even Marta was now silent. I could hear only Mirek's voice from a distance of about half a meter, purring quite pleasantly into my ear.

"If you let me, I'd caress your nipples for hours. Terribly gently. That's the way they like it, see? And I would feel how they got beautifully hard. Because they would like it so much, my caressing. Just look at them, sweet little things, just hearing me talk about it is making them grow. And I, I know exactly how to play with them so wonderfully . . ."

Suddenly I was linked to Mirek by the thin ribbon of his voice; he was drawing me to him with that voice as if by a leash; his voice wrapped around me and bound me to him. I could see that there was no escape.

And meanwhile Marta, feeling neglected, clawed off her top and, hopeful, bared her chest to the sun.

•

It wasn't in the least bit important what was or wasn't going on. We couldn't even think of getting acquainted in the public atmosphere of Room 7, so Mirek rounded up a car somewhere, and we drove off to a little hotel just outside of Baden—and Mirek, because he could see how it excited me, undressed me slowly, almost without touching me, as if he were removing a molting lizard's skin. After that we sat naked next to one another and he did not try to seduce me with his cuddling, not at all. He just wrapped me up in his voice as if in a cloak, a silkworm's cocoon in a mulberry bush; he bound me up so that I could not speak or think, but only slightly, ever so slightly, tremble. We were almost at opposite ends of the wide, clean bed, him tying me up in his voice—and only much later holding me lightly by the tips of my fingers, by my lips, by my breasts. He filled me with his voice for such an endlessly, unbearably long time, and probably that's exactly why he succeeded in neutralizing that black hole in my soul, so that when he finally filled me with himself and kept talking to me and whispering, there appeared within me an aroused but peaceful haven where the two of us could indulge ourselves until morning.

•

But even that was not important. What was important was that beautiful birch outside the window in the morning, actually just a small section of its trunk, and not even that so much. What made me wonder was the fact that I was noticing details, small things, the likes of which had never found their way to me so quickly before.

The delicate sweat on his back. The fragrant smell of his hair.

The small group of dark brown freckles on the back of his neck, reminiscent of the constellation of Cassiopeia.

Mirek was coming into me . . . not as a whole, not like a chance dream chaser. He was coming into me in illogical fragments. At first as the touch of words. Then as the scents of caresses. Finally as the music of penetration.

It occurred to me—that very first day—that I had fallen in love.

●

Although even that wasn't the most important thing. The main thing was that all night, until morning, he gently held my right nipple, so that this touch, which ran along nerve filaments deep into the center of me, was my very last perception before falling asleep, and the first when I woke up with him.

His fingers held my nipple like an infant's mouth, and this prolonged caress connected me with my own secret inside; I had heard that it could happen this way in motherhood, but I had never suspected that it was possible to awaken with such a feeling: a feeling of peace, calm, and completeness. And that in order to achieve all this it was only necessary for sleeping Mirek to gently rub my right nipple between his thumb and forefinger.

17

Room 7 in the Henhouse was screwing happily once again. The long-standing couple of Hanka and Zděneček were gently rocking the bed supported by cabinet doors. Marta, whom Josko had already managed to dump, was now getting laid, to her slight embarrassment, by an earthy Tomcat from Ostrava, who was about 155th on her list. Baška, who had come home unexpectedly that evening, had vociferously ejected Bára from her bed, and the latter had stretched out on the notorious, sex-worn bed right by the door, the only one that wasn't buttressed by doors, and on it was experiencing the complexities of love with a newly discovered Hungarian. His avowed name was Tibor, but we had nicknamed him Nixproblem. The expression *Nichts Problem* was the only one he ever used in a foreign language, and he used it constantly. Mira had brought someone over from the Hilton, and was doing the deed with him on her old bed, the one right next to Marta's, the one no one else wanted. I held Mirek's elbow and took in the evening's activities. Mirek and I had somehow not succeeded in including ourselves in the universal rhythm of screwing. The atmosphere was a little too thick with the erotic. And the electrical charge of his elbow beneath my hand was quite enough for the time being.

I held Mirek by the elbow and vigilantly followed all the various couplings. After a short period of exertion, Marta's and Mira's lovers succeeded in correlating their rhythms, and the iron heads of their beds banged together in unison. Baška was taking purposeful, deep breaths, no doubt under the assumption that if she feigned sleep she might succeed in dozing off for real. Or perhaps

she was trying to be as far away as possible. At the moment
Hanka and Zděneček were probably doing best of all. They
weren't very noisy, but when you imagined yourself in their places,
you could sense just how beautiful it must have been for them.
But I was not a lone ship lost at sea tonight. I was holding Mirek
by the elbow.

"Wait a minute, come on, wait a minute," Bára was now attempting to restrain Nixproblem. "This mattress is rubbing the
skin off my butt," she explained hopelessly. "I can't take it anymore, I've had it. Tibor!"

"*Nichts Problem, bazmeg, nichts Problem,*" he mumbled and
the uninventive, relentless rhythm of his screwing continued to
shake the room. Even before this his effectiveness and endurance
had become the subject of general discussion: the gentlemen unan-
imously envied him, and the fair maidens imagined how it might
be with him. Only Bára insisted that it was no big deal, that all
she really got out of all that screwing was a boil on her butt.
Marta's Tomcat had already long ago finished up with a satisfied
pant. Mira's newest find had just pulled it out in time beneath
the blanket and was now searching under his breath for a handkerchief. Hanka and Zděnek were cuddled together and every
time Zděnek breathed a little too loudly, Hanka pleaded with
him: "Zdě-eneček . . ."

Through the partially open window above our heads scraps of
music flowed into the room from the Hilton like messengers from
foreign lands.

Suddenly, Nixproblem's persistent screwing was joined by the
stomping steps of two pairs of policeman's boots. It was impossible
to mistake that sound. The steps clattered up to our floor—and
we could hear someone pounding on the Albanian girls' door.
"*Türe öffnen! Polizei!*" Through the wall we heard the echo of
confusion, "*Guten Abend, alles OK—oder nichts?*", and then a
flurry of voices, female and male, loudly protesting in Albanian
half-German. But the further development of events beyond the
wall quickly ceased to interest us. Panic set in in Room 7. "Shit,

the cops!" Zděnek hissed as he began looking for his boxer shorts. From Mira's and Marta's bed flew two white shadows of the male sex. They were not looking for their boxers. As experienced camp skirt-chasers they both had kept them slung over one leg as a precaution. "Hurry, hurry, hurry, get into the cabinet!" Marta cried with presence of mind, and she hid her lover among some sweaters. Mira's suitor flew into another cabinet, and Mira deftly slammed it shut. These two were safe. Mirek's first impulse was to stick his head under the covers, as if he hoped that my embrace would shield him from the Austrian cops. Finally he hid beneath my bed.

The pounding was now on our door. *"Polizei! Öffnen! Kontrol!"*

Marta immediately went running for the door, on the way ejaculating: *"Ja-Ja!"* It sounded like a hen's cackle.

"Hold on, Christ, God, I've only got my shorts on halfway," Zděneček hissed at her. Completely in vain. As if in revenge for all the wrongs she had suffered at his hands, Marta was already turning the key.

Even Baška had jumped out of her bed, looking around to see what was going on.

Only Tibor-Nixproblem kept right on pounding away, despite Bára's protests, and he had to be extracted by authority of the law.

•

Just a couple of minutes later we watched from the window as three wistful male figures trudged—under police escort—across the yard. Nixproblem, who had been caught in the act, Zděneček, for whom no cabinet had remained, and Mirek, who had been sniffed out from beneath my bed, had all been forced to leave the room immediately. The cops had wished us a good night, praised Baška's nightshirt, then clapped the green door shut behind them.

Mira's friend liberated himself from his cabinet and went back to bed. And Marta watched with satisfaction from the window as the three male figures receded across the camp yard, remarking with joyous sadism: "*Ja, ja, ja, nach Hilton marschieren!*"

After which she dragged her lover out of her wardrobe and aroused him into performing an encore.

18

I had already been living about a month surrounded by the Traiskirchen refugee camp—but at the same time I still did not belong to it. I functioned here about like someone who, without the slightest warning, falls suddenly into a cesspool. The thought process of such a person is not complex: it quickly becomes evident to him that he is up to his neck in shit. And then he does everything he can to try to dig his way back out. But if he is not immediately successful, he faces a decision: he can keep suffering miserably among the excrement. Or he himself can become shit. Then he can feel right at home in the cesspool. And I would say that this is exactly what I, through Mirek, managed to do.

When Mirek officially led me to his Hilton cubbyhole for the first time, I became, without the slightest inhibition, an accessory to acts of which I wouldn't even have dreamed just two weeks earlier.

And I felt infinitely better.

·

It seemed to me now that all my life I had only been able to feel at home in the world with the aid of men's touches. Could it really be that—beginning with, let's say, the adventure on the boat on the Vltava, which in fact had been more *Franta's* adventure than mine—it had always been some man who had brought me out into life and among people?

That was probably why I now needed Mirek. Because he was not just a chance dream-chaser. Through Mirek, to whose per-

ception I had attached myself in the course of one night in a little
hotel in Baden, I had access to the Hilton. The genuine article.

●

The doors of the room—painted that unsavory gray-green,
which I of course knew all too well, but whose essential camp
nature I had never understood as deeply as I did today—swung
wide open before us, so I saw everything. The crammed and
stinking space with a bunch of little cubbyholes, within which the
smarter, cleverer, braver, or better-armed lived, while the others
lived up top, on their roofs, more exposed. I saw their faces as
they turned toward us with lazy half-interest. I saw the rickety
table, standing alone in the middle of the room, the spit-covered,
filthy gray floorboards, littered with flattened cigarette butts and
polished only in the pathways along which characters such as
Edita Open House went sliding from one cubbyhole to the next.
Jamming splinters into their heels along the way.

But the most conspicuous phenomenon in the room was the
wallpaper. Pink all over. The boys had papered the walls, wardrobes, and ceiling with naked crotches cut out of porno mags;
from behind the clutter in the corner, composed of unwashed
mess tins, flattened Kronenbier cans, and discarded socks, poked
several more shapely female bodies, and the light switch, the kind
you twist, formed the end of the somewhat overfondled tit of some
lusty blond wench. This wallpaper of pink groins was not in
perfect condition; all daubed with glue, smudged and torn as high
up as eager hands could reach, it was coming unglued from the
walls. But it still worked. The vertical mouths of pussies could
be seen in every corner, and one look at the rickety table was
enough to make it clear that the cards dealt out upon it would
also have to bear photos of naked beauties. This surplus of syn-
thetic womanhood had a slightly narcotic effect on me. Mirek
expected this. He gave me a little prod from behind.

On the broad windowsill stood a pot, containing—judging by
the stench—coagulated dinner leftovers from a couple of days

earlier. Into the pot a spoon dipped from time to time, at the other end of which sat a creature of indeterminate sex, although its voice eventually marked it as male. It was, in fact, the hirsute Band'urka, on whose chin, when he turned slightly, appeared long, shaggy Slovak "whi-i-iskers." "We-e-elcome," Band'urka said extremely sociably, rising from his perch.

The top of the table in the middle of the room was so slanted that it seemed the glass Band'urka's hand was filling with Ballantine's must sooner or later slide across it and shatter on the floorboards. The opalescent surface of the booze was evidently the only consistently horizontal plane in the room. I grabbed the fragrant whisky in its unsavory looking glass and decided that I would derive equilibrium from it. I was the only female in the room, if you didn't count the aura emitted by all those pink things, and everyone took notice of me for this reason. Even the legendary Legionnaire, who was just stretching out on the roof of his cubbyhole in order to get a better survey of the buzz in the room, greeted me—"Hi, pussy!"—and waved his foot at me in an almost friendly manner.

I tilted the Ballantine's in its glass and observed its surface, how it shifted in accordance with the earth's gravity, the only consistently horizontal plane in the room. How is it possible, I asked myself, that people drink alcohol from a perfectly level surface, and end up unable to walk straight?

"And what d'they call you?" the Legionnaire asked with the lofty air of a supermale, afterward taking a long drag on a cigarette he held with four fingers. From his movements, his diction, his dulled voice, I could tell he was not entirely sober.

"Quit messing with her, please," Mirek remarked with a superior air, but it was clear that he was pretty scared of the Legionnaire. I nudged him in the ribs. Inconspicuously, I thought, but Band'urka chuckled.

"So you ha-a-ave another ne-e-ew one," he thrusted in Mirek's direction, sticking his glass into his whiskers.

I had heard about him from Mirek. I knew that he was an

amazing dancer; that when the fever caught him, he would leap
from the wardrobes and walk on his hands and twist and so on.
I also knew that he had been in the camp a good four years. He'd
fucked everything up. No one would take him. First he had applied to Canada, but before they had time to invite him for an
interview, he took off for Germany to see if maybe that wouldn't
be better. When he returned, he found he had missed his chance
with Canada, so he applied to the Down Unders, who didn't take
him; and when you didn't get Canada or Australia, then the
Americans were certain to turn you down, so things didn't look
too rosy for Band'urka. But once—a long time before—when
they had been at a disco in Baden, Band'urka, climbing the walls
and spinning around on the floor, had unleashed such a dance
craze that every girl in the place went crazy over him, Slovak or
no, *Flüchtling* or no; but Band'urka—Band'urka had wanted no
part of it. "I ha-a-ave a wife and child a-a-at home," he said,
and he took off. And when the girls went running after him in
a big mob, he hollered: "I a-a-am a-a-an Easterner, the-e-ey
wi-i-ill ne-e-ever ca-a-atch me!" And they didn't. But Mirek, on
the other hand, now that was a different story . . .

"I don't want to hear about it if you don't mind . . ."

(It wasn't that I was jealous, not at all, it was just that it had
been unthinkable for me at the time to imagine that someone else
before me had been allowed to perceive the camp through him.)

Band'urka poured himself another shot, then stuck the glass
into those whiskers, its contents disappearing in an instant.

"Where's Ládík?"

"Oh, Ládík . . ." The voice came from behind the blanket of
the opposite cubbyhole. "Ládík's got some *Arbeit*. Paper hanging.
Professionell Tapezierer. He nailed this job for a hundred an
hour, man, never mind that he'd never seen any wallpaper in his
life. He was standing out in the day-labor pack and he snagged
himself this lady over forty and now he's making a hundred an
hour papering the walls of her pussy. Just hope he doesn't fuck
his dick off from all of that . . ."

"Him of all people, with all those pimples . . ."

"Well, sure, some forty-five-year-old painted cow . . ."

"They can be damned nice sometimes," Mirek pronounced knowingly, and now I was jealous.

"Did you hear, they locked Checkerboard up."

"Oh? Who's that?" Stupid me.

"Checkerboard? Jesus Christ, is it possible you don't know Checkerboard? She doesn't know Checkerboard, that's impossible! How can you *possibly* not know Checkerboard? Haven't I told you—" Mirek scolded me; but the blanket of the opposite cubbyhole parted slightly, a face emerged, greeted me—"Hello there, kitten"—and lit into Mirek: "Cut the bullshit, for God's sake, how could she know Checkerboard? Has she ever even *been* to Blue Beach?"

It turned out that Blue Beach was a certain stretch along the bank of a pond not far from Traiskirchen that was open only to people with tattoos. And Checkerboard went there to pick up girls. "Let me explain it to you," the face in the cubbyhole said with a grin. "They call him Checkerboard because on his entire body, except for his face, you can't find a bit of skin, not one bit, that isn't colored in blue. He got himself tattooed in jail, where else, right, and now he looks like Picasso's blue period. It starts with initials of women he's had on his chest and ends with the little bee he's got tattooed on his dick. He really loves to pull that one out and show it around to the girls; he says to them, 'It's buzzing for you, honey.' I only saw it once, and it was this small."

"Pour me another one, dammit," the Legionnaire ranted, giving the nearest two-dimensional woman an erotic slap. "Nobody to fuck, I feel like getting hammered."

"You're already ha-ammered," Band'urka answered, but he got up anyway, grabbed the waning bottle of whisky, and brought it over to the Legionnaire's throne.

"And right on his collarbone he's got—" Mirek started to say.

"Hold on, I'm getting to that."

"Pour me a decent shot, dammit, I was in the Green Berets."
The Legionnaire's experience with the Moravian plum brandy
had taught him the magical powers of this incantation, and now
he used it in nearly every other sentence.

"And he also boasted," the face in the cubbyhole continued,
"that the last time he was in jail he gave this one guy a couple
of Pervitins to tattoo a wolf right on his butt, so that whenever
he shits, the wolf opens its mouth and the shit comes right out
of it."

"And he wanted to prove it to us right then and there."

"But none of us felt like getting shat on, so to this day we don't
know if he's telling the truth, girl. What's your name?"

I told him.

"I see. Okay. I'm Jirka. He's got pictures all over his body,
hearts on his hands, and flowers, you name it, intertwined snakes
on his legs, that wolf on his butt that opens its mouth—all beautifully done, except for the one on his back—"

"Yeah, on his back he's got . . ." Mirek shouted and started
to guffaw.

Band'urka: "Oh yeah, his ba-a-ack . . ."

"So you see, he wanted to get a gorgeous blonde tattooed on
his back, with big tits and all. Well, he had to pay up front, I
don't even know how much they wanted for it. Then he lay down
on his stomach and the artist starts tattooing him."

Mirek: "Ha-ha-ha hahaha!"

"So he's lying there on his stomach and gritting his teeth and
suffering, it isn't so painless, you know, to get a blonde with big
tits tattooed on you. And when they've been sticking him with
needles for an hour, Checkerboard asks them: 'Is it almost done?'
All the other jailbirds gather around, and the one who's doing
the tattooing gives them a wink, and they all yell out: 'She's
gorgeous, what a fuck she's going to be, one tit's already done,'
and they stroke his back. And Checkerboard wants to get a look
at her too, but all the others tell him not to fidget, or the other
tit will come out crooked. So he suffers for another hour, then

he asks: 'Well—well, what's taking so long?' 'What a belly button she's got!' they all holler in chorus. 'You're gonna have the most gorgeous beauty on that extended butt of yours anyone's ever seen.' So he suffers another whole hour, and now the guy who's tattooing the blonde on him tells him he should just lie like that for a while so the colors don't run—which he thought was pretty strange. But the tattoo guy takes off, so Checkerboard gets right up and goes looking for a mirror. He had it all planned how he would be able to beat off just looking at his own back in the mirror, that was the part he looked forward to most, and all the guys in the cell were asking him just to turn his back with the beauty to them, so they could beat off, but he wouldn't do it, he wanted to be the first. He couldn't find a mirror anywhere, so he stood up against the wall and tried to look over his shoulder and see his own back, but he couldn't see shit, of course. Then later on it struck him that all the guys in the cell were laughing kind of strangely, and when he got his hands on a piece of something shiny, he discovered that instead of a chick with big tits he had this big Stalinist proletarian, with medals and all, pitching dirt, with a shovel tattooed on his back, and right in the little hole over his butt, right where her pussy hairs should have been, in big capital letters he had tattooed: 'Glory to the Communist Party!' "

"And then," Mirek said when he had finished laughing, "then right here on his collarbone he's got a whole § tattooed on him, so that when he needs to look respectable he's got to wear a shirt one size too small and almost strangle himself with a tie so you can't see it. So one time Checkerboard's pretending to be a millionaire . . ."

"And he got nailed for it, too. He doesn't speak much German, and still he tries to finagle money out of some bitch. What a perfect marriage scam worker!"

"But when he . . ."

"But when he undid the collar of his shirt, or I don't know, maybe she did it, that § came right out at her, she nearly shat in her pants . . ."

"But really, at that point . . ."

"Girlie, let me vul-ga-rize it for you," came the Legionnaire's voice from his perch. "He fucked her, whether she wanted it or not, then he clubbed her in the head, took her money, and ran for it. But when she came to . . ."

"She could tell the cops what tattoos he had and that he had a strong Slavic accent. So they went after him and found him. They dragged him right out of his room. Now they've got all his pictures in their records. They played with him like a model, filmed him from every angle, it was almost too much to fit in their mug books. He told us about how . . ."

"Yeah, that's how Checkerboard tells it . . ."

The doors of the room flew open and two guys came in. I dimly recalled that they were two of Marta's former Tomcats.

They said hello. Mainly to me. And they winked at Mirek.

"See you've got a new kitten," one of them said.

Mirek half shut one eye and measured me through the lash. He'd been drinking plenty that day, too. The cozy warmth of his cubbyhole was calling out to us with a strong temptation to sin; our eyes met for a second over the surface of the Ballantine's, the only sober plane in the room—and all the way across the tabletop I could feel Mirek's arms embracing me. I suddenly touched the camp through him. Exactly the way I wanted it. Mirek drank up in a hurry, in long gulps. I followed his lead; the whisky burned in my throat, but only moderately, and its aroma drowned out the other, intrusive odors. And thoughts. I could feel Mirek's warmth terribly close to me, and his breath; I recalled the constellation of freckles on his neck—and suddenly I wanted him badly.

"Goddammit, pour me another," the Legionnaire said. "I was in the . . ."

"No more."

The Legionnaire yelled: "But I was!" He flipped a cigarette butt out of his mouth and was getting ready to climb down from his perch.

Jirka crawled out of his cubbyhole with a sigh. "Christ, do I have to?" He opened the enormous lock on his wardrobe and pulled out a half-full bottle of Ballantine's. He looked at it longingly, then tossed it backhand to the Legionnaire. The shadow of the opalescent surface flew across the wall and all those beauties like a spot of reflected sunlight.

Half a meter from my foot the floorboard smoldered, singed by the tossed cigarette butt. I stretched out and ground it out with my shoe. I nodded in slight embarrassment at Marta's ex-Tomcats, who were spreading those obscene cards out for a game of whist. And I flew to Mirek behind the blanket as if into the protective depths of an ocean.

•

The lights were still on in the room. The Legionnaire was bent over backward in his throne, polishing off shots of Ballantine's: examining the bottle against the light of the swinging bare bulb, sticking his little finger suggestively into its neck, and performing extensive examinations of the crotch seam of his pants with his left hand. "Damn, cunt, I wouldn't mind having a go myself," he remarked tactfully.

The Legionnaire was no longer of any interest to me. Not in the least. Because I wasn't looking at him from the surface of the warped table. I was peeping out through a narrow slit in Mirek's cubbyhole, and I felt fine.

"Give it a rest, Legionnaire." The satisfied voice of Mirek, who was snuggled up against my back. I could feel his breath on my neck and it excited me.

"What a stupid hothead," Jirka, my new acquaintance, agreed, peeking conspiratorially into our cubbyhole.

"Butt out, for Chrissake," Mirek dressed him down. "What if we happened to be—"

"Well, we probably would've heard that, no?"

"How do you know, Jirka?"

"So little passion today? That we wouldn't even hear it?"

"There are some things in this world . . ."

"I was in the Green Berets!" a grand voice proclaimed.

"I really think you've had enough," someone said.

"And you know they don't take singles in Australia? I applied, and that was a mistake—"

"No shit, Sherlock—"

"They didn't take me either," I called out in an injured voice.

"It's a good thing, too! Otherwise you wouldn't be here!" Mirek whispered. This time for my ears only. And he caught me by the breast, as if to tell me I should stop talking.

The mattress suddenly sagged. Someone had sat down on Mirek's bed outside the cubbyhole wall.

"They don't want me either!" one of the ex-Tomcats complained about a meter from my head. "They're all a bunch of fucking bastards. I'll probably just stay here in Austria and—"

"Give me that fucking whisky. I want to get hammered!"

"We haven't got any more, I'm telling you, ferchrissake, want me to squeeze the bottle over your mouth?"

"You motherfucker! I was in the . . ."

"Right, right, we all know that already."

"Just ignore the shitface." One of the Tomcats, attempting a conciliatory tone.

"Who're you calling a fucking shitface?! Just you w-w-wait, when I co-ome after you, then . . ." said the terror of *Zimmer zweiunddreissig*, and as he climbed down from his throne he got his leg tangled up in the covers, caught the cuff of his jeans on one of the iron rods that connected the upper and lower bunks, and fell in a shaggy ball of blankets to the wooden floor with a loud thud. The room was drowned in a sea of swearing.

"Haven't we got a drop of that puke-water left?" resolute Jirka asked irreverently. "Maybe he'll get alcohol poisoning and finally croak."

"Stupid fucking tyrant. Idiotic bastard."

"Better watch out for him. Because."

"He's a stupid fucking deserter, that's all he is. He ran away from the Legion, shat his pants there. He can't even set foot in

France, they'd court-martial him in a second, and he's got more than a million francs there in the bank. Over a million!"

"And you believe that?"

"He's a chickenshit. Nothing more."

"Hey, how do you know what he went through over there? You can't even imagine—"

The tidal wave of obscenities gushing from the Legionnaire's lips slowed but did not stop.

"Get him ba-ack up on the bed. He'll ne-ever make it himself." Band'urka, charitably.

With one of the Tomcats' assistance, the Legionnaire collected himself up off the floor, spat, examined his limbs, and climbed into his cubbyhole. "In the Green Berets," he mumbled to himself. "Watch out for me, in the Green . . ."

But no one was listening to him. Since *I* was the only genuine female in the room at the moment, a very flattering erotic sultriness revolved around my presence. It was not a bad feeling, and I basked in it with enormous pleasure. The tone of the Legionnaire's earlier greeting had not been lost on me. I knew that I was not two-dimensional; I knew that I had an inner depth, the reason for Mirek's embrace. I looked at the half-rotted wooden floor across which Edita the Open House (like so many others) had traveled with lightning speed from cubbyhole to cubbyhole. Because even Edita had not been two-dimensional. Mirek caressed me in all my dimensions, and I was suddenly gripped by jealousy. Through the slightly drawn-back corner of the blanket that formed the wall of our cubbyhole, I peered out, into the world that had now sailed away from me to a distance of hundreds, thousands of nautical miles. I looked at the boys spreading the cards out on the table, rapping them against its warped surface and muttering curses. I knew absolutely nothing about whist.

I looked at Band'urka sitting by the wide sill of the window, gazing thoughtfully out into the darkness, and pulling on his whiskers.

I listened to the Legionnaire grunting in his bed.

It was good to be here, and also to be with Mirek, that too. It was infinitely better *not to be* that lone ship lost at sea. To feel that I was Mirek's. To experience deep inside how we belonged to one another, or at least how I belonged to him. Precisely at that moment—in that little cubbyhole—there came to me (as it only rarely does) a sense of the absolute rightness of all things. Not just the way I was feeling. Not just what was going on in my immediate surroundings, the things I could see by peering past the felt blanket. But even things much farther away, ones I couldn't see but knew about. Things I had never seen, but some-day might. Maybe even things that existed, but which I would never see or perhaps those that had been or would be. All of these enormous space-times in the distance now sent me their positive energy. And I stretched out in Mirek's cubbyhole and it was enough for me just to exist.

I was aware of Mirek's hands, which were crossed over my breasts and tremendous as burdock leaves, so that I fit within them completely, like a gondola in its slip. Mirek's strength was in his voice, and his tenderness was in his hands. He freed my hair from its rubber band, so that it would not pull at my scalp, and it seemed as if he were making love with each strand of my hair, with each one individually, as he spread them out across the pillow. "You will be my own mermaid in here," he said to me, and I acquired strength, fantastic quantities of strength, from his embrace when he entered me from behind, tenderly and in-toxicatingly slowly: as if I were the sea and he were the keel of a ship.

•

The camp cops went by the door on their metal-soled boots. A persistent buzz and clamor reached us from the neighboring room, our door opened and shut a few times, but no one came in; after that someone could be heard fighting near the toilets, and Jirka, who went to have a look at the brawl, reported that it was no big deal, just the Romanians from Room 28 punching each other in the face. The Legionnaire staggered off to the bathroom several more times, and one of the Tomcats took the opportunity to offer his help. Apparently he was the one the Legionnaire had burned for that bottle of plum brandy a couple of weeks earlier: since that time he had displayed a nearly religious respect for the Legionnaire, even when the latter was hurting with the runs. The Legionnaire, when he was sober, amicably called him "Dickhead" and asked him small favors.

As the sleep of the righteous descended on him, the Legionnaire gradually ceased his cursing; his mumbled imprecations of "Fuck, piss, shit" now rattled the air only occasionally. And just when it seemed to us all that there might finally be some peace and quiet, he tried to get up, and since the Tomcat didn't get over there quickly enough, the Legionnaire went sprawling on his back right next to his cubbyhole, belched, burped, and moaned a few times, raised his head, trying to curse, then puked upward into the air. It was like a geyser. I watched from my position as the whisky-scented stream gushed every imaginable color about half a foot upward from the Legionnaire's mouth, then cascaded onto his face like a vomitfall. The Legionnaire retched, and Mirek made a couple of stalwart thrusts, fearing that he would lose his hard-on. The Tomcat, with much lamenting, jumped from his chair, stood for a couple of seconds in confusion over the filthy, choking Legionnaire, decided not to touch him, then—suddenly inspired with a brilliant idea—ripped a naked bunny from the wall and with her help turned the Legionnaire onto his side so that he wouldn't drown in his own puke. After that he wiped his hand on his pants and retired for the night to his top bunk perch.

The lights went off just then. And in the dark the powerful smell of the Legionnaire's vomit penetrated upward to our noses, disrupting our bedtime activities.

"Good night," someone tossed into the ether.

"G'night," mumbled Mirek from behind me.

"I'm not talking to you. G'night, pussycat."

"Good night," I said—and by my voice it must have been evident that indeed it was.

"They always have such beautiful voices while they're at it."

"Stop drooling." Mirek from behind.

"Girlie, let me vulgarize it for you, as our Green Beret might put it. I wouldn't mind it if you and I—"

"For God's sake who's going to clean that shit up?"

"Let him clean up his own puke . . ."

"Oh yeah, sure, that I'd like to see."

"Well, are *you* planning to do it, Jirka?"

"That little boy Friday of his will take care of it."

The voices gradually fell silent. I lay in Mirek's cubbyhole and he stroked me magnificently from inside. Slowly and enticingly. So that it would last as long as possible. And also so that we wouldn't make the bed creak too much. I was melting in his arms. Mirek whispered: "Now pay attention! Watch how it works!"

I paid attention. Because the room was silent only for a moment. I could hear the distinguished gentlemen settling their butts into bed. Then a couple of snores. The Legionnaire's gurgling, at times verging on a choking sound. Then the creaking began.

Entirely different from the collective creaking of Room 7. These were tragically solitary creakings.

Mirek quickly embraced me tightly and chuckled into the back of my skull. So I understood how it worked.

●

For a long, endlessly long time, Mirek thrust pleasure into me with his ship's keel, and I felt like shouting. Shouting with pleasure, joy, love. Of course I was more or less silent, I didn't dare emit so much as a decent sigh. But it didn't really matter. We would do our shouting later, tomorrow, the day after tomorrow, while looking at our little airplanes in the sky. Despite the fact that Mirek wasn't interested in flying anywhere. We always found some remote corner of the camp where we could lay down on our backs—but not to make love, never; we looked up at our airplanes and sang, called out, shouted into the heavens. Sometimes with words, sometimes without. Recalling past pleasures and anticipating those still to come.

19

And so life somehow continued on like this. We marched in place and looked forward to our airplanes. But Mirek made everything seem so much easier.

The period I spent with Mirek, when I was seeing the world through him, was unusually complete, but I couldn't possibly explain why. In reality we had very little in common. We were both from Prague, true, and so we could talk about places we both knew; about a pub I recalled having been in a few times with Standa, for example, but at the same time I had never suspected that behind its polished taps—as Mirek now confided—there bustled an *extremely* hospitable barmaid. In a remarkable way Mirek brought me closer not only to the immediate surroundings of the camp, but also to the Prague we both knew, or rather to the Prague he knew and I didn't.

This was precisely Mirek's greatest strength: the power of his recollections. That is, for the most part he existed in a reality entirely different from the one he was in direct contact with. Mirek, who had an unsurpassed ability to usher me into the camp—Mirek himself *did not live* in the camp. That external, genuine, and therefore meaningless reality concerned him no more than the feel of my body right now, as he crossed his hands over my breasts and held me. My breasts had existed for him far more genuinely on that one and only day when he had not yet known them, before he knew their feel in his hands . . . the day the grasshopper landed on me in the depression between them. And the worst part of it was that I knew all this, I suffered because of this dimension in Mirek—and I was jealous of another time.

Because this dimension within him stretched out in two directions: forward and backward. I knew that when touching me, instead of feeling my body, Mirek already felt other bodies, the bodies of the future. But although the future—in contrast to the present—was very real, it was still the past upon which everything hinged for him.

You could scarcely say that Mirek was impaled on some certain point of his past—one to which he continually returned in his recollections. It seemed, rather, that he was living in a state of delay—that he could only begin to value people, things, and landscapes once they had passed from him. He sighed over some Luděna he had gone out with here, before I had turned up in the camp. He recalled her painfully, because she had flown off somewhere on him and in this way had become desirable. Of course, when he later received a letter, for all intents a love letter, he did not answer her. He did not wish her to exist for him in any material form, even on another continent. She was not in the slightest way important to him as a living woman. And doubtless she had not been even when he had been with her. She had become substantial only through her departure; this was how he needed her when later, as we embraced, he sighed to me, a being too concrete and too near, about how sensational she had been. The consciousness of happiness reached Mirek with a delay of several days, several weeks, or several years, so that most of the time he could happily suffer and torture himself, a condition which by all accounts agreed with him enormously. As a result we lived in a kind of perpetual absurdity. While I, through Mirek and by means of Mirek, was experiencing the great, intoxicating *here* and *now* of Traiskirchen, he himself lived in the boundless *after* and sweet *before*, in the bewitching *elsewhere* and memorable *there*.

·

When he lay next to me, I knew that a too powerful past prevented him from feeling the happiness of that *now*, for which he was in any case unprepared. I knew that while he had driven off that dream of *mine* almost entirely, at night he tossed and turned and talked in his sleep; I knew that he was besieged by throngs of nightmares, that he muttered "Marcelka" under his breath. And so I would wake up and with painful clarity see the room, the camp around us, the blankets of the sleepers, and the moon's silver light . . . all the *heres* and *nows*; I would lean over Mirek, jealous of his dream, jealous because he was now right beside me, nearly naked, sleeping, defenseless—and still, in his dream, he was visited by alien, distant realities in which I had no place. And then, bent over his lips, I would long terribly to kiss him, to inhale the words he mumbled in his sleep, to awaken him and make love to him, to feel him inside me—it was not at all a matter of pleasure, but rather of knowing that I could envelop him in my lap, that whether he liked it or not he would have to immerse himself in me, in my reality.

. . . I would lean over Mirek, who sighed at me in his sleep, and I did not want to allow him to escape into his dream reality, I wanted to awaken him . . . But with dreams it works in reverse: when we are awakened in the middle of a dream we remember it—otherwise we do not. And so I preferred to let him conclude his experiences in his dreams; I listened to his breathing and did not dare to move in the slightest, so that he would not come to —so that in the morning he would remember absolutely nothing of his nightmare from that other reality.

●

I was dressed in a nightshirt reminiscent of an American great-grandmother's. It was a washed-out flannel shirt with a red-and-white flowered print and a lace collar, like a shirt for a half-ton baby elephant: so enormous that I could wrap it around my body four times—or else spread it around my knees and hide my legs in it all the way down to the soles of my feet. It was a formless nightshirt from a Charity shipment, one of the items even the Romanian women hadn't haggled over in the YMCA building, so I found it lying on a table.

It was the nightshirt that shielded me from the eyes of all the men who came traipsing through the room; it shielded me from the X-ray flashlights of the camp guards, who since the last raid considered it absolutely essential to inspect us almost daily, always around midnight or one in the morning, to assure themselves that we were *ganz allein*. We had learned to shove our lovers into wardrobes swiftly; each of us had for this very purpose a corner reserved in her own cabinet. Then it was safe to jump out of bed and open the green door for the cops, and that nightshirt shielded me from the eyes that groped in place of hands. The hands would instead be resting, hanging from the uniform belts, which were buckled through the wrong hole, having been themselves only just recently hanging over the back of a chair in the Hungarian girls' room.

My hideous camp shirt protected me, my disgusting shirt, which Mirek had nicknamed Baba Yaga, after the fairy-tale witch, suggesting that perhaps I should wear something a little flimsier. On the other hand, he found the shirt quite flimsy enough, almost nonexistent in fact, since from its bottom hem he could stick his head up inside as far as he liked.

So perhaps the shirt was to blame.

For the fact that Mirek never gave me a proper kiss.

He always stuck his head far up into it, his buttocks forming a hump like a camel's under the covers—and he caressed me with his lips from the neck downward, circling with his tongue those nipples he loved so much, conversing with them happily like a nursing baby; and it made my throat go dry, but I couldn't do a thing; my arms were imprisoned in the flounced sleeves of Baba Yaga, bound by yards of horrid soft flannel. Mirek would hide beneath my shirt, moving across my body down to my lap —and he would kiss it passionately, as if kissing the raspberry red mouth of his Beloved.

And, hidden in the tunnel of blanket that bristled on Mirek's back like a dinosaur's hump, imprisoned by the nightshirt, I simply had to lie there, without sighing—and kiss Mirek with all the longing of my *other* lips. And either it was really true or it only seemed to me that with those other lips I desperately expressed to him the longing of my real lips to kiss him, just once, *finally*—and that he intentionally failed to understand this. So that my real lips, the ones used to speak of love and stupid things and asylum or high-heeled shoes, my first lips, were as isolated, distant, and deserted as a coral atoll in the Pacific. (I took lipstick to bed, just to touch up my mouth a bit, so that my crimson lips would tempt him, so that they would express by means other than speech my need to join with him, to drink him in.) My coral lips were amputated from the rest of my body by the lace seams of Baba Yaga, and Mirek wanted it that way, he wanted me decapitated, not in a bloody way, but in a comfortable way; he wanted my body to surrender to him, but he wanted as little as possible to do with my lips, head, and brain.

And so night after night, as soon as the lights went out, Mirek stuck his head under my shirt and conversed with me. He conversed with my cunt, whispering sweet nothings into it, saying that it was beautiful, enchanting, magnificent as a child's face, and that he knew exactly how and where to kiss it. Oh yes: those two understood each other, all right. Unfortunately, they left me out of the picture.

20

In front of the entrance to the AFCR office (in which sat Míša: the reason why we all applied there, because Míša was a good-hearted woman, she chatted with each of us, bringing us the scents of America and making us Viennese coffee), several people were shouting each other down in Czech-Slovak-Polish.

The loudest among them I recognized as—yes, it was none other than Olda, my acquaintance from isolation. "I'm telling you, miss," he was just declaring to the entire crowd. "If I had so much as suspected that these chestnuts were such *morons*, such *incredible* morons, I would've preferred to stay at home and be persecuted in Czechoslovakia. A person gets just a teeny bit drunk—what else is there to do in fucking *moronic* Austria except get drunk in order to forget what a bunch of idiots you're living with—and instantly these cops of theirs are all over you, dragging you off to an interrogation. '*Nichts sprechen Deutsch*,' I tell them, but that does no good, they're already getting an interpreter, and what an interpreter, the kind where you've got no idea *what* he's putting into those chestnuts' heads, and I tell you, afterward he says to me in the doorway, 'You can kiss Austrian asylum good-bye.' Jesus, I didn't do anything all that bad, turned over a couple of tables. When I get mad, you know how it is, and I had good reason to be pissed off, after all, I should have killed her, that bitch, carrying on behind my back with some balding, fat, stupid old hotel manager, but I'm nobody's fool, I just took one look at her. 'Where did you get that blouse, you whore,' I scream at her—and she's got the balls to say right to my face that this girl she does some cleaning for gave her the blouse, said she didn't wear it anymore. 'She didn't give you *shit*,' I yell. 'You got it whoring, the price tag's still hanging off the rag,' and Božena says, 'Well, I guess she hadn't worn it yet.' But let me tell you, miss, I'm not some stupid sniveling idiot, I'm the head of a goddamn family after all, and I'm not going to let anyone ruin my family harmony, so I gave her a good wallop in the butt. And she was lucky I don't have the same passionate nature I had when I was younger, yeah, my ex, when she screwed a friend of mine I broke four of her ribs—this one paid for it only with a black eye—and these chestnuts dare to say that I committed assault on my wife—"

"Oh, well, assault, these Austrians are kind of touchy when it comes to that, you should've taken that into account beforehand—"

"But I'm telling you, what assault, you tell me, if you had taken a tumble with some Austrian, wouldn't you deserve a shot in the mouth? And all they can do is keep harping on the same thing: 'Kiss asylum goodbye,' they say. And they kicked us out of the pension on account of it, not that it was worth a shit living there—the minute Božena got back from the hospital we had to start packing up! And just look where they stuck us! They took us by transport back here, back to this filthy, lousy, stupid camp, and stuck us in a building with the Gypsies! Come have a look sometime, miss, and see what it's like there. It's like the fucking Soviet Union there, if you'll forgive my saying so; the second you turn on the light in the bathroom whole divisions of roaches this big go marching off in all directions right before your very eyes . . . And it stinks, all the toilets are clogged up; just tell me, how's a person supposed to raise children under such conditions? And those half-niggers there are always fighting, screw them, I say, but here I am rotting almost a year in this idiotic Austria— and now they just throw me like a used rubber among this sort of *Lumpenproletariat*. But me, I'm the head of a damned family, do you think I'm going to let my kids grow up to be savages? Well then, miss, you're mistaken, I'm going to Vienna first thing tomorrow morning and complain to the United Nations, and I'm going to tell them everything, how they're treating me, me, a dissident! When I'm done with them they'll be this big!"

•

Behind the closed door of Míša's kingdom, with a mug of coffee in my hand, I seemed to be in another world. Míša sat behind a desk, with her beautiful eyes and friendly smile, an oasis of peace, quiet, delight—and most of all, concerns of an entirely different order.

Although she visited the camp day after day, its tribulations did not get under Míša's skin. The problems, "reasons," and screwups that were vitally important to us were for Míša merely another source of the undying inspiration she derived from the surrounding world. Míša never got mad at anyone. She never shouted at anyone for lying to her, never gave anyone long narratives about their responsibilities—and she never asked anyone (with the hostile, almost threatening tone of voice employed with gusto by the Austrians) why we had come here and what gave us the right to be here. Míša simply let herself be fascinated by the endless accounts of our adventures, and in her amazed eyes people like myself searched for the narrow escape routes that reduced all possible concerns, "reasons," ordeals—life in the here and now—to almost surreal absurdity. Míša sat behind her desk with her head inclined to one side like a bird's; she had a kind word for everyone; and because it did not affect her personally, she filled out applications to America, Canada, Australia with divine equanimity, tapped appeals into the typewriter, and arranged our reasons for flight from our homelands into neat, easy-to-read columns: one, two, three, four.

"Dear sirs"—she was at the moment transcribing a letter, written in the heavy hand of a manual worker, that lay on the desk before her, making corrections as she saw fit. Meanwhile, she mumbled some sort of incantations to herself under her breath, by the sound of which the experienced ear could discern

American west-coast English (Míša had arrived there with her mother at the age of eleven). "Dear sirs, my reasons for leaving are that I am a professional bathroom tiler, and who has the money to pay for that these days except criminals, black marketeers, butchers, and Communists? But I am a rightist, I didn't want to work for Communist swine, and when one of them wanted me to moonlight tiling his bathroom, I quoted him a higher price, but he found out that I had done a tile job for his non-Communist neighbor for less—and of course, why not, he was an old friend—and so the Commie reported me to the plant, saying, and this, dear sirs, is my reason for leaving, that I was stealing tiles. And grout and cement and everything, but it really wasn't true, you see, do you know how much I had to pay the guard at the gate to let me carry the stuff through . . ."

"Dear sirs, we have been exchanging antigovernment books with people our own age, under twenty. When I finally had a chance to read Kerouac, I realized that I had to hit the road."

"Dear sirs, although I left my wife and two children behind, I did not do so for the reason of wanting to escape my familial responsibilities, but because there is no one in Czechoslovakia who can provide for them. I have always been a faithful husband and a responsible person, all my neighbors will attest to this, above all our superintendent comrade Soukupová, who lives on the ground floor and leans out the window all day and therefore would see anyone who might come to our apartment. But when the aforementioned wife simply had to have a car and a summer cabin, and how I ask you was I to make enough for that, that was my reason for leaving, because both of us, my wife and I, refused to become members of the Communist Party. We could have made a bundle, but after all I have my pride, and so in short I had to flee, what other choice did I have in that situation, and I would have taken my wife with me, certainly, but what could I do, they wouldn't have allowed the whole family to go, and so with this purpose in mind I said 'I do' to Marie Řepíková, here in Austria. With her help and tireless efforts the two of us plan to attain happiness and material prosperity as political émigrés in Canada."

"To whom it may concern," Míša tapped in English translation into the treacherous keyboard of the German *Schreibmaschine*, head tilted to one side like a pensive dove of peace. "I was persecuted in my homeland because I served as a . . ." Here Míša stopped and, thinking out loud, pronounced into the air: "Because I worked as a dealer in foreign currencies, by which means I made it possible for the working people of Czechoslovakia to buy imported goods in Tuzex foreign-currency stores and elsewhere, in this way helping to propagate Western culture and thinking, and the ideology of anti-Communism among the broadest masses of exploited workers . . ." Míša paused, toyed with the word *dealer*, which reminded her, as an American, of streetcorner drug dealers, rejected the phrase *black marketeer*, grabbed a pencil from its holder, and clicked it thoughtfully against her teeth. "There was no way to do business there, just *no way*, see?" the originator of this request for asylum blabbed, moving a wad of gum into his cheek, where it now formed a mobile bulge. He was a newcomer to the camp, still without the patina of experience, who wanted at all costs to try his luck on the other side of that great pond. "There was just *no way* to be an entrepreneur. Understand? Write 'Western goods,' Míša, write it; they were confiscated from us for ideological reasons, Western currency was stolen from us by the state police, who put hidden cameras in windows, trees, or traffic booths, and used them to destroy our business, they even used secret policewomen who would come on to you under false pretenses, but as soon as you started up with them"—here he slipped back into expressive Prague diction—"not only'd they rip you off blind down to your underwear, but then they'd narc on you, 'nough to make you shit your pants. Isn't that a good reason? Write this: 'With this purpose, dear sirs, I would like to be accepted.' Wait a second, that's stupid, I mean they *have* to admit me to the United States of America, the land of free trade, which I will promote by my contribution to it." The black marketeer looked around proudly, cracked his gum, then parked it back in its previous place behind his jawbone. "After all, anyone who can manage under the Commies can make it in the West with his right hand tied behind his back!"

"My reasons for leaving, like, since," the next charge began, clearing his throat. "Since back in '52 they took away my grandfather's pub, I wasn't in the world yet at the time, mind you, he wasn't so young at the time either, and his heart couldn't take it. I heard the whole story from my father, who should have inherited it from him, but how could he when the Commies took it all away? And after that he couldn't even look at it. The whole village saw how they ruined us, they made an Agitation and Propaganda Center out of the pub, hung a big banner on it, and no one ever set foot in the place again. Well, and Father couldn't bear to see it, after all in my grandfather's time they poured the best draft beer in the whole region there, and now for it to just be deserted like that, and those, esteemed sirs, are my reasons for leaving."

"Míša, look here, I've got very good reasons. Health reasons. You can write this down for them: 'For the purposes of the retention of, if you will pardon the expression, sufficiently solid stool, I have had no choice but to leave my homeland.' Look here, Míša, I'm over thirty. And every day for at least the last fifteen years I've had to put up with all that shit."

I looked at Míša tapping away at the typewriter, head to one side like the dove of peace, I took a sip of coffee from the big mug—and I felt calm and at peace. In the wake of such reasons for leaving, my adventure with the boat and the bass seemed almost persuasive.

"Esteemed sirs, at the beginning of my humble letter allow me to respectfully ask how for God's sake is it possible that you have refused me asylum in the U.S.A.? We had good reasons for leaving, my whole family and I, you've got it all there in black and white, but then you say we are not suitable candidates. My whole family and I have discussed your reasons for refusing me and my family with a representative of the American Fund for Czechoslovak Refugees, and she pointed out to me where we apparently had our misunderstanding. Where I was supposed to say that I had nothing against citizens of other races I signed everything in all honesty, but I added that I can't stand blacks, which is true, but after all the consul was white, I can't help it if I was raised in conditions of backwardness. Thanks be to God I've never seen a black man in my life, even though there were a few staying at the university dorms in Prague and the girls all went after them, which I don't understand why, because they've all got lice and they stink, but accept me in America, I'll sign anything you want me to, after all it's already our second year, four people living in one room in a pension. I beg you, don't leave my family to rot in poverty and misery on account of those blacks, all the others either got Austrian asylum long ago or flew off to some other continent in order to begin new lives, so why should my whole family and I have to be stuck here?"

"In regard to the nature of my criminal offense I ask the members of the Australian commission to please take into account that I was wrongly convicted according to paragraph 132A for pilfering Socialist property, but who didn't steal there, everyone was doing it, every single person in that plant took things, whoever doesn't steal from the state is stealing from his family, and was I supposed to go hungry? I request that the members of the commission take into account the extenuating circumstance that I sat out a nearly two-year sentence, unreduced, in the prison in Ruzyně, only one package a month, and they censored every one of our letters, you say *I* didn't suffer under the Communists?! I have always thought that Australia was a country whose bountiful nature and hospitable people gave people whom life had taken down the wrong track the opportunity to work their way back up from scratch and build a decent house and buy a nice car. After all, the original population of the Australian subcontinent was made up of social outcasts of Anglo-Saxon origin; I request the members of the commission be so kind as to take into account . . ."

Míša sat there with an intent half smile, pecking rough drafts of these stories into her machine, and I knew that in the evenings, back in her apartment in Vienna, she composed from them justifications that fit together as perfectly as the pieces of a puzzle: one, two, three, four, five.

21

On the windowsill, motionless, only his birdlike profile turned toward us, knees up under his chin, sat the runt Boris, supposedly Míša's newest admirer. Dressed in a white T-shirt with the English inscription FUCK YOU! carefully emblazoned on it in black marker (which had unfortunately bled quite a bit on its first washing), shorts created by ripping off the legs of a pair of faded blue jeans, red-and-white-striped socks, pink tennis shoes, and roller skates, Boris was experiencing his Daily Thirty Minutes of Punk.

He was practicing, he said, for America, where he intended to become an active member of the counterculture. His glassy gaze fixed on the camp yard, he seemed to be almost totally disengaged from all earthly matters. Nevertheless, suddenly Boris's heavy eyelids shuddered and the two stiff locks of hair that sat above his forehead like an owl's ears jerked. It seemed as if he was emerging from his trance, although his Daily Thirty Minutes were far from up. "O-o-ove-e-er the-e-ere, look!" he stammered in Slovak, slowly raising his finger and aiming it at a target in the camp yard. We all converged on the window. At the end of Boris's extended index finger there shuffled from the direction of the gate an unfamiliar female figure of truly astounding proportions. She was just passing through the shadow beneath the linden tree over by the YMCA building, dragging two over-stuffed plastic shopping bags, on which the almost offensively red-and-yellow inscription BILLA gleamed in the distance. Boris raised his finger slowly from the moving figure, turned half of his body toward us, lowered his roller skates from the windowsill, and in a high, dull voice announced prophetically: "The Ma-a-ammoth is comi-i-ing!"

•

The Mammoth half sat, half lay on the notorious bed right by the door, the only one that was obviously vacant: completely bare, sagging, and not all that clean. The two red-and-yellow shopping bags with the inscription BILLA HEUTE FREUT EUCH LEUTE were lying on the wooden floor of Room 7, also not all that clean. From those bags the Mammoth was pulling yogurt after yogurt—in strawberry, bilberry, raspberry, and vanilla flavors—tearing the lid from each one with a single pull, and plunging into it with her camp-issue spoon of scratched aluminum. The contents of each spoonful disappeared in a flash. The empty yogurt containers the Mammoth scattered to all four winds. And the echo of each toss segued into the rummaging sounds that came from the bowels of the red-and-yellow Billa shopping bag, which was emptying out with remarkable speed.

At the table sat Wild Bára, who had no *Arbeit* just now, her shocked gaze fixed on the Mammoth from beneath her conjoined eyebrows.

I closed the green door behind me, and was forced to share Bára's admiring gaze.

The Mammoth paid no attention to us. She kept digging into her yogurts, tearing off the lids with a scraping sound and tossing the emptied containers. She looked satisfied. Her right hand was fully occupied with eating yogurt, while her left leafed through a glossy magazine, which—judging by the preponderance of interwoven pinks—must have been some pretty hard-core porno. At the same time she hummed a song, whose words were unintelligible as they emerged from her stuffed mouth but whose melody sounded familiar. The Mammoth must have been Czech.

"Hi there," I called out from the door, and—perhaps recalling Nad'a the Good Samaritan—I stretched my right hand out to the Mammoth and said: "Call me Jitka."

"Janička," the Mammoth answered jovially, throwing a container in the direction of the refrigerator and, in a continuation of the same motion, reaching for a new one. "Hey," she added between two gulps. "Have you been here long, girls? I'm so goddamned glad to be in Austria! I've never stuffed my face like this in my life."

Bára continued to sit at the table, her square jaw resting on her hands. She was thinking so fiercely that the thoughts made a little bulge over her brow and wrinkled her temples. I noticed that the red of her stockings, although softened by their wavy pattern, was still a shade more offensive than the lettering on the shopping bags. I would have liked to cheer her up somehow.

Janička gave a whistle as she turned the page. The next container went flying toward the wardrobe and stuck to the top of it. Janička reached into a bag. She pulled out a bilberry yogurt. She raised it to her lap and snapped the top off. "Want some, girls?" the Mammoth called out hospitably. "What a fool, I should have bought more."

I shook my head automatically. It was clear to me that Janička had prepared for herself just the sort of reception she required. As a naturally gluttonous soul, which her figure seemed to indicate, she had to welcome herself to the camp with gluttony—a gluttony of yogurt, at least. After all, yogurt had not been so easy to get one's hands on in Czechoslovakia. Pornography even less so.

I waded through the drifts of empty yogurt containers to my bed beneath the window. The next container was catapulted over the divider that Hanka and Zděnek used to isolate themselves from the rest of us, when they had it working, and landed on their bed. Janička groped around reproachfully for the last yogurt. The lid snapped off. "So tell me, girls," she said, her mouth full, still leafing through the magazine. "Are there any guys here worth mentioning? On the way in from the gate I laid eyes on a couple I wouldn't mind bagging. In Czechoslovakia, even in Prague, and that's no countryside village, there's no one to screw, isn't that the truth?"

I can't remember what we said in response. Probably not much. All I remember is that from that moment on I began to be terrified by the sounds that accompanied the arrival of night.

●

Janička, alias the Mammoth, became the heart's desire and darkest nightmare of the entire male population of the Hilton.

She provoked them.

She performed stripteases. The only such performances that inevitably sent Zděnek fleeing to the bathroom.

"Why are you always running away?" we tried to soothe him. "The Mammoth has enormous tits. You should have a look at them sometime."

"I've seen it before, thank you very much," Zděnek answered. "They're the Mexican kind."

"The Mexican kind?"

"That's right: slung low at the belt."

Nevertheless, Janička did not let this stop her. She barely paid any attention to Zděnek. She had no intention of taking anyone else's man, she was too good-natured for that. Janička simply (and with boundless delight) took her place among the few single women the Henhouse had to offer the Hilton—she meant to take full advantage of this opportunity.

And so she paraded around naked, equipped with her Mexican tits, day after day in front of the curtainless window. She sauntered beneath the Hilton windows with as provocative a gait as her figure would allow. She went with great enthusiasm to breakfast, where, standing in line for the mess hall, which could consume a good hour, she could take in the whole buzzing scene with her enormous, ultramarine, sleepily horny eyes.

She made acquaintances.

She mingled.

She led, dragged, or carried men home, indulging with them in the games of love, regardless of the time of day, on the screwed-out, not particularly clean bed right by the door, never even bothering to put sheets on it. Not long after her arrival the legs of the bed began to buckle, the springs squawked in a voice that grew more and more anguished each and every day, and Janička—surrounded by the camp, by all those males and a mountain of comestibles—flourished ever more bountifully.

So much so that somehow it seemed she couldn't get enough of anything she needed.

We knew nothing of the Mammoth's inner concerns, of course, but still it was clear that even a herd of thoroughbred stallions couldn't have satisfied her. What she had begun a few days earlier with those yogurts she now continued with the men of the camp. She brought them home in droves, sucked them dry in a blink of the eye—and sloppily discarded their shells.

In short, she was a kind, hospitable, and omnivorous soul who readily accepted anything, at any time, in any form—and, whenever possible, used all of her bodily orifices.

And so all sorts of interesting creatures began trickling through the room—to everyone's amusement, especially Miss Marta's. The turnover was rapid, since none of them could withstand the assault for long, although Janička was supposedly a real ace in the sack.

Only the Hungarian Gábo, slight of figure though supposedly very well endowed (he had been born in Slovakia and so could communicate with us, and he even served as a linguistic bridge between Room 7 and Nixproblem)—only Gábo assured us that while Janička was the a-a-absolute e-e-expert when it came to blow jobs, wi-i-ith scre-e-ewing itself it was somewha-a-at worse, at least in his case. When he climbed up on top of her, he felt as if he were atop a mountain. To let *he-e-er* be on top, oy, oy, oy, Gábo would shi-i-it hi-i-is pants in the fear that she would flatten him. We-e-ell, and so what i-i-is left on that fucked-to-death camp bed? To screw her from the side or from behind, and eve-e-en then he'd have to put a ci-i-inder block under himself, just to get to the right spot through all tha-a-at fa-a-at. For a while he tried it with a pillow underneath, with the moral support of the whole room, which closely monitored Gábo's session, providing commentary on every creak of the bed and guessing how many times he would fall out of her with a thud and on which try he would succeed.

Finally, though, even the industrious Gábo wandered back through the semidarkness to the Hilton in the middle of the night, like many others before him, used, abused, and defeated, mumbling into his mustache Hungarian curses and Slovak pronouncements to the effect that you couldn't sleep i-i-in one be-e-ed with a fa-a-at a-a-ass like that anywa-a-ay.

Janička, who in spite of her numerous experiences still seemed not to understand the spatial complexities her dimensions posed for these men, sent them all—one after the other—packing back to the Hilton with the same gesture of her muscled hand she used to scatter emptied yogurt containers.

The camp simply washed away all her inhibitions, that is, if she had ever had any.

She kept on feeding herself yogurt, rolls, salami, marmalade, as well as numerous dinner leftovers brought to her in battered mess tins by her past, present, and would-be lovers—lovesick, yet flushed with fear—bribing her in the manner of male spiders, who humbly bring their chosen one flies so as not to end up between her pincers. At least three or four times a week Janička would allow a new suitor access to her rutting, elephantine body. Only rarely did one last longer than a day. Nevertheless, although it was clear from the very beginning—at least to the rest of us —how each session would end, Janička always stuck to the unwritten script. Regardless of the age, looks, nationality, or physical dimensions of the suitor, Janička always worked herself into a high passion—and the second a gentleman picked her Mexican nipples off the mattress Janička began to purr with satisfaction, like a Zetor tractor given a good, solid kick-start.

22

Stinking Jezebel stood in the doorway of the Henhouse washroom—and gave off a sweet smell. She gave off such a sweet smell that the scent poured down the corridor, seeped under the door of Room 7, crawled into the corners and crannies and under the beds where it overpowered the decomposing odor of laundry soaking in tubs, and—in almost visible cloudlets—flowed upward to our noses. Jezebel tore off her clothes, threw them in the corner, splashed water over herself in the sink, and with an equanimity all her own lathered herself in soap bubbles. Stinking Jezebel's violet scent mystified Room 7. Finally we sent Hanka into the washroom to investigate; there, pretending to dig out a corn on her big toe in the sink, she attempted to find out how it was possible that Jezebel did not stink today. She found out nothing. Of course, after Jezebel had washed the sweat and dust and perfume off with soap suds—perhaps more thoroughly than ever before—then her intrusive, musky, oily odor began to mingle with the still-persistent scent of violets. And, finally, Mirek brought the news from the Hilton that it had happened to her again. For the second time, at least. Namely, some Albanians had dragged her off to one of their rooms at the Hilton, and so that their fucking would not be inconvenienced by having to hold their noses, they had covered her with several flacons of perfume stolen from a pharmacy. "One whole corridor of the Hilton still stinks of violets!" Mirek reported to me. And he added: "You know, girls, those fucking Albanians seriously don't know what to do with all their energy. Now me—if I were a woman, I'd be shitting my pants!"

●

"Maybe I shouldn't come to visit you at the Hilton anymore,"
I whispered to Mirek that evening after lights-out, when Mirek
in only his undershirt and I in Baba Yaga had crawled under the
quilt. "Since you say it's so dangerous!" And Mirek mumbled on
about how, yes, we certainly had to be careful, but I had nothing
to be afraid of, because I had him with me. Probably he liked it
better when—at his place at the Hilton—I didn't have Baba Yaga
with me. "Better," he said to me, "better not to go around the
corridors much by yourself. But otherwise you'll be with me, and
I'll protect you!"

Perhaps a little awkwardly, I formed my mouth for a good-
night kiss. Mirek only touched my reddened lips with his index
finger and stroked them absently. Then he plunged beneath the
covers and—as it had happened every night here in the Henhouse—he vanished from the world into the folds of my Charity
nightshirt.

23

There are things, thoroughly nasty things, which we somehow cannot believe will ever happen to us—and they don't happen.

There are other things, which we likewise cannot believe will happen to us—and they happen. But sometimes an entire incident merges with reality only for an instant, and, as it remains without consequences, it falls very quickly into oblivion, in our own heads. This seems to occur with events that are too horrendous or unprecedented for us to comprehend. Then their momentary reality (although historically undeniable) so contradicts the common, everyday reality that the former is completely vanquished by the latter, quotidian reality. And perhaps it's good that it happens this way.

·

Everything takes place incredibly quickly. The four of us— Mira, Band'urka, Mirek, and I—are climbing up the central staircase of the Hilton in the direction of *Zimmer zweiunddreissig*, when we suddenly hear a couple of whistles. Footsteps, noise, and a blur of bodies are moving in our direction at the speed of light. Before we know what's happening, we've lost the power to use our own legs—and suddenly we find ourselves being carried off.

It is not only the ability to use my own legs that I have lost, something similar has occurred with my senses: I cannot see, hear, or feel, nothing; only somewhere deep inside my head am I transsensually conscious that on the door of the room into which we are being dragged is scratched the number 42; it hangs there surrounded by a vacuum, as if it, too, is legless. All at once something inside me takes a mental plunge backward in time, to the number 44, just two doors farther down, where things turned out so miserably for Ekrem and me.

The power of the imagination is truly incomprehensible, because suddenly nothing of what is going on around me interests me in the least—and during that single instant from the sight of the closed door with the number 42 until the moment when one of the Albanians kicks that door wide open (causing the number 42 to fly out of sight), I experience all at once everything that happened a few weeks ago, everything thrusts itself into me at once, including the colors of the caresses, the scents, the sensations, and the sounds; everything happens as it was meant to, Ekrem is making love to me as he should have—and that moment cuts into me like a sharp razor, it stabs me deep in my belly with a pleasure it didn't have, although it was meant to.

And then one of the Albanians slams the door shut with a kick. The action is suddenly moving too quickly for me, all the people are operating about six times faster than I. But that is not the main thing, the main thing is that sound that goes right through me, high, disturbing, unremitting. It dawns on me that it is Mira. She is screaming insanely in the arms of the Albanians. An Albanian is smiling. And Mira, carried, adrift as if borne by a surging wave, now appears as a small angel sitting on a cloud of Albanian arms. I notice grins on the Albanians' faces, Mira's screams can't help us, the green door is bolted behind us, and two boys, acting in perfect concert, are already dragging wardrobes up against it.

It takes me awhile to stop hoping that simply by pressing up against Mirek's back—or Standa's, or Tadek's, or someone's—I could make this dream evaporate and everything would be fine again.

Time has slowed down, so that even that instant just before we were carried through the door lasts an eternity for me, literally; but, on the other hand, everything around us is moving faster than the eye can follow, and therefore there is simply no time to take any action. I can hear Mira screaming, I can hear —as if it were also a sound—my own silence. I have no idea what is going on with Mirek and Band'urka, why they aren't saving us, why they aren't fighting for us. I see only Mira, in the arms of the Albanians, screaming, screaming, screaming . . . That sound envelops every sense, has a color, a feel, a taste—and Mira, hanging there, in the blue raincoat, the immaculate pink sneakers, with the blond hair that she actually has not washed for several days (so that I can sense the rain and sweat emanating from her hair), looks like a little angel, like a cherub, like Cupid on a cloud. Her lips parted, she is screaming . . . screaming . . . screaming . . . And the memory of that sound becomes etched in every pore of my skin. I long for a chaser of dreams. And then the situation does become real after all, I am suddenly sitting on a bed and someone is tying my wrists with a clothesline.

•

The coarse feel of the rope now connects me with reality. I become critical. At first olfactorily. Several of our jailers would be better off using that clothesline to hang their socks. Although —who knows? Perhaps we do not smell so sweet to them either. But probably we do, at least a little, otherwise we would not be here. I try to find among all these other odors the smell of Stinking Jezebel's sweat, or that of violet perfume. They are not here.

But I am unable to think logically.

Like a stupid sheep, like a cow, who has let herself be caught, I am sitting in *Zimmer Nummer zweiundvierzig* of the Hilton, and two Albanians whose words I cannot understand are tying my hands behind my back with a clothesline.

•

The best I can do is gather fragmentary perceptions.

The coarseness of the brand-new clothesline. Of course they have tied it too tight. I am irritated by their lack of professionalism. Already, after only a few seconds, the rope is beginning to tear the skin on my wrists. Someone turns the lights on. Tattered sheets have already been hung over both the room's windows; only in one little patch of windowpane that remains exposed can I glimpse the image of the bare bulb and our double reflection. I catch sight of Band'urka, who gives a yell, leaps high into the air, and strikes the back of one of the Albanians with the soles of both his shoes. "Fucking Shiptars!" He knocks the guy to the ground. He kicks him. Mira still has not stopped screaming. And the Albanian Zolo, the king of all the Shiptars (the one who is supposedly in charge of everything going on here, who has bodyguards, who walks around with a dagger at his belt so enormous that even the cops fear him)—King Zolo holds Mira's chin between his thumb and forefinger and strokes her jaw, as if lulling a crocodile to sleep, and Mira's throat, as she screams, extends in Zolo's hand like the vocal organ of a tree frog. Zolo strokes her chin with two fingers, as if hypnotizing an alligator. And then he stops stroking her, covers her mouth roughly with his palm, and pinches her nose until Mira loses her breath. Mira goes red in the face—suddenly it is so quiet that I begin to perceive, almost painfully, how one of my captors is breathing in my ear.

It is insanely quiet.

And we all watch Band'urka as he gives another yell, steps away from the man he has just hit, jumps up, and hurls himself at Zolo. Zolo steps aside—and like an old, experienced fighter slides his hand down to his belt. My perceptions are running at two temporal speeds again, so that, on the one hand, everything moves too insanely quickly for me to rise to action—and, on the other, my *perceptual* speed is slowed down, Band'urka's motion and Zolo's reaching for his knife are as slow as in a nightmare. It seems as if the horror that clenches my throat lasts God only knows how many hours—and at the same time it is all compressed into several seconds. Another Shiptar, who has been standing behind Band'urka, grabs an iron bar, one of the kind that connects the upper and lower bunks; it is army green, I see it glint in the light of the naked bulb by the ceiling, I see the movement of the bar, I see it broken down into a million frames, the million frames of a slow-motion horror film. I see the graceful movement of the bar, like the flapping wings of gulls on the Vltava, I am conscious that the bar is scuffed, its paint peeling, and I scream at least a thousand times in my soul before that bar hits Band'urka's neck. Band'urka bellows like a wounded lion. The grip of the two men who are holding me loosens slightly, they jerk upright in unison, and so do I. I try to tear away from them, I kick out all around and hit them in the shins, trying to wrench myself loose, but of course it does no good. I am disappointed in myself, at how easily I have become reconciled to the circumstances. But so far there has been nothing to it. I am in no pain, although it is unpleasant to be held in the grip of those two who are guarding me. Their hands are sweating. Whenever I pull, they reflexively grip me harder. No one kicks me back.

Band'urka is now stretched out against the wall by a wardrobe, and two Albanians are holding him by each wrist and raising him up in the air. Band'urka kicks out in empty space and rages: "You fi-i-ilthy Shiptars! You fucke-e-ers! You worthless rapists! You filthy scum!" And angry spittle flows like noodles into his beautiful Eastern whiskers—the ones we love to run our fingers through whenever Band'urka lets us—and intertwines with them. Someone grabs a chair and hits Band'urka across the shins with it several times. Band'urka hisses with pain and curses: "You fucke-e-ers, you fucke-e-ers, just you wait, we'll ki-i-ill you!"

"Tie his legs!"

I hear this command: perhaps in this chaos I have learned to understand Albanian. The coil of clothesline that up until now has been connected to my wrists is sliced with a long dagger. And we are all looking at Band'urka. Four men hold him and a fifth wraps his entire legs, from ankle to thigh, with long, sweeping, circular motions. I can see how skinny Band'urka is: the rope cuts into his pants, which stand out from his thighs like a string of balloons; it strangles him; he looks like a toothpick—and Band'urka curses them: "You scum! You cunt-faces! Fi-i-ilthy

Shipta-a-ars!" And as he stretches out his fists and tries to jerk
free, the angry veins in his forearms stand out like a procession
of snakes. This makes me recall the British sailor who helped me
cross near Trieste—and the tricolor snakes on his arms. Suddenly
it seems to me that now, once again, I am crossing some kind of
boundary, that another border looms ahead. I recall the snakes
on the sailor's arms, the perfect little circle in his ear, through
which I gazed at the entire globe, bewitching and round, as if
through a telescope. Or do I no longer remember correctly? The
dream and reality are blended so completely that every single
little real thing now recalls a symbolic element of the dream. I
try blinking several times, but I decide that I am not sleeping.
Band'urka curses: "You fucke-e-ers! You sons-of-bi-i-itches!"
and those interwoven snakes now lead the way for Band'urka
through the gates of hell.

The Albanian Zolo smiles with the tranquil superiority of a
Shiptar king. He looks at Mira as she breathes deeply, forgetting
to scream. Everyone now gazes at Band'urka, hanging there like
Christ, two men lifting him by each arm—a wonder his arms are
not torn from their sockets—and kicking out with his bound legs.
It looks as if they might in fact want to crucify him. And Zolo
takes a stance, legs wide apart, in front of Band'urka on the
shattered wood floor (whose dirty, dusty odor now creeps upward
to my nose, accosting me), folds his hands on his chest—and in
Serbo-Croatian, so that all will understand him, he pronounces:
"Zolo wants blood!"

Band'urka tries again to jerk free. It is easy to see how much
he doesn't want to die; he clenches his teeth, spits, and when the
Albanian approaches him with his long knife and runs it across
his throat, Band'urka's eyes tighten to slits and he holds his
breath. He cannot breathe, he does not want to be here, he is
trying to recede into himself, away from that knife; he strains to
dissolve backwards into the white, phosphorescent wall upon
which he is being crucified, and droplets of sweat appear on his
wrinkled brow beneath his hairline.

The Albanian runs the dagger across Band'urka's throat,

across his nose, below his ears, symbolically plunging it into both slits of his eyes. Band'urka is exerting himself to be as far from here as possible. To be as absent as possible from this ritual of sacrifice. His own sacrifice. Sweat runs down Band'urka's forehead—and I can sense from it how now, just before death, Band'urka is truly experiencing his own existence.

The Albanian runs the knife across his throat again, pressing on it, but not cutting. Band'urka's eyes bulge slightly from their sockets; he is suffocating from the pressure of his own blood. The blood, which will gush forth if Band'urka is to die.

But instead of that, the Albanian severely slices his forearm. He opens his arm in a long, gaping wound—and from it gushes that blood. Its hot smell flows through the room, filling it before the first drops have time to hit the floor. I am again confused by the distortion of time. I never expected that blood, when there is a lot of it, could have such a beautifully sweet smell. Its smell affects you all the way back deep behind the tongue, as if Band'urka is becoming one with us. It seems to me that I can follow each drop along its journey toward the floor, can hear it splatter into a red fountain. It seems to me that each drop falls slowly, incredibly slowly, simply creeping toward the floor . . . that at any time I could leap forward, catch a drop in my palm, and somehow return it to Band'urka. After this, I begin fearing for myself.

Because Zolo still stands there, legs spread wide, in the middle of the room, arms folded on his chest. "No one will be harmed," he says in Serbo-Croatian. "If you obey."

Only then do I notice in the corner behind a wardrobe my Mirek, silently and inconspicuously cringing—my chaser of dreams, my teacher, my love. It does not suit him at all. He cringes there, puny, quiet as a mouse, sweating so much from fear that I can smell it from across the room, and his eyes—sullen, rolled upward, a rabbit's eyes—flit timidly around. He cringes behind a wardrobe, as if he weren't here, as if what is occurring in the room does not concern him, as if by pure accident he has walked through the wrong door at a movie house—and now his only fear is that the horrifying monsters on the screen might reach out and grab him.

●

"Zolo wants a woman," Zolo announces in Serbo-Croatian, glancing possessively at Mira. I wince from fear and wait. Although—as yet there is nothing to fear. The two men hold me with a rather dutiful air, although the one on the left does huddle up next to me from time to time, as if acquainting himself with my body while awaiting his turn. And beneath his touch I am conscious that I am a woman. Femaleness radiates from me through every pore; nothing can be done about it. Not by me. Nor by Mira. Nor by Jezebel. Nor by the drunken Polish girl. I know perfectly well that my body happens to offer a lot—alluring curves, discoveries, and surprises, which make us interesting for them. My body—

When I shut off my thoughts like a water faucet, the huddling of that man on my left seems almost pleasant. I know that the only thing I don't want is pain, I do not want pain . . . Beyond the window covered by bedsheets hung over a broom handle flicker the branches of a tree. I look at the dancing flecks of shadows on the sheets, and suddenly it occurs to me that this tree shaking in this way could not possibly have its roots a floor below us, in the camp yard. It has to have its roots in bedrock, in the humus, in the foundation. Its roots must reach all the way to the center of the earth; it is in fact a magic tree.

The power of the magic tree is such that, instead of dying, the pale Band'urka is gripping the gaping wound in his forearm with his left hand. Two Albanian samaritans are actually tearing a narrow strip of sheet in order to bandage Band'urka's wound. A third carefully grounds the blood into the dusty floor. I try to imagine that swinging tree, as if its roots were now growing into me. Into my center.

Now I can hear Mira screaming. All of us fix our eyes on her.

I, the Albanians, Band'urka, whose blood is still seeping through the bandage on his forearm. Zolo undoes the button on Mira's pants, carefully pulling down the zipper. Two others hold her arms, pinning her to the cross of the bed, just as Band'urka was pinned to the cross of the wall. Mira tries to kick out, but someone clasps her ankles. They undo the laces of her pink sneakers. They draw her pants off rather carefully, lift the elastic band of her panties, and pull them off her. Mira lays there like that, in her waterproof blue jacket, exposed only from the waist down—and all of us are looking at her. Band'urka through eyes narrowed to slits like a tiger's. Mirek, from behind his wardrobe, with bulging eyes. The Albanian Zolo with satisfied affection. The blue coat covers Mira's belly; she is naked only from the waist down, because they only want to use her from the waist down. And we are transfixed by the thrill of the wild hunt. Mira's squeals drown out everything else.

And I know that my turn will come, too, but that strange thrill still will not leave me. The thrill of the hunt. Even though we two are the hunted animals, caught in the trap. Mira scrapes her nails into the wall. I look at her as she lies there spread-eagled, and I say to myself: So, she's first. Is that what I will look like, too?

Zolo is in no hurry whatsoever. He caresses Mira from the ankles upward along her white legs. I observe all this whiteness: the white sheets on the windows, Mira's white legs, the white wall against which leans the pale Band'urka, wordlessly gripping the white bandage through which his blood seeps. My eyes are burning from the naked bulb in the room. Or perhaps from the cigarette smoke. Mira screams and screams. And Zolo grips her thigh above the knee roughly, so hard that his knuckles go white—and he runs his other hand up into her crotch quite tenderly . . . He is discovering her, searching her, opening her —and as though she can understand him with some sixth sense she has down there, he leans toward her belly and quietly whispers some tender Albanian words. We all watch this. And Mira's face suddenly loosens, becomes filled with calm; she has been thoroughly pacified, as if Zolo has played a harp whose strings have the power to make her trust him, as if he has torn open an envelope with a parchment inside, on which in ink prepared from oak gall is written the text of an ancient pact whose terms still apply.

And the great Zolo, Zolo the avenger, Zolo the king, Zolo the man, merely smiles complacently, gives a little twitch of his wild, swarthy, and actually quite handsome face, reaches with his left hand for the belt on his jeans, and unhurriedly unbuckles it.

●

One might have thought they would have finished with us pretty soon, but they didn't. I had already heard that when the Albanians caught themselves a woman and dragged her here to the Hilton, they tied her with her legs up on the bed, so that they wouldn't have any difficulties with her, and fucked her. Of course, I had never been present for any such event until now, but from the stories of the better informed I had gotten the impression that it lasted no more than a couple of hours total. But I guess I had misunderstood these stories, because I myself had not been lying on my back on a bed with my legs spread and tied to the tops of bedposts painted with green lacquer. To tie my legs they used the same clothesline they had used to tie my wrists—and, indeed, that had been *yesterday*!

It was clear to me that not that much was going to happen to me, that we already had most of it behind us. We were not in a den of maniacs. We were simply in Room 42, at the mercy—or lack of mercy—of men, some of whom, although not all, were armed with long daggers. Nevertheless, they did not want to injure us. It was just that we somehow served their purposes right now. It was uncomfortable, to be sure, but it wasn't terrifying anymore.

My hands were free. I could have somehow deftly raised myself up, untangled the clothesline, and freed my ankles, rather clumsily tied to the pipes, which actually felt quite pleasantly cool.

It was stuffy in the room. The windows were closed, but in spite of this our jailers walked and stood around in buttoned-up shirts, as if they were ashamed of their nakedness, though not of ours. They undid their pants only when they wanted to use us. And even then the more timid ones gave a little look around first. One of them, for example, unbuttoned himself only once he was right up close to my crotch, so that he could hide himself from the others' eyes in my three-dimensionality.

My hands were free, I could have easily untied the clothesline, clumsily knotted around my ankles, which were located somewhere above my head, touching the insides of the pleasantly cool iron bars. I could have undone the clothesline easily, but: there was no point! Being tied up was not the issue here, the men had not secured us in this way so that we two females, Mira and I, would be unable to defend ourselves, so that we couldn't escape. We could have, both of us, easily undone these makeshift bonds, and then the men, running over, would have—probably without a word of reproach—once again patiently wound them around our ankles. But there were about fifteen of them against us. They didn't even need to tie us up. Even if there hadn't been two wardrobes pulled up against the door as a barricade, which our jailers dragged aside only to allow a few outbound excursions.

For water, brought back in mess tins, with which to wash us off.

Trips to the bathroom. Sometimes. Since more often than not they urinated in the corner into a Kronenbier can, their backs turned in humility to us two women.

For breakfast, lunch, and dinner, someone always squeezed out through the door, entrusted with the white meal tickets for Muslims. A rhythm could be discerned in their comings and goings. It was our second day stuck there.

So I'd had the time to realize the symbolic value of the fact that I was lying here, in all my glory, naked only below the waist, legs spread wide, my bare, yes, *womanhood*, that's the word, on full display. We lay here as if in a museum case, stripped and impersonalized, like the pink close-ups on the glossy pages of a porno mag. We were part of the decoration of the Albanians' room, just as those two-dimensional, magnified, spread-eagled beauties had been on the wallpaper of Mirek's room. Of course, we were more useful than they. We were three-dimensional. They could do more than look at us. They could touch us. And enter us.

Nevertheless, we were not *women*. We functioned here only as the female principle, the idea of a woman, like close-ups depersonified by their accessibility. We were three-dimensional cutouts from magazines, hung here as decoration.

On a bunk in the corner of the room sat Mirek and Band'urka, pale as ghosts. They had been sitting there like that since yesterday. Band'urka, defiant, and Mirek, terrified, hunched over on the bed, waiting for this to pass, because the Albanians would not let them leave: so they couldn't go running to the cops. The day before, each of them, a knife to his throat, had been forced to swear that he would keep his mouth shut until the day he died. And so they sat here, Band'urka nursing his sliced arm and soothing it with Slovak terms of abuse as though it were a tearful child. They smoked Yugoslavian tobacco, with which the Albanians kindly supplied them—and, just like Mira and I, looked forward to an end to all this.

I lay stretched out on the bed, legs tied above my head, and it was apparent that nothing worse awaited me than having to serve a while longer as a three-dimensional decoration. One boy came and sat next to me on the bed, touched me as if I were a picture, and grinned, half in satisfaction, half in embarrassment. It occurred to me that they were not as experienced as they had seemed earlier. That perhaps—like Ekrem—they would not have known what to do with a body that had not been depersonified. It would have been too much for them.

The Albanian lit himself a Camel and with a philanthropic gesture indicated that we would share it. I felt the moisture of the cigarette on my lips. I took a drag and choked on it. Then I froze.

Because in the door of *Zimmer zweiundvierzig*, in the space between the two wardrobes stood . . . yes, it was Ekrem, and he stared. With an eerie ecstasy, with the most beautiful eyes I had ever seen in my life, he stared at the three-dimensional pictures.

24

Something seemed to be missing when I went out into the camp yard, into that bizarre angularity, almost uncomfortably infused with afternoon sun. Since the time of my capture, almost forty-eight hours had passed. Something was missing, perhaps the clothesline with which my feet were suddenly *not* tied to the cool bedposts; perhaps I was overwhelmed by a sense of release: the consciousness that I now *was no longer* in anyone's power, that I was responsible for my actions. It was the same feeling I had experienced in Italy: you are alone with your freedom and you don't know what to do with it.

I gradually checked my whole body, one part at a time. I realized that my belly hurt, that my back was strained; I bent down to feel my ankles, only slightly chafed. The swollen sensation in them was eclipsed by the absence of the clothesline. I felt like crying.

My sudden freedom lay upon me like the weight of centuries. The moment they had shoved us, all four of us, out through the door, this freedom had flooded over us like a tidal wave. We merely nodded at one another—and scattered to the four winds. The guys disappeared somewhere into the bowels of the Hilton. Mira, apparently to the Henhouse. And I—with indecisive but long steps—strode out of the building and out through the camp gate.

I walked past the guard booth and the public telephone that was permanently besieged by horrific lines of *Flüchtlinge*, because it was supposedly broken and ate fewer shingles than the others near the camp. I walked down the alley of chestnut trees, in whose crowns the leaves already shone gold, preparing to fall. Along the wall a couple of men still stood, their faces nearly burnt from the sun, apparently the remainders from the morning's day labor lineup, who had been waiting a good twelve hours to see if some chestnut might drive up and offer them *Arbeit*.

And I walked down that narrowish path, hailed by the snapping of fingers, the clicking of tongues, winks, sighs, and numerous hellos, *Guten Tag*s and *Bitte*s—and I don't know what other words in I don't know what dialects. I walked among all these nationalities—and out of nowhere, suddenly I ceased to be afraid of them, they were acquaintances, so unmysterious that I almost could have started talking to them. I walked along the country lane that ran through Traiskirchen, as far as the gigantic billboard with the inscription WILLKOMMEN IN TRAISKIRCHEN and, God knows why, with a picture of a black cat stretching; I walked past the gingerbread cottages with their pastel stucco, past the gardens of people who did not want us in their village, not one bit, and everything was so clean, so pretty and sleepy, that it made my eyelids heavy. My eyes were suddenly somewhat different; at times it seemed as if I changed my eyes as I did T-shirts or panties; I had new eyes now probably because just two hours earlier I had been hanging on display like a picture; and on the front lawns of the gingerbread cottages of the sleepy village called Three Churches, I was searching for the sunny remnants of myself. Meanwhile, the sun was sinking toward the horizon, shading the colors into twilight; an old man rode by me on a bicycle and—almost as if I weren't an immigrant at all—called out *Grüss Gott!* and pedaled on. And at the other end of Traiskirchen there was a building site where the workers had just poured the concrete for the foundation of a new little cottage, and there I saw a cat, black and shimmering. It was precisely the same cat that was on the sign that said WILLKOMMEN IN TRAISKIRCHEN—except this one was real; it jumped lissomly down from the wooden foundation frame and walked across the moist concrete, which to its surprise sank beneath its paws, so that the

chain of footprints which stretched across the surface of the
concrete grew closer together when the black cat turned its head
and looked back at its own path. Then it sat on the other side
of the wooden frame, the sun sparkling in its fur like diamonds,
and stretched, purred, and licked its paws, immortalized by that
little walk.

I walked through the village of Traiskirchen—and all the feelings that grew from behind the barricaded door of Room 42 were
fading, falling silent, becoming irrelevant. There are things, altogether foul things, which we cannot believe will ever happen to
us, and then when they do, they soon evaporate from our lives;
they come to us—and then disappear forever.

And so, on that day, I became convinced that this was precisely
what was happening to me. Despite the fact that I hurt all over,
was dirtied and sullied from those two days, despite the fact that
I could still feel the bruises on my ankles and, above all, the
absence left by the removal of the ropes that had bound me . . .
the experience was already lost, squeezed out by my rational
consciousness. So that when I returned to the camp and climbed
over the fence behind the Gypsy building, it almost seemed that
such a thing simply could not have happened to *me*.

●

Unfortunately the rumors had spread through the camp along
their mysterious, imperceptible conduits—and at a speed faster
than that of sound.

Consequently, the reactions of the refugee camp's inhabitants
took me unpleasantly by surprise.

First, I met a couple of Czechs on the path by the medical
building; I nodded to them amicably, and they stared at me with
blank eyes, as if I were a ghost.

But that was not all.

Good Morning came toward me across the lawn, greeted me
from a distance, his grayish pink palm raised toward the sky,
wished me a good morning (although the sun was just setting),

nodded his graying, silvery head several times, and examined me with the saddest, deepest, softest brown eyes.

"I'm so sorry about what happened to you. Can I do anything to help?"

"L-l-like what, for instance?" I stammered.

Good Morning was suddenly embarrassed. He nodded for a while, swallowed a couple of times, and cleared his throat; he rolled the whites of his eyes, and then, as if English could not express what he wished to say, he just stared into me with those velvety eyes.

So that in his feltlike brown pupils I could make out the improvised walls of those cubbyholes in the Hilton when the sun shone through them . . .

I saw how the twilight was reflected on the lustrous skin of his face and swallowed up by his eyes. "I could interpret a dream for you, okay?" Good Morning said.

And so he led me off to the little room he had managed to wangle for himself after fourteen years in the camp, sat me down on the couch, and talked with me by candlelight, since they did not provide him with electricity. The candle was magic. "Tell me everything you want to tell me," Good Morning said, and the flame of his candle flickered like time itself. I told him. I faltered along the way and many times could not recall the right word, but none of this mattered in the least, because Good Morning's thoughts were connected to mine by the light of the bewitching candle that flashed across his face, reflecting into my eyes as if from a glossy black mirror. I was linked to his thoughts by the touch of his velvety hand; I was attached to him by his deep brown eyes with irises like soft felt. So I told him everything. I ended with the cat and the yellowed leaves falling on the congealing concrete. Because they were dying, their imprints would remain on that surface, like the fossils of trilobites—

—and then I must have begun to cry, because Good Morning lifted my damp face from his shoulder and directed his eyes deeply into mine. He stared into me so deeply that I could feel the pupils of his eyes, their delicate feltlike texture—like the eyes of a snail on their stalks—entering my head, sensing my thoughts—and wiping them clean of my tears. Good Morning stroked the skin of my mind with his soft gaze as if with his fingertips; he touched me for so long inside my head that—in the light of the waning candle—the ritual scars on his temples were transformed into the symbol of the Egyptian sun god Ra. Then he released my hand from his grip and said, "You know, it is a terrible shame that what you are telling me is true. Because if it had all been a dream, I could have interpreted it for you so terribly well."

25

On my bed below the window, from which the bedding had been rather carelessly stripped, sat Janička, alias the Mammoth, looking very much like she had already taken it for her own. Of course, before I even had a chance to think anything of this, Zděneček made a face at me from the table. "So, did you have a good time?" he asked me. And before I had time to react to this, Miss Marta, beautifying herself in front of the mirror, noticed in the reflected view that I was taking down the toilet seat left to us by Anežka—and she turned around and remarked that I should leave the seat where it was, that this was the way diseases were spread.

Hanka got up from the table in a flash and with a somewhat merciful half smile came at me across the room. "You're not going to give up now, Jituš, are you?" And as if she wished somehow to get closer to me, but did not know how, she gave me a thump on the shoulder.

·

"Mirek was here, he'll stop by again tonight," a voice announced from my bed.

"They took Banďurka off to the hospital, if you haven't heard. He's got pus dripping out of his arm, and the stench, it's—"

"With a wound like that he should have gone to the doctor right away, instead of waiting so long, it's like I always say—"

"Marta, he was being held *hostage* those two days!"

"Mirek will be back tonight, he promised he'd stop by—"

"You already said that, Janička."

"And Mira, well she . . ." Hanka blurted.

"What about Mira?" I said in alarm.

"Well, she went back."

"She went back where?"

"Where else, for Chrissake? She went back to Bratislava. To her mother's—"

"—so she can huddle under her skirt and cry."

"It won't do her any good, anyway . . ."

"She can tell the cops there about it . . ."

"Sure, they'd love to hear it: a nineteen-year-old looker returns from a camp in Austria; raped and abused, she returns to the Commies' welcoming arms. I can already see her, they'll parade her all over the TV, and with tears in her deflowered eyes she'll tell the whole world how those Albanians diddled her," Zdeněk piped up. "I don't know, my little bedbug, but I'd say—"

"Shut up already, Zdeněk, you don't understand, you're a man, so what do you know about women? Mira was pale as death when she got back here, she didn't even want to talk to anyone. Look, I said to her, at least go wash up, right, and she didn't make a sound, just kept looking all around her like a cornered mouse, as if she expected those Albanians to come rushing in any second—"

"Well, you can never be too sure, bedbug, after all—"

"And she paid absolutely no attention to us, she just went over to her wardrobe, started taking her stuff out, and with every little T-shirt she took out, she howled: I'm not stayi-i-ing here! I'm goi-i-ing home!"

"Like that's really going to help. Her life will be a living hell till the day she dies. They'll have her slaving away on an assembly line, and they'll never let her travel anywhere ever again."

"It's like I always say: from the very beginning that one never knew what she wanted. She never took care of herself, God knows how many men she let get under her skirt, and how she *changed* here in those couple of months! It's no wonder they singled her out and something like this happened. She wasn't even here half a year! Just look at me: I've been here in this camp over sixteen months and—"

"And you never, ever change. Which is why I'm so sick of you." Zděnek interrupted Marta's speech, continuing in a bored voice meant to mask his curiosity: "Now, girls, you're making such a big deal of it. First with Mira, now with Jituš, and you all look like you're going to your own funeral. Nothing all that terrible happened to you, right? It's not like you were still virgins, judging by the croaking, that is, creaking, coming from your beds, and what's a couple of lovers more or less, really—"

"Mirek said there were at least fifteen of them!" chimed in Janička-Mammoth's baritone, which beneath its matter-of-fact surface seemed—almost without a doubt—tinged with envy.

"So there, you see, Janička," Zděnek said, beaming. "See how long it takes *you* to collect *your* fifteen, and what we have to listen to here. These two had 'em lined up like tenpins, a couple of times in and out, next customer!"

"Zděnek, stop that, you're disgusting!"

"But, my little bedbug, don't get cross, I'm just philosophizing. No one's ever raped me, except for you, but it just seems to me that—"

"Men are morons, like I always say."

"But, bedbug!"

"Next time you can go join the girls, if you think you're so smart! Imagine yourself lying there, opened up like a book—"

(It was clear to me that Hanka was the one who understood best, but why did these words still hurt most coming from her in particular? I went and sat next to the Mammoth on the bunk.)

"Well, I didn't really say *that* exactly," Zděneček said, clearing out, and as always when he was embarrassed, he went to sit down on the floor to occupy himself squashing roaches.

"—and if they got you pregnant, the kid will have fifteen fathers with daggers thi-i-is lo-o-ong in their belts, not to mention diseases, and he tries to tell me—"

"It's like I always say: you can never be too careful. Not that I have anything against Jitka, but first she's over at the Hilton with God knows how many of them, and now she's going to live here with us *in the same room*. I'm not saying, Jitka, that I've got anything against you, but if I were you, I'd go to the doctor and get a good, thorough check-up *tomorrow* at the latest . . . Look after yourself a little, because you ought to be thinking of other people, too, after all you're not the only person on earth—"

Pretending that I didn't notice the nature of the gaze Marta had fixed upon me, I fumbled around on the shelf for the rubber hose with the slit in one end, and as if unconscious of the fact that this was the way diseases were spread, I set off with it boldly to the washroom.

●

And afterward, when I could finally wash myself in that stream of clear water for which I had so longed, I took the matter very seriously, cleansing myself from the soles of my feet to the crown of my head, from the bottom up and from the top down; nevertheless, however much I washed, newer and newer dirty spots kept appearing on me, faster and faster, and there were more and more of them.

The parts of my skin that had not yet been wetted were almost painful. My teeth cried out to be brushed. My hair begged to be scrubbed with shampoo at least five times. My toes pleaded to be scrutinized, each one separately, the tender folds of skin between them soaped clean, so that not a single reminiscent particle, not a speck of dust from Room 42, might remain.

One after the other, all the parts of my body each demanded my undivided attention; the more I soaped my body, the more loudly they cried, trying to drown each other out, begging, pleading—

—the dirty spots, which at all costs had to be cleaned (now, now, now, right now!), moved around on my body, now here, now there, they escaped and swerved away from the soap; they contracted, but did not disappear, they condensed—

—so that in the end that feeling of being *stained* settled down right in my center, a little knot of my tangled sorrows—

—and this little knot took up residence in the filthy, slimy black hole inside me, somewhere above my navel, but inside, in the chest cavity, right there, where nothing could ever wash it away, even if I could shed my skin like a lizard, even if I scrubbed my aorta with soap suds, the inside of my stomach, the creases of my brain . . .

I realized finally that I was *stained*. And this idea filled me with shame.

·

The world had been reduced to the glowing yellow bulb below the ceiling, intrusive odors, and voices. I had ordered the Mammoth out of the bed below the window, the bed that was by all rights *mine*, then stretched out on it, as is: without sheets. I covered my head with my handkerchief and tried to be as far away as possible.

I reached into my center—and tried, with Good Morning's caressing hands, to find, within my heart, within my soul, deep under my skin—

—what? What exactly was I trying to find? From those depths I was trying to grasp the places that were not empty, the caresses that had been and were to be. But instead of the loving, warm caresses with which Standa had touched me (for three years, a whole three years, Jituš, can you even imagine?)—instead of these, I found within myself only dank monsters, slimy seaweed that entangled my ankles, pulling me down, down into sordid cesspools.

"Jituš? Are you asleep? How are you doing? Wake up, d'you hear me?"

I guess I really had succeeded in falling asleep at that moment, because I hadn't even heard the scratching at the door. Mirek was sitting at the foot of my bare bed, smoking a cigarette with his left hand and removing the meditational snot-rag from my eyes with his right.

I blinked into the sudden excess of light. And an unexpected salty stream jerked halfway, not fully, *only* halfway up and out into my eyes, and it stung. Because it was happening again. Despite how Mirek had looked behind that wardrobe back then (back then—yesterday!), he was entering me again—illogically, by means of all my senses.

The touch of tobacco smoke. The color of words.

Because I already wanted him again. I wanted to have him next to me, in one bed with me, beneath an army blanket . . . I wanted his skin against my skin, that music of caresses.

"I brought you all a little something to drink. Care to join us, Jituš?"

I was sitting at the table, tilting the burning surface in my hand. I observed how it danced before my eyes. The yellow bulb no longer protected me, I felt there was too much light on me, combined with the eyes of the others.

At the table the talk revolved mostly around me. All sorts of foul things were being dragged out of me—as if out of a cesspool—into the light of day by means of an enormous ladle; these things were examined with disgust, then thrown back into me with an extravagant splash. I desperately wished that Mira were there, that there could have been two of us for this, as there had been in Room 42. Had not Good Morning already disclosed to me that when a man reached the age of forty-two in his country he was supposed to be wise? The number 42 was pursuing me. I didn't know how much wiser I had become in *Zimmer zweiundvierzig*. I knew only that I didn't want to get any wiser, because getting wise was painful.

I rested my nostrils on the rim of the glass and let the dense scent of the whisky pound its fist into each and every olfactory cell. I imagined the cells absorbing shot after shot in the nose. I traced the individual wisps of Ballantine's as they swept my throat clean like a broom. Jituška, you're starting to lose your mind. The alcohol was connecting me to my own center—no, not that filthy, stained one—it was connecting me to my own *spiritual* center, the one that recollects and looks forward. Mirek, who was sitting next to me at the table making some sort of very important speech, became amplified within me, the way he had been before, and his constellation of freckles suddenly appeared on the tips of my fingers. Mirek tossed back a shot and continued: "And so I went to see him, in Baden, and I'm telling you, I've never *seen* such a pale Slovak, he was whiter than a sheet, they're going to operate on his arm tomorrow, that Albanian cut through a tendon or something, and it pulled up back behind his elbow, so they're going to try to fish it back out tomorrow. But you know Band'urka, right? 'What are you ta-a-alki-i-ing about? I'm pe-e-erfectly fi-i-ine!'—and while they're trying to explain it to him, he's already packing up his stuff, ready to head back to the camp: *Nichts sprechen Deutsch!* he says to them. So then they stuck him with some kind of injection, so he'd give them some peace, but sedatives have no effect on Band'urka, he just kept plotting how as soon as his arm healed he was going after them, one after the other, he would just wait and then rip them to shreds, 'I'm an Easterne-e-er!' he says . . ."

Only then did I notice the Polish girl Baška sitting on one of the beds, her jacket still radiating cold, concentrating fiercely in order to keep up with this rapid conversation in Czech. Her beautifully shaped, rosy lips were whispering something that seemed to be a prayer to the Polish God. She must have just returned from Vienna, still not fully in the know about the matter.

And she stood up, walked carefully over to the table, and tugged at the sleeve of the depressed-looking Hanka: "*Przepraszam . . .*" Hanka rose and sat down next to Baška on the bed, where the two of them began to whisper in Czech-Polish. I saw Baška cross herself, and although I couldn't hear a word, I could see with my peripheral vision how Baška's eyes followed the entire event as it unfolded, although now it was over: she squinted her eyes sideways at me, her lips trembled, then she glanced in the direction of the Hilton, which continued to overflow with mystery and music; her gaze returned to my profile, then stopped on the half-closed doors of Mira's emptied wardrobe. A light draft blew through the room, the doors swung feebly on their hinges, and I turned together with my glass toward Baška, so that I noticed that her pupils—as if from the wind—were also swaying feebly. Then our eyes met—and Baška lowered hers in embarrassment.

I turned back to the table, took a sip of the Ballantine's—and I felt Hanka's compassionate gaze hit the back of my skull like a slap. Marta was fixing her face in the mirror, checking the powder on her chin, pulling at an invisible hair, and, with a long, red, hooked fingernail, scraping away a bit of black mascara that had peeled from her lash. Zdeněk fidgeted uneasily and swirled his share of Ballantine's around in its glass with a circular motion, as if trying to cool a cup of tea. From the bed that creaked and groaned beneath the Mammoth's weight could be heard the smacking of lips and the tinkling of an aluminum spoon against the inside of a mess tin. Janička was finishing off the dinner leftovers.

"He was dumb, what can I tell you, just a regular dumb Slovak," Mirek was saying with irritation, and he turned to me: "Tell them, Jituš, did it make any sense to *fight*? I, I was afraid—"

"Yes, you were, I noticed that," I agreed. Zdeněk laughed, but Mirek continued: "I was afraid that if we tried to defend the girls it would just make them madder. Didn't Band'urka just provoke them more? They mangled his arm, God knows how long he won't be able to work, and I'm telling you, he doesn't even realize *how badly* they mangled it, so badly that the tendon pulled up behind his elbow." Mirek impotently waved an arm, *his* arm, an arm that had *not* been cut open. "And the girls, they didn't defend themselves, right, Jituš? The girls knew that it was the only rational thing to do, after all, nothing really terrible happened to you, but sure, fighting makes sense when it's one or two of them, even three I could have handled, but against fifteen . . ."

Mirek slapped me on the shoulder, as if seeking support. I said nothing. My eyes fell back in time. Once again I saw Band'urka against the white wall, hanging there, crucified, dark drops of his blood cascading toward the dusty floor with a roar like Niagara Falls.

"In the end, it couldn't have been *too* awful for the girls, at least the way I saw it," Mirek said, and he looked to me for sympathetic agreement. But I was unable to tell him to go to hell at that moment. Because in the starry heavens shimmering beyond the window, I could see the constellation of freckles on his neck, and I wanted to press up close to it.

"It simply didn't make sense to *fight*," Mirek added contemptuously. The word *fight* came out sounding like *bullshit*. "All he did was piss them off, and that's exactly what they wanted: a fight, blood. Maybe if he hadn't gotten them so worked up they would've let us go sooner—"

"If I'd been one of those Albanians," Zděnek said self-confidently, "if I'd caught myself—as an Albanian, I mean—some woman, I'd have kept her in there at least a week, until she fell in love with me and followed me around like a little dog, but I'd have to do it well to her, of course, aren't I right, my little bedbug?"

"Zděnek, shut up!"

Hanka pulled some train tickets out of a mug filled with soapy water and a little vinegar. This was Hanka's recipe for removing the inky stamp from them while preserving their whiteness. Hanka now carefully rinsed the tickets in a mess tin filled with clean water, examined them against the light of the bare bulb, and carefully inserted them between sheets of blotting paper which she then placed on the seat of her chair. She poured the water from the mess tin into the mug to rinse it out, hesitated, squinted in the direction of the door, but she didn't feel like going to the washroom, so she poured the water out on the floor. She

held out the mug to Zdeněk, who trickled some Ballantine's into
it for her. Then she sat down on the chair with the damp blotters,
ever so gingerly—so they wouldn't slip out from under her—and
ironed the tickets with her butt.

"You could have gone outside to pour that out," Marta grumbled. "Who needs to smell that, that stench." But Hanka paid
no attention to Marta.

She grinned at Zdeněk's warning that her butt would catch
cold and start sneezing, and sat attentively enthroned upon her
drying tickets.

"That bodily warmth, that's better than any iron," Mirek
added, modeling two ample cheeks in the air.

I looked at his fingers and felt a little faint. Despite the fact
that there was nothing unusual about his hands. Except that they
knew me. Except that I knew them.

And so I at least looked forward to lights-out. To Mirek embracing me with those two hands that knew me. No, he would
not make love to me, no, he would just caress me beautifully,
and perhaps he would hold me tenderly by the nipple all night,
so tenderly that I—

Footsteps echoed in the corridor. The door opened, and
through its rectangular opening entered the unkempt head of
Nixproblem. "Bá-ára? Bá-ára?" he bleated questioningly.

"*Nichts* Bára, *nem* Bára," answered Zdeněk, who had apparently picked up a little Hungarian in the camp. "Bára *Wien
fahren*. And don't come around here! *Bazmeg!*"

"*Nichts problem!*" Nixproblem said, and the door closed.

"Well . . . well she . . ."—Marta drew a breath, about to
speak a vulgar word, but settled on a more respectable
expression—"starts up with him here . . . and then all sorts of
creatures come crawling. It's like—"

"Well, Marta, you've had a couple of guys in here that I—"
Zdeněk began his favorite game, but Hanka cut him down with
a look: "Just drink and stop shooting your mouth off!"

"Well now, bedbug, aren't we being the perfect lady today . . ."

"Just where is the Wild Woman?" I asked, in order to change the subject.

"Bára is in Vienna, haven't you heard?" Hanka said, her butt parked on her train tickets. "Bára found another completely fantastic apartment in Vienna—"

"But not an apartment, it's not an apartment, it's a *house*, right," Zdeněk corrected his love. "On *Corneliusgasse*, she said—"

"So she packed up her potato sack and took off to live there. This time there's no guy."

"And no electricity, water, or gas, either, is what I heard."

"So what, if she likes it there."

"If she doesn't like living with us," the Mammoth added.

"Well, no wonder she doesn't want to live here, with this lot," Zdeněk said, thus provoking Marta, who mumbled something about how certain people who had absolutely no business being in the room ought to be marched directly back to the Hilton under police escort. I was beginning to feel at home again.

Janička the Mammoth climbed down from her bunk and looked out the window.

"Who are you keeping an eye out for so hopefully?" Zdeněk asked inquisitively.

"Well, Gábo, of course, who else?" Hanka answered with a chuckle. "Her little Gábo, with a pillow under his arm."

Janička turned away from the window, distractedly gathered one Mexican breast in her hand, and said hopefully in Hanka's direction: "He should have been here by now . . ."

"Maybe he's *never* coming back, maybe he's sick of you already, Jana," Marta remarked cruelly. "And if I were you, I'd—"

"Maybe you should wave your tits at him out the window," Zdeněk suggested. "You know, like a white flag."

"And then the whole Hilton will come streaming over here, see?"

"It already is, anyway," Hanka the realist answered.

Mirek topped me off. But I was a little sorry that he wasn't paying much attention to me otherwise . . . He didn't even put his arm around my shoulders—even in the most noncommittal way. I sat feeling abandoned at the table and suddenly, together with the whisky, a burning, searing sadness flowed into me. It grew and grew, and it made me drunk.

"Maybe you should try parading in front of the Hilton with your shirt unbuttoned," Zděnek advised the Mammoth. "You walk by two or three times, the Albanians come running out, they seem to have a healthy appetite at the moment, and two hours later you're carving another fifteen notches in your bedpost. Just try to tell me you wouldn't like to see what it's like."

Janička turned toward Zděnek and said nothing. Significantly. And so he called me up as a witness, stretching his hand across the table and slapping me on the forearm: "Well, tell her, Jituš, wasn't it worth it? At least a little?"

"Shut up, Zděnek, you're really disgusting!" Hanka roared at him again.

Mirek's lack of attention now seemed almost a provocation. Perhaps he didn't realize how much I needed his warmth right now. Or else he didn't care. Which bothered me even more.

And so I raised my eyes from the Ballantine's and pronounced thoughtfully: "I've been wondering if we shouldn't report it. Not that I expect anything to come of it, probably nothing will, but we can't just let the Albanians run around raping women like this, and—"

Then, with playacted preoccupation, I looked directly at Mirek.

The effect was immediate.

Mirek's eyes bulged out of their sockets, so that for a moment he again reminded me of that sweating rabbit; then he grabbed me by the shoulder and aimed his whisky breath at me: "Jituš, have you lost your mind?!"

And he launched into a monologue I didn't care to hear. So I remained silent. But not Hanka.

"I think she's right, Mirek, she's right!" she responded, taking the offensive. "It definitely should be reported. Just try being in a single woman's shoes in this camp. Or maybe you just don't care that there are animals running around this camp with knives this big tucked into their belts, catching one of us every day just for sport—"

"But, bedbug, I'll protect you!" Zdeněk, a bit drunk.

"I'll tell you why you don't want to report it, Mirek! Because you shat your pants so bad you still have shit behind your ears! Because you don't care what happens to the girls here, you just—"

Mirek put his glass down on the table with such a thud that the Ballantine's splashed out of it. His eyes bulged even further out of their sockets and he went red in the face. "I'll tell you why!" he roared. "I'll tell you! Because *you* weren't lying there stretched out like a frog, it wasn't *you*, so why are you sticking your fat butt into this in the first place? I'm telling you, maybe I was shitting in my pants, but *you*, Hanička, you would've shit so bad they'd have to pour perfume on you like Stinking Jezebel. *Because!* Because they weren't holding a knife thi-i-is bi-i-ig up against *your* neck, so hard I can still feel it on my Adam's apple, want me to show you?" Mirek bounced up from the table, it was a wonder he didn't knock his chair over. He pulled a long bread knife out of the cupboard and fenced with it before Hanka's eyes. "Are you interested in a demonstration?"

Hanka fidgeted on her train tickets. "Mirek, what are you doing?" she gasped in alarm.

"Go to hell with that shit," Zdeněk suggested, remaining seated.

Meanwhile, terrified Miss Jituška threw herself on Mirek's elbow and tried to twist it. We fell together to the floor. He got up immediately and shook me off like a bothersome fly. And I went rolling across the floor, my nose rammed into its dusty odor, my tears fell, wetting it, and I started sobbing.

•

That night (because the dreams had been set loose again) I dreamed about a bell.

Or, more precisely, about myself *as* a bell, because my entire body was transformed into a bell, I could feel the resonating chamber within me, my ears rang with the sound of my own alarm.

The transformation of my body was not the worst part. I rang metallically, coolly. My tears and dreams froze on my inner, resonating surface in the form of small hillocks, salty as the ocean crossed by Columbus with his fleet.

The frozen tears dissolved into frozen blood, which melted and pulsated: the bell was a heart, hot and aching . . . I woke up.

And everything probably would have been fine that night if I hadn't seen—through the diffuse darkness—Mirek in Marta's bed, huddled together with her, and I had no choice but to watch, turning my head, staring . . . So that I saw, not really saw: *felt*, because I knew Mirek, and this gave me X-ray eyes that burned through the camp military blanket to those two bodies, the body of Marta and the body of Mirek, *my* Mirek, who now held Marta by the nipple, tenderly rubbing it in his sleep, so tenderly, just as I had known it, so I knew how nice Marta must have felt inside that night . . . I knew that in the morning she would wake with a feeling of inner fullness, that pleasurable consciousness of motherhood, almost as if an infant's mouth were sucking the milk from her breast.

I envied Marta that touch, that *single* touch, the structure of those fingertips on her skin, I envied her that awakening as I tried to fall asleep again, to shape myself again into that bell. But it would not work, so that instead of a clean, resonant surface, my insides felt like a cesspool, decomposing and fetid, infested with worms and covered with algae.

26

So I packed up my sleeping bag, a few T-shirts, and a hundred or so schillings—in a word, almost everything I had—in my backpack; I left my wardrobe unlocked, since those thieves could have just picked my joke of a lock with a pair of nail scissors anyway; I put my camp ID on the shelf, answered in the negative a few questions revolving around the theme of whether you too, Jituš, weren't perhaps packing up and running back to the Bolsheviks, climbed over the camp fence, and walked off toward the access road, which led to the highway, which led to Graz.

And it was such smooth sailing that I didn't realize I had no passport until I was almost at the Italian border.

But being on the road helped. It helped a lot.

Because when I was moving *forward* along that ribbon of the open road, it didn't matter in the least that I was actually *retracing* my own footsteps back to Venice; it didn't even matter that it was almost fall and drizzling.

I got out coolly two or three kilometers before the border, and I didn't even have time to be surprised at what fabulously smooth sailing it was going south through those hills and forests, among the fading raspberry thickets . . . Before I knew it I was once again on the pavement, which glistened from the fall rain, reading the signposts giving the number of kilometers to Milan and Rome, and sitting in a white coupe next to an insane Italian, who of course spoke neither English nor German, but who kept reaching for my knee and constantly asking if *Italia* was *bella*.

•

In Venice I searched out a certain apartment in the Lido. Betsy was no longer there. In her place there was now a Dutch girl by the name of . . . but the name didn't matter, we never called her that anyway, it had too many sounds we couldn't pronounce. The Dutch girl was young and had long, straw-colored hair, a white complexion, and red cheeks. And she was nicer than Betsy had ever been. She stretched her whole hand out toward me right away, and when she heard that I was coming from Austria she asked me whether I wanted to speak English or German. "I'd rather speak English," I said, and she grinned at me. Dana the Kurd ran out to the store to get a bottle of white wine. "That is to celebrate the fact that you have arrived," As told me in his belabored English.

The blond beauty called her father every so often. She always smiled when she was on the phone. What she said, I have no idea, she spoke Dutch, of course. I do know that the checks from Amsterdam kept coming. It was not difficult to deduce on whose account we were sponging.

And so we lived happily this way: three Kurds, myself, and the Dutch girl. The world was becoming a healing place again.

●

And since I was already in Venice, I said to myself, why not go a little farther, have a look around. And so one morning I found myself on the highway interchange outside of Mestre, standing and looking into the sun, which had just come up—and it stung my eyes; then a dense cloud came rushing over and it started to rain. I had nowhere to go for cover, I realized, and at the same time, looking into the sun, I saw how each droplet formed a little silver pearl before exploding against the asphalt. I turned around—and there it was! The rainbow. It stretched across the highway like a five-colored bridge, and I said to myself, Jituš, remember, this is not a symbol, it's morning, so that rainbow *had* to appear over the West, it's a law of physics . . .

But all this only did so much good. I stood, drenched, by the soggy highway, from which rose little columns of steam, and I knew that I'd have to go as far west as I could in pursuit of that rainbow.

·

There's probably no point—right, Jituš?—in trying to choose from among the tangle of adventures what was important and what was not, what happened here and what happened there, just as there is no point in classifying the types of dust that settled during that time on my body and on my sleeping bag; there is no sense in classifying the types of dust: which is from Naples, which from Mont Blanc, which dust I brought back from Paris, where I spent my nights like the homeless, sleeping on the grates of *le Métro*. That journey lasted several years, from Jitka-the-girl to Jitka-the-woman, or at least it seemed that way to me; I actually spent several weeks on the road, and I wouldn't have wanted to return to the camp at all if I hadn't been flooded out of southern Spain by the rainy season.

But I really ought to begin from the beginning and tell it in order: the tunnel through Mont Blanc, the mustard-colored lights on the cars in France, the beggar by the *l'Opéra* Métro station, who had PAS DE CHANCE tattooed on the stump of his arm, the Spanish border, Barcelona, the Sierra Nevada with its black cliffs that glinted whitely in the light . . .

But how can I tell it in order? How can I begin, when everything, the entire journey, entered me all at once? Not like a day, but like a mosaic of all days; not like a thread, but like a tangled ball of many threads.

Jumbled filaments, byways, roads, connected in a web, gnarled and intricate. I was making my way across this web to the West, onward, while the sticky, elastic fibers tried to bind me, like a sparkling spider web, and drag me back. *Homeward.*

But my erstwhile *home* now occupied a space in the distant past, somewhere out there on the other side of the barbed-wire fence; it was the flowery, springtime landscape that opened only in the wake of the semi that had taken me away.

The filaments of recollection followed me and harassed me, leading—as if I were a marionette—from the soles of my feet, from my hands, from my brain, to someplace far beyond the horizon, like endless silvery ribbons, entangling me at the crossroads whenever I had to leave someone; they stretched me out like a butterfly and pinned me across the part of Europe I had traversed; the farther I got from my flowered land, the more the fibers tugged at me.

And this was interesting: the more I touched things, stroking rocks, cornerstones, cathedrals, the tires of semis (because I wanted to store these sensations, steal them, carry them with me like amulets, and console myself with them day after day)—the more I tried to do this, the more the reverse happened: the soles of my feet became worn by all the asphalt, they eroded, and in the same way the tactile skin of my hands eroded. It was not just that I did not succeed in carrying all those sensations away in my hands: it seemed to me that I actually left my skin on the touched objects, that I was spreading the skin of my fingertips all over Europe, and through its nerves I could still feel all its pain from a distance.

So I probably would have felt pretty miserable if I hadn't arrived one fine day at the finger-shaped mountain of Montserrat.

•

On the side of it stood a monastery, perhaps not uninteresting, but crawling with tourists, crappy souvenirs, and bustle, so I kept on climbing up the narrow path between scrubby young oaks, higher and higher. It was afternoon. Only when I was quite high up did I become conscious that the entire, extensive massif, which jutted out over the landscape like a ship at sea, was composed of—

—yes, it was true, of rotund sandstone columns decidedly phallic in shape, towering over the landscape like an erotic forest; to the right, to the left, in front and behind, wherever your eye fell, erect phalluses jutted toward the sky. It was beginning to get dark and the haze was thickening below me. I tried again just to touch the rock, still warm from the sun, but I feared in advance the imprints that my hands were leaving all over the world, and so, in the fading sun, I merely climbed up to the top of the largest, highest sandstone finger, spread out my sleeping bag, waited for dark—and fell asleep.

When I woke up in the morning I found myself floating on a crimson sea. My little summit had been transformed overnight into an island, gently and safely sailing through the fog, which like oatmeal enveloped everything below me with its impenetrable brocade, stained red by the rising sun. I sat on my little island, in my ship, on the flying carpet of my peak, and all around me, as the sun climbed higher, the surface of that, yes, that orange desert grew more and more orange; it was the desert I remembered from Berlin, except that this time it was *not* a desert, but a sea, not even a sea, but a fertile amphibious wilderness, like the background in a Dali painting, where you can only tell where the desert ends and the sea begins by the ship launched upon the water. No, it was not a desert.

This was the orange of ripeness, of monks' habits, of the skins of sweet tangerines stolen from gardens in Castile. I sat on that highest of Montserrat's islands, and wispy columns steadily peeled off, evaporating skyward from the viscous orange fog. So that bit by bit this whole sea was dissolving, revealing the upward thrusting phalluses, scrubby oaks, open spaces, the land—

(the land spread out below me, fielded with orange groves)

—and the tangled, silvery spider-web filaments of my recollections and nostalgic longings. Those painful fibers of my pasts, my previous *selves* and other, potential *selves*, were dissolved and torn in a series of inaudible explosions, releasing me from myself, curling up nicely into little balls, like tame little grass snakes.

That morning, when the orange desert had finally dissolved, I was suddenly someone else.

Perhaps I did not know it for sure at the time. But then a couple of days later in a port town somewhere in Andalusia, I lay my weary bones down to sleep on a stone ramp near the water and awoke just before morning. The sun was coming up over the sea red as a propaganda banner (where were the hammer and sickle?), a light breeze ruffled the surface—and on it directly in front of me were reflected dozens of yellow and white masts of swaying sails. The rippling surface chopped the masts into sticks of firewood stacked up and tumbling over one another. Against the sun I could see an entire forest composed of the compact, whole, slender masts of the boats themselves, while in the reflection I could see only the shattered ones, as if in a cracked mirror.

I just lay there, staring. And then two fishermen (carefully, so as not to step on me) made their way toward their boats with armloads of nets, smelling of salt.

27

I didn't have my camp ID with me, so I had no choice but to climb over the fence behind the Gypsy building, and then I was again walking across that familiar courtyard, on which the puddles were already freezing, sparkling crystals of ice forming around their perimeters. The trees had been bare a long time, and their fallen leaves were steeping in the puddles, smelling of decay. It was winter. Very little music now filtered through the closed windows of the Hilton. The camp looked entirely different from how I remembered it—and my present self could not believe that one of those former selves could have ever lived here. The camp looked small, and it was difficult to grasp how at one time—that is to say, a few weeks earlier—such an enormous sadness could have filtered from it into me.

.

The room welcomed me with its familiar smell, supplemented by a multitude of odors from the washed-out panties, bras, and T-shirts, which now that it was winter were hung out to dry on the peeling ribs of the radiator, between which dust crackled and burned.

There were dozens of burn marks on the walls, since in my absence they had acquired the habit of roasting cockroaches with cigarette lighters.

Perhaps this had something to do with the fact that Zděneček no longer sat in his usual place, crushing them day after day with his shoe. Zděnek and Hanka had split up, and Zděnek had taken off for Germany because supposedly it was "better" there. Meanwhile, behind her felt wall, Hanka was carefully tending to none other than Nixproblem; she was learning Hungarian on his account, and during the night, whenever Tibor breathed a little too loudly, she begged him not to snore, because, Tibor, they'll throw you out on me, and what will I do here without you?

Marta still spent her nights clucking and listening to the music broadcast by Vienna radio.

Baška, who hadn't yet managed to get her Vienna lover to marry her, counted her shingles up mentally and tried to summon sleep by means of regular breathing.

I lay down for the time being on the ruin of a bed by the door, because on my bed (on *my* bed!) beneath the window some young swain was trying (literally) to climb Janička. Apparently he didn't succeed, because the springs sighed, the young swain gave a short hiss, and Marta clucked.

"Everest denies another attempt!" Mira's lover commented.

Some mother was now spending her nights on one of the beds with her seven-year-old son. Officially she lived in a pension, but she was secretly living here in the camp, because she had found some work in Baden. She held her offspring's head beneath the covers, apparently holding her hands over his ears too, every five minutes commanding him: "Sleep! Pét'a! Go to sleep already! Do you hear me?"

And in the corner of the room, just below the ceiling, an admiral butterfly with bewitchingly dentated wings was trying to sleep and hibernate.

•

The guy I started going out with after that was affectionate and nice. He even paid for me in the pub when we stopped in for a *Viertel* of wine. He was openly enthusiastic that he "had" me—and apparently he really thought that he somehow owned me, that we were going to fly to America together and open a pub. In many respects he was much more pleasant than Mirek had ever been. Nevertheless, I just smiled condescendingly at his rash declarations of love. Because the whole thing was so tenuous, so insignificant, that I don't even remember his name now. I did not need him to chase away the dream.

•

I went to drink coffee with Míša at the AFCR once more, and no one wanted to believe all the adventures I had met with on my journey. But this didn't bother me. That evening, beneath the blankets, I recalled the silvery filaments that still led from me back to Paris and to Andalusia and to Montserrat, connecting me with the Europe I had just sniffed around in. But they no longer bound me. Everything was fine, mostly because they had finally called me to the American Embassy in Vienna and, after a whole day of my waiting there, interviewed me and told me I had been accepted by the United States. By way of celebration my lover of the moment invited me for a *Viertel* of white wine and could not shut his mouth about how in Washington or in Frisco we would open a pub and cook Czech dumplings together.

I didn't take him seriously, of course; nevertheless, my acceptance made *me* so jubilant that the next day in the YMCA I successfully battled with the Romanian women for a flowered blouse.

•

And once, on my way to dinner with a pile of pink meal tickets and clattering mess tins, I spotted Wild Bára heading for our room across the yard with her jute bag.

I almost wouldn't have recognized her if it hadn't been for that bag. Because instead of her long, tangled black hair, Bára was now sporting a very unlikely blond do, which, it was apparent even at a distance, was already going black at the roots. I called out: "Bára!"—and she stopped and looked toward me. With one hand she raised her bag, which had been dragged through mud and winter streets, over her head. With the other she made a vague gesture of greeting, which I imitated without thinking. "So you're back?" we both said at the same time. Except that she, being from Moravia, extended the "o" sound in the word "so" slightly longer than I.

"Girls, I'm telling you, you're not going to believe what I'm about to tell you," the Wild Woman was saying about an hour later, now seated on the bed. Her boots were standing by the door; gallons of water and melting salty snow were streaming from them onto the wooden floor. She kept the drenched soles of her patterned red stockings under herself, drying them with her butt. It was an impotent, submissive pose. In general, everything about Bára breathed impotence. And, of course, she was stuck with that bed by the door again.

"Some people imagine that it's all so simple," Marta was saying. "They think they can just go off wherever they feel like, then come right back to our roo—"

"And what do you think this camp is for?" Hanka countered aggressively. She was enthroned on Nixproblem's lap, cuddling up to him lovingly, as if they had belonged to each other since the dawn of time. Tibor was winding a lock of her long hair around one finger with great concentration and continuously nodding his head, pretending he understood everything. Every so often he uttered his favorite phrase. Nixproblem had taken over Zděneček's role in the room, except that he didn't haggle with Marta and he didn't smash cockroaches with his shoe. It would have been difficult to get him to leave, because every effort in that direction was answered with his standard "*Nichts problem!*" Consequently he maintained a rightful place by Hanka's side, and for his sake Hanka had cleaned out her wardrobe and stashed her things under her bed. During police raids most lovers could be easily hidden simply by pushing a few clothes in the wardrobe to one side, but Nixproblem was quite a substantial specimen, and when the nighttime invasions occurred, Hanka worked up quite a sweat cramming him into her cabinet.

"So tell us about it, Bára, tell us what happened to you," Hanka now said sympathetically. "It wasn't the place with that guy this time, so what went wrong?"

With her newly bleached head Bára now looked totally different, but she still preserved the same gestures as she spooned up the leftover potatoes from a dinner tin. She still put her elbow out to the side like a country girl, smacking her lips as she ate. Then she lay the tin down on her lap, tossing the spoon into it with a clang. She wiped her mouth with the back of her hand and said in embarrassment: "I already told you, girls, that I was in Vienna in this house, but it was a crazy kind of house. We were there with no gas, no electricity, and no water, but I'm not complaining, I'm not new to that kind of stuff. They had these buckets right by the door, on the third floor, and you had to go all the way to this pub on the Mariahilferstrasse, the manager already knew us there. *Wasser, bitte*, I would say, and he would just make a face and show me into the kitchen, but he never got mad when I would go there ten times in a row, which was always when Ulrika wanted to take a bath. There was a whole gang of guys living there, but just us two girls; the guys didn't pay any rent, they were all muscles and tattoos, and they called themselves *die Lumpen*. They called Ulrika *unsere Halbhure*, and they appreciated her because she was the only one of them who worked: whenever they ran out of *Geld* they dressed her up and sent her out on the streets, and she would return with a few hundred, and then the next day I'd be carrying a ton of water so she could wash herself from head to toe in the tub; she'd just say *Ich will rein sein*, and off I went with the bucket. And so, I'm carrying water, and that's no big deal, after all, I've done stuff like that before, I was even pretty happy, I was going to cook and babysit for this Slovak woman, and whatever I made I put into the communal fund, and they always said, Bára, *du bist gut, gut Arbeiter*, but maybe I could also bring them something *zum essen*, since I was already over there, cooking, why couldn't I . . ."

The door opened and through it stepped my lover of the moment. The prosperous American barman, that is. He sat down next to me and started fawning. I kissed him behind the ear so he would leave me alone. Marta gave a snort. And Bára continued: "So they wanted me to steal something, but I didn't understand

the word they were using, and so Wolf, his real name was Wolf-
gang, but that reminded him of Mozart, and he hated Mozart,
so we only dared call him Wolf, like the animal, and he wore a
wolf's head around his neck on a leather thong, so Wolf says
zapzarap, and did this with his hand, so I say I can't because
they'd fire me, and Wolf says I have to contribute something to
the communal wealth, carrying water isn't enough. 'You live here
with us, eat with us, drink with us; it's either *zapzarap* or *Halbhure*, take your pick.' So what was I supposed to do, I'm no
virgin, I say to myself, Ulrika came up with some peroxide, said
she was going to doll me up, well, they did this to my head,
dressed me up in a whore's clothes. They bought me this horrible
black . . ." Bára indicated the skin-tight leotard on her body
with her hand; I could see her shaved eyebrows beginning to grow
back together. "And they stuck me out on the street. So what
am I supposed to do, I hit the pavement, and more than anything
I'm afraid of talking money with anyone; Wolf told me not to go
with anyone for less than three hundred, I'd be stupid to go for
less, but I'm telling you, girls, the pumps I had on were pinching
me so bad that by the time I made it to Mariahilferstrasse there
was no skin left on my feet. I couldn't even walk, I was in so
much pain, I was almost crawling, I was so destroyed, and then
some guy comes out of nowhere, '*Zwei hundert*,' he says, 'okay?'
So like a fool I nod, I was almost looking forward to him taking
me someplace where at least I could lie down, but instead of that
he gave me such a slap that I'm still dizzy from it. So I'm feeling
totally out of it and start making my way home, and there's Wolf
at the door: '*Na, wieviel hast du, na?*' So I've got to tell him the
truth. '*Nichts*,' I tell him and describe what happened. And he
says: '*Du Trottel*, what did I tell you, you can't go for less than
three hundred, he was probably someone else's pimp, if you'd
told him *sieben hundert* he'd have left you alone, but as it is
you're competition.' Then he got out a bong and said we were
going to smoke some hash, they always had some on them, one
of them was smuggling it in from Holland . . . and he said my

feet wouldn't hurt then and I could still make some *Geld* whoring that night. So what am I supposed to do, I smoke it, and zap, right back out on the street. I go trudging back, and some Arab appears out of nowhere, and it's not like I speak great German or anything, but the way this guy spoke it was horrible, out of the whole sentence the only word I could latch onto was *blázen*, and because I was stoned I thought he was calling me an idiot in Czech, but, of course, he wasn't speaking Czech. 'Who are you calling an idiot?' I say to him, and he just kind of smiled and pulled me behind this gate, and then he took the thing out . . .'' Bára looked around at her audience. "Girls, at that point I realized how dumb I was, because in German *blasen* means blow, and you've never seen anything so enormous in your life, I swear to you. So I'm scared shitless, but as soon as I open my mouth to object, he takes advantage of it. The whole thing's in my mouth. So what can I do, I bite into it hard, and he bellows like an ox, and he starts chasing me, so I throw off those shoes and go tearing home, but there's Wolf, and he says to me through the door: '*Wieviel hast du?*' So I had to tell him, '*Ich nichts habe,*' I say, '*Problem.*' '*Was Problem?*' he says to me right away. 'I haven't got . . . haven't got any shoes,' I say. 'So go beg for some, *du dummes Ding!*' Just what am I supposed to do, it's winter. I go huddle in the hall until morning, when they're all sleeping, and Ulrika gets back and lets me in, but when I try to explain what happened to me, she just says: 'Pack up your things and get out of here, you're good for nothing, we only let you stay here out of Christian love, anyway.' So here I am again."

Bára rearranged herself on the bed and carefully massaged the soles of her red stockings. Then she raised her hands and with a sigh ran them through her unlikely head of unkempt blond hair.

"Well, I'm sorry, Barunka," Hanka said from behind Nix-problem. In the meantime Bára's jaw dropped, her face contorted, and she quickly armed herself with a pillow so she could hide her head.

•

One of the secondary phenomena that accompanied my acceptance by the United States of America was the sudden flood of suitors who had heard about it. The door would unexpectedly open and in would march admirers—Czechs, Slovaks, and Poles—all of them with the intention of sweet-talking me. It would begin with declarations of love, continue with roses, probably stolen from the local flower shop, and after several *Achtele* of wine were bought for me, this America-lust would reach the point of promises that as soon as the guy in question could scrape it together, he would pay me as much as a thousand bucks to marry him right away. It seemed that everyone wanted to get to America, and everyone hoped that I would help them do it.

•

Then one fine day there was a scratching at the door of Room 7. "*Herein!*" Marta yelled, taking pride as always in her German. Hanka—who was sitting on Nixproblem's lap and, since language was lacking, lovingly stroking his whiskers—added: "Through the door!" precisely the way her Zděneček would have been certain to do a couple of weeks before. The door opened and through it stepped my love.

I knew, of course, that Mirek was still in the camp, but I hadn't seen him since my return from Spain. It had not even occurred to me after all that had happened to head for room *zweiunddreissig*; I figured that my love for Mirek had already been exorcised, that he had been buried and forgotten on one of the crossroads formed by those shimmering, fine threads that I didn't wish to recall.

But here he was standing in the doorway. "Hi, gang," he uttered, noticing no one. Except me. "Hey, Jitka," he said, almost embarrassed.

"Hi," I said, and I was sorry that at that moment I had no visible work to occupy myself with. Because Mirek was having his effect on me again. He was unraveling those filaments of memory, carrying me away from the *here* and *now* a couple of months into the past, to the time when . . .

"Jituš, I only just heard that you'd gotten back . . ."

I said nothing.

"I heard you made it all the way to Spain . . ."

"And she brought us back a big fat zero!" Hanka added from behind Nixproblem.

"So I said to myself . . ."

"What did you bring us, Mirek? Come on, show us!" the Mammoth said hopefully.

"Jitka, come outside! Come into the hall."

"To tell you the truth, I don't feel like it. I'm just fine where I am."

"Come into the hall. I have something to say to you."

"I'm happy right here."

Nevertheless, Mirek, milady's court chaser of dreams, had so perfectly unraveled my filaments of memory that barely an hour later we found ourselves in a pub; Mirek ordered some cans of beer to take out and started talking my ear off.

•

"Well, kitten, who'd have thought that we would see you back here this year!" fawned my old acquaintance Jirka from Room 32. Mirek held me wrapped in one arm and a red-and-yellow plastic shopping bag full of beers in the other. A gloomy looking Band'urka sat on a creaky chair by the table; he waved at me, and I could see that along his forearm ran a long pink scar that wrinkled at the elbow. An extraordinary stench was crawling through the room, since at the moment the Legionnaire's indentured servant was just cooking up his master's socks in a mess tin.

I gazed around at the pink wall decorations in the room and I felt a little queasy. But Mirek had already thrown the bag down on a chair and begun to pull beers out of it.

"We're going to have ourselves a regular celebration today. I've taken care of the beers, so everybody grab one, and if we run out, I'll go get more."

"Hu-u-uh?" Jirka gaped in mock amazement, reaching for a can.

"Just take one," Mirek offered hospitably. "Here, Band'-urka!"

"Tha-a-anks a lot," said the latter, deftly snapping the pull tab, causing a little gusher of foam to stream upward.

The indentured servant wiped his hands on his jeans and handed a can up to the Legionnaire on his perch.

"So I hear you've been on a little vacation," Jirka immediately engaged me in conversation. "Weren't you afraid? All on your own?"

I took a deep breath, sipped my beer, and launched into an account of my Travel Adventures. I didn't try very hard. And no one was listening to me anyway. Ládík poked his head out of his cubbyhole, he'd heard of me by now. I recalled that he was the one who'd been papering walls for a hundred an hour. Professionally. He said: "Hi there!" And he immediately added: "You didn't happen to stop by Czechoslovakia, did you?"

"Are you crazy?" Mirek snapped. "Jituš is no undercover cop. Jituš is—"

"That's not what I meant!" Lád'a pacified him. "I just meant that there's one Czech here in the camp who's been back to Prague a few times using a stolen Yugoslavian passport. He let his mustache grow so he'd look more like the Yugoslav in the picture, and Yugoslavs don't need visas, so the only thing he has to do is say a few words in Serbo-Croatian. And, of course, he had to be careful not to let the cat out of the bag when he was in Prague; he couldn't go home, but he met with his parents in a park. And since by Czech standards he had a fair amount of cash, he was a big spender, and the girls . . . Well, when he got back he complained that he had no skin left on his knees from fucking!"

One of the cubbyholes issued a sigh of admiration and envy.

"Yeah, the Poles do that too . . ."

"The Poles, sure, but those Romanians!" Jirka interrupted Lád'a's speech. "I knew one who helped all his buddies swim across the Danube down by the Iron Gate. He did it at least ten times, there and back, he knew all the currents . . ."

"Don't they ever shoot at anyone down there?"

"Down there? You'd better believe they shoot at people, and one time one of them got it in the thigh, almost went under, but the guy pulled him out! As long as they don't kill you, getting shot isn't so bad, and they give you asylum in a second for that!"

"Oh sure! A guy can be persecuted as much as he wants in his own country, but if he hasn't got a bullet in his leg, fuck him!"

"Tell me about it! I don't know how much truth there is to it, and I don't want to spread rumors, but I heard that somewhere near Graz in southern Austria there's this old deserter from the Albanian army who's still got one of their rifles, so for a price he shoots those Shiptars from Kosovo in the arm or leg so they can claim that they fled Albania. It's the only thing that works, but the price keeps going up, supposedly he's running out of ammunition."

"That can't be true!" I spoke up, feeling myself blush. "Who would let himself get shot in the leg just for the sake of—"

"—just for the sake of asylum? I think I know a few who would! Once they've been stuck here for a few years . . . What about you, Band'urka?"

Band'urka grumbled something and nursed his beer.

"Hold on a second, I . . ." Mirek had been trying to say something for some time, but he kept getting interrupted.

"I'd probably let someone shoot me in the head to get asylum!" Jirka piped up from his cubbyhole. "I've appealed ten times now, and they keep shitting on me like a diaper. But I heard the Yanks took you."

I confirmed this. "So, the rumor mill works sometimes . . ."

"No need to be embarrassed about it. I'd better treat you right, so maybe, even though I'm old and gray, you would do me the honor of giving me your hand in marriage: She took him as her spouse just as he was practicing for his final swan dive into the grave . . ."

"Quit messing with her, Jirka, or I'll fix it so they can put you in that grave right now," Mirek finally succeeded in getting a word in, adding: "I would like to—"

"Ach, all the be-e-est to you in America!" Band'urka said, measuring me grudgingly from behind his beer can.

"I would like, on behalf of everyone here, to congratulate Jitka. That's another reason I bought this beer, so that we can drink to her. Three cheers! Hurrah! Hurrah! Hurrah!"

Three feeble hurrahs rang out and faded into the corners of the room.

"Gimme a beer over here! I want to get hammered!" the Man of the Legion hollered. But his Tomcat slave had meanwhile headed off with the Legionnaire's socks to the bathroom. Consequently there was no one there to give him his beer.

This exasperated the Legionnaire. "Call that dickhead back in here!" he commanded Jirka.

Jirka went to the door and opened it. "What's his name again?"

The Legionnaire: "Dickhead!"

Jirka, halfheartedly: "Dickhead!"

The Legionnaire: "Louder! I was in the . . ."

Jirka shouted: "Dickhead! Com'ere!"

The boy arrived two seconds later. The Legionnaire pointed wordlessly at the plastic bag, and his slave fished a can out of it. "I want to get hammered today!" echoed from above, and I could hear the can pop open.

"We must drink to the fact that one of us, Jitka, has had a stroke of good luck and will soon be crossing the great ocean."

"And kissing us goodbye, not that she'd want to take us with her!"

I suddenly felt endowed with New-Worldly powers.

"Well, it's true, guys, I can't take you all with me . . . But I am looking forward to it, I admit."

I could feel the beer going to my head, perhaps even more quickly than the Ballantine's ever did.

"But maybe you could take just one of us? Right? Just out of Christian love . . ."

"I've been feeling like a pagan for a few weeks."

"A bacchant, perhaps?" Jirka offered learnedly. "Shall we celebrate in the manner of Dionysus? Beer, women, and song?"

"As far as I can tell I'm the only woman in here . . ."

"Don't tell me you can't handle—" Jirka began, but he stopped.

Band'urka lifted his gloomy face. "Ach, I would ha-a-ave bought you somethi-i-ing, for your celebration, but I ha-a-aven't had a-a-any work since . . ."

"You should be glad you have a chance to rest," Jirka chipped in. "Just look at Ládík over there, he got some *Arbeit* for forty an hour, picking grapes and—"

"I don't want to hear about it!"

"And he stuffed his face with so many unwashed grapes in the process that he got poisoned by the blue vitriol they use as insecticide. We had to wait on him hand and foot for two days while he just lay there puking up bluish green stuff. I keep forgetting to ask you, was your shit blue too . . . ?"

"You and your shit fixation!" commented someone.

"But I think it's just as much our fault, that we're stuck here like this," Mirek said self-critically. "Just look at Jitka: America took her, and after all she's a woman . . ."

"She's a woman, exactly! If I were a woman, then . . ."

"Then what?" I said, going on the offensive.

"Then I'd put on a nice see-through shirt . . ."

"I'm sure that would help in your case . . ."

"You can be my fairy-tale princess with a golden star on your behind," Mirek was chattering in my ear. "And every day I'll take off your clothes and wonder at it . . ."

The talk came around to the quality of Austrian beer, the Ballantine's that Mirek should have bought but hadn't, the asylum that everyone in the room should be granted but wouldn't, even if they stood on their heads and yodeled. Miss Jituška, who was supposed to be a big star (because America had accepted her) and whom this treatment didn't suit at all, had drunk up the contents of God knows how many cans and was now bent over backward trying to gulp down the last drop of Kronenbier, which as if on purpose rolled around against the inner surface of the can, absolutely refusing to flow out into her mouth.

"So you should teach us how to get across borders, no?" Jirka fawned. "You must have crossed a bunch of them. How'd you manage it? From Austria into Italy, then across France to Spain . . ."

So I let myself get caught up in my celebrity, and I told him how I had hidden myself in semis, simply saying I had no passport, and how no one ever asked why it was that I didn't. "The best one had been on the way back into Austria from Italy. I already had five illegal border crossings behind me, so I should have been seasoned by then, but it was just the opposite; I told myself how embarrassing it would have been to get caught at that point, to get myself sent off unceremoniously back to the camp in handcuffs, and forget about America . . . And so I was shaking pretty bad; I was riding with this nice, young driver, and he laughed at me for being afraid. He said to me, 'Come on, lie down here on the cot, I'll cover you with blankets and put a crate of Coke on top of you so they won't even notice, I'm telling you, they won't even look in the cab, I'm friends with all the border guards . . .' But it turned out that he was a little too friendly with the border guards, because he sat there for two hours getting drunk with them on this Sicilian moonshine raki he'd brought for them, while I was sweating blood lying there on his sleeper in that heat, two whole hours without moving with two blankets and a crate of Coke on top of me . . . And when the driver got back it was like getting raised from the dead, and I loved him for it, even though he still stank from all that booze . . ."

"You . . . *loved* him?" Mirek blurted out.

"Well, he must have liked it, having a girl in his cot, right there on hand, wouldn't you have liked that, Láďa?"

"Me? Leave me alone, fuck off, I'd screw a light socket, so long as it didn't kick!"

"You . . . *loved* him?" Mirek articulated laboriously, grabbing onto my arm.

"So you never made it to Germany?"

"Germany, no."

"That's what I'm most interested in, you know, how you can get into Germany, if it's hard, I mean, because people who've been in the camps in Germany say it's a lot better over there."

"But there *aren't* any camps in Germany . . . ," someone says.

"Okay, I mean in those . . . pensions or shelters or whatever it is they live in there. It's much easier to get work, especially for whites; they don't force you to run out and marry some girl before you can live in a pension, the way these crazy religious nuts here do, and they don't stick their noses in your business so much . . ."

"You can get to Germany, no problem," the Legionnaire's servant piped up. "All you've got to do is crawl through the barbed wire and—"

"Christ, what an idiot you are, there's no barbed wire between Austria and Germany," Jirka immediately cut him off. "You just walk across on a nice little footpath."

"Yeah, right! Didn't you hear how they brought back that whole band of Poles?"

"Sure—but did you hear the whole story? They were wasted; it was freezing, so they took some Wodka Wyborowa with them on the road, and they were crawling on their hands and knees by the time they got to Salzburg. They forgot which way was north and were going around in circles . . . They deserved to be caught! I'm telling you!"

But I was no longer capable of thinking about everything that was going on around me. Only about him. About *my* Mirek. It seemed to me that the constellation of freckles on the back of his

neck was the third of my magical signs. Perhaps I should tell him
about those two mornings when . . . I leaned against his arm and
could feel him . . . I loved him! Mirek raised the blanket over
his cubbyhole and I leaped inside as if it were Noah's ark.

The other guys, who had inherited the remainder of the beer,
made a few more comments. Mirek pressed me in his arms and
waited for them to turn the lights out. He giggled a little at how
it was always the same. But soon we were no longer noticing those
sounds. Not in the slightest. And I trembled in his arms, shaking
with love, I sprinkled my love over him like golden rain. "Mirek,"
I said to him, and I wanted to tell him about those two miraculous
mornings, but he covered my mouth with a kiss. "You make me
so high!" he kept whispering. I was shaking my love off on him
like a Newfoundlander after a swim, and he did not take it into
himself, he just let its golden droplets flow over his surface,
allowing himself to be voluptuously gilded with them, basking in
them, warming himself . . .

"You make me so high!" he whispered to me all night.

But by then he was lying to me. He was high, all right, but not
because of me. He was high on all that swill that was now, toward
morning, beginning to seep out of every pore of his skin—and it
stank.

●

"I don't have the money for rings, I haven't got enough for
cigarettes even, since I bought all those beers," he said to me.

"What do you mean?"

"Jituš, I've realized that I want you terribly much. I realized
it when you went away. When you were away I . . ."

"I believe you, that's just the way you are."

"But you really pissed me off that time. Saying that I should
have *fought*. Like that stupid Slovak. Do you know how long he
was in the hospital?"

"Mirek, stop, don't talk about that anymore."

We were wandering around in the freshly fallen snow by the

camp wall. It must have been close to freezing, because there were little black puddles of water standing in the footprints left by the hares. Between the grapevine furrows there were some thawed places through which shone the black-brown earth. I squatted and dug into the clay with my fingers.

"Maybe I should tell you . . ." I began, considering whether I was capable of telling him about the symbolic importance of those two mornings, those two awakenings. But Mirek was already babbling on, so I had no chance. A flock of rooks alit on the bare field a little way away from us. We headed closer to them and I could see how the world was mirrored in the blue reflections from their wings.

"It wasn't so simple for me, you know. God knows how many filthy Albanians . . ."

"And Marta. Why did you have to choose her . . ."

"And how many guys did you sleep with, on that trip of yours, don't you want to brag about that?!"

"God, now we're fighting . . ."

"I just want to say to you that . . . that I want to start over. You know I'm still married, I've got two sons, and it's not like I don't miss them, I'm not saying that, but . . ."

We had reached the sunflower field. They had already been harvested, but a forgotten one still jutted up out of the earth near the field's edge, half pecked out by a goldfinch that flew from its top as we approached, twittering angrily.

"Well, I was thinking, to put it bluntly, what if we tried to make it in America together, you and me? Things aren't going so well for me here. And you're the only one that . . . I don't know English, but I could learn it, I can already speak some German. I didn't really want to go to America, but since you're going there . . ."

I was beginning to feel a little cold and he noticed this. He took my hands in his palms and breathed on them like a donkey. That's how he suddenly appeared to me. As an ass.

"So you want to marry me?" I asked him. But Mirek, absorbed with himself, didn't catch the spiteful tone in my voice.

"I'm already married. But if I started the divorce proceedings right away . . . Maybe if you waited here in the camp until the divorce came through, then . . ."

"Mirek," I sighed. I was suddenly above it all. How simple life was! "Mirek, I know it sounds stupid to ask like this . . ." I stared at the forgotten, bent sunflower that was still nodding a little from the goldfinch's departure. "Mirek, *do you love me?*"

He gazed into my eyes in surprise: "I think the world of you!"

"No, that's not what I'm asking you, I know that already," I said with magical naïveté. "I mean, you see, after all this . . . Do you love me like you've never loved anyone else before . . . ?"

Mirek looked sincerely into my eyes. But his gaze did not burn into me the way Good Morning's pupils were capable of doing. Because he said: "Jitka, I'm no good at talking about these things, but I love you. Terribly much. I've been in love a couple of times before, but you, you I really love!" And he was not even conscious that the very effort of saying this caused his eyes to bug out of their sockets and that he had again begun to remind me of a sweating rabbit.

●

I saw Mirek off to Germany. He was glad to go. He had long ago decided that fortune would never smile on him in Austria. At least I was able to help him out by getting him past Salzburg on the highway hitching, so he wouldn't have to pay for the train. According to our watches it was not all that late, but still the trip had taken us almost the entirety of that short winter day. We immediately took off across the new-fallen snow, away from the highway and toward the border. There was not that much snow. Just enough to soak our camp-issue winter boots. Most of all it reflected the rays of the sun into our eyes like silvery wires. We walked through a small forest, then decided that we had to be in Germany by then. All that remained was for Mirek to walk across a snowy clearing to the highway.

Mirek and I said farewell in that clearing. I offered him my hand to shake, probably just so we could show each other that there were no hard feelings . . . But Mirek pulled me to him and did not want to let go. And then he walked off across the clearing, into the distance. I knew that the fact that I was staying, turning back, made me concrete for him, substantial, because Mirek had never lived in the *now*.

His walking off into the distance across that snowy plain caused me to fall into his past; I believed that he would remember me because we would never see each other again. I followed him with my eyes as he receded, placed him in the proper compartment, and for me, because I *did* live in the now, he was ceasing to exist, disappearing. Meanwhile the sun had slipped down to the horizon and tinted the clearing orange. I looked out toward the West, in the direction of the orange fleck of West Berlin, which still lay buried somewhere out there and somewhere inside me. And I realized the burden of emptiness within Mirek. Because without a doubt there was nothing in his heart except that orange desert.

28

The last months of waiting were the worst. Because I was once again positive that I did not belong in the camp, that I was moving on. Meanwhile, in the *Flüchtlingslager* at Traiskirchen, the unsuccessful, disappointed, hopeless, and discarded slowly congealed, like the grounds settling to the bottom of a cup of coffee.

The silvery trails of the airplanes shone gloriously in the winter sky. I was waiting for my own now, knowing that it was coming for me. I threw my head back and looked forward to America. I looked forward to landing there.

Some ten years later it finally dawned on me that, wherever you are, the world beneath you is never round, you always see only a piece of it, delimited by the horizon. Even when you're sailing in the middle of the ocean. Even when you're climbing a high tower. Even when you're flying in a jumbo jet toward the West, and everywhere below you, above you, and around you day is slowly and endlessly dawning. And so for a while I played with the globe as with a multicolored inflatable beach ball. I felt my way through the jungles of big cities and peeped into real jungles that emanated urgency and fear. I managed to convince myself that I was really a journalist. And meanwhile I drank tea with monks from the most delicate of cups, cups through which the light shone. I wandered across the rooftop of the world and looked down into the abysses, in order to know boundlessness. The world *really was* round, but you couldn't see it from any one place. Part of it was always missing.

So I returned to New York and found myself a man. And once, after an argument, in order to appease me, he took a marker and drew this picture on the wall:

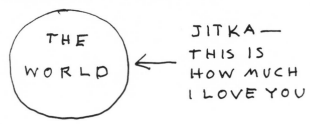

—and I knew that he meant it.

I was looking at that globe one day when it seemed to me that I could feel its roundness within myself. Because my period was late, and my nipples were growing swollen and sensitive, as if in preparation for an infant's mouth.

I remember (I think) those few weeks of expectation and uncertainty, the few weeks of recollections and reminiscences during which it is so easy to touch your own inside. There's (probably) a tiny human being inside your womb that asks you in alarm: "Are you going to let me live this time? Or will I become just another scar?"

A blur of scrambled memories is attacking me from the depths of my own past. Standa. East Berlin. Good Morning's stroking eyes. The round world which I have circumnavigated, and which is now reflected in my own pupils just as on the rooks' black wings.

I still haven't been to the doctor; we have no health insurance. But I am allowing the world's roundness to grow within me. It's pleasant, I feel no need for change. And although streams of fugitives flow in one direction across the earth, although people murder one another, shoot one another, and die of hunger, I'm not going to worry about that. Because a tiny new life is flourishing right in my center, connecting me (and Gary) with our distant pasts, and promising to connect us with the future.

Bronx, New York, 1988
Paris, 1991
Prague, 1991
Manhattan, New York, 1992
Prague, 1992

DATE DUE

GAYLORD			PRINTED IN U.S.A.